WABENO THE MAGICIAN

·The MCo·

WABENO THE MAGICIAN

Norwood Press
J. S. Cushing & Co. — Berwick & Smith
Norwood Mass. U.S.A.

This Book is Dedicated

TO MY SISTER BERTHA

CONTENTS

vii

LIST OF ILLUSTRATIONS

FULL PAGE

ix

I

The Dream Fox

IT was the first week of March. Time for the grass to be greening along the edges of springy meadows, for the Pussy-willows to stretch out their silver-furred paws, time for the cheerful little Marsh Frogs to tune up toward sunset. But instead of these spring signs and sounds, snow was falling around Happy Hall, as it had done for two whole days, until the paths were quite buried. Great drifts swept over the violet frames, and clung to the woodshed roof. The pines and spruces at the north of the house

B   1

shivered and bent their heads to the fierce wind;
and a flock of newly arrived Robins huddled in the
hemlock hedge, wondering what had become of
their friend the Sun, who had given the signal for
their journey, half suspecting him of having
played them a shabby trick.

Tommy-Anne was sitting on a foxskin rug
before the fire in her bedroom, with no other
light besides what the logs yielded. She was
allowed a "go-to-bed" fire every chilly night,
and the fireplace was a frame in which she saw
wonderful pictures.

A great many things had happened since the
Christmas Eve four years before, when Waw-be-
ko-ko, the Snow Owl, came to the Christmas
party, and Tommy-Anne halved her name with the
little brother. People often called her Tommy-
Anne still, in spite of the fact that Tommy was a
sturdy little chap, strutting about proudly in his
first knickerbockers, and puckering his lips to
make his very first whistle.

In fact, this double name caused great confusion in the house until the day when Tommy-
Anne took matters into her own hands, saying,
"I can climb better than ever, because my arms
are longer; I ask as many questions, and I'm
only just beginning to understand a few of the

whys. I like outdoors much better than indoors, and dogs better than cats and dolls; but, as I'm a girl, I want to be called by a girl's name, so *please*, father-mother, call me Anne. Then, perhaps, by and by when I grow up and have to wear long skirts and turn up my hair and tread on every step of the stairs and *always* go *through* gates, I *may* like to be called my whole name, Diana, after the hunting lady with the young moon on her head."

Meanwhile Waddles had been growing into quite a sober, middle-aged dog, with many affairs of his own and even troubles to attend to — troubles that he considered far worse than Aunt Prue's broom or his old enemy, the Miller's cat, for Aunt Prue did not live at the house now that Anne's mother was quite well and strong again, and the Miller's cat had one lame front paw, and seldom dared dogs to fight with her.

Waddles' first grievance was that he could not take his usual naps in the study scrap-basket, as Tommy kept his blocks in the comfortable old one, while the new one was high and tipped over easily, in addition to being made of rough, prickly straw. This was a slight grievance, however, beside other things; and as Waddles walked slowly up stairs, and along the hall to Anne's

door, that snowy March evening, his heart was
very heavy indeed. "As like as not she has
gone to bed," he whimpered to himself, "and I
shall have to wait another day to tell her." ·

As she heard the patter of his feet outside, Anne
started, put a fresh log on the fire, saying, "How
can I *ever* tell him?" Waddles nosed the door
open, but only enough to squeeze his plump body
through, and then pulled it as nearly shut as he
could with his paw, for what he had to say to his
mistress was for her ear alone. To be sure Tommy
was supposed to be in bed, but then he was always
turning up unexpectedly. Waddles snuggled up
to his mistress, who began smoothing out his
velvety ears after her old habit. He was tempted
to curl up and go to sleep ; but no, he must not.
So he sighed, turned his head on one side, and
gazed first at the fire and then at Anne, with a
most pathetic expression in his soft brown eyes.

Anne clasped her hands around her knees and
returned the look, thinking in perplexity, "How
can I break the news to him?"

"Mistress," said Waddles after a while, as Anne
was beginning to be interested in an angry dispute in the chimney between the wind that wished
to come down and the smoke that was struggling
to go up, "I'm *very* unhappy and it is partly

your fault, too, though I'm sure you never meant
it.   Do you remember the night when Tommy
came and you were so pleased that you turned
reckless and began giving him things? First you
gave him half your name, then you gave him half
of me — the back leg half, so that I could 'wag
my tail to amuse him,' you said.

"At first it worked very well; he didn't say
much of anything, and I could go up and sleep in
your mother's nice warm room where his crib was,
whenever I pleased. When the warm weather
came I followed his coach to all the cool shady
places. Then, after a while, he took an interest
in my tail and used to shout and give me crusts
of bread to make me wag it. Of course I only
took the crusts out of politeness, for you know I
never eat them.

"Pretty soon after this, when he could run
about, he began to pull my tail and sometimes

trample on my ears, when I lay stretched out
asleep.   Still I did not whimper or complain
because he wore girls' clothes and had such puppy
ways, but since he has worn those pantikins I can
bear no more. *He* wants to wag my tail.   The
other day he tied a string to it.   He wishes me to
run races with him directly after my dinner, and
go to sleep under his chair at breakfast when the
Earth has so much news to tell me, and perhaps
there are tracks of a Weasel or Scent Cat all
around the barn.   Then twice he has shut me in
the woodhouse just as you whistled.

" My patience ended yesterday.   You know the
duck leg your father gave me after dinner?   To
be sure it was a trifle tough, but otherwise good
eating, so I thought that I would bury it awhile
to ripen.   I had barely laid it down, to look for a
place where I could scratch a hole, when I saw
Tiger slinking down the orchard wall looking
narrow and sly as ever.   I growled — he stopped.
Then Tommy ran up and called, ' Tum here, thin
cat, here's a dood bone fatty Waddles tant eat,'
and he threw *my* duck leg to Tiger.

" For a minute I meant to run away, down to
the Horse Farm, for they say that a woman lives
there who is very good to dogs, but we've been
friends so long, and you wear the Magic Spectacles

and know my language, that I couldn't go without telling you, so please, mistress, take back my hind legs and let me *all* belong to you again," and Waddles raised his head and bayed dismally to hide the fact that he was nearly crying.

"You dear old Waddlekins!" cried Anne, standing him up before her until their noses met.

"Of course I'll take you back, for I've often missed you dreadfully when I've been for long walks and had to leave you behind because Tommy wanted you. Yet when Obi offered to get me one of the pretty spaniels from the Horse Farm, I could not bear to let another dog take your place. But we must be patient with little brother, because you know the Three Hearts have given him to us to take care of until he can see through the Magic

Spectacles himself. Father says, he is a *responsibility* — the first real one I've ever had. Do you know what that means? Well, it is this way.

"Before Tommy came, if I was careless about anything like getting my feet sopping wet, tearing my frocks and forgetting about meal times, I had wet feet, or scratched arms, or felt hungry, but that was all. Now, if I do these things and Tommy sees me and does them too, I'm responsible for him, do you see? So responsibility is a thing that makes you mind what you do and isn't altogether comfortable. Waddles love, I might as well tell you first as last, — you are going to have a responsibility too. A new dog is coming to live here to-morrow, or next day, or whenever the snow stops. You will have to help train him and teach him to be neat and eat his food off his plate and sit on his own mat, and not get up on the sofas, or lie down or dig in mother's flower beds, besides all the other things you've learned."

"A new dog here!" yelped Waddles, bristling and springing up as quickly as if some one had cried, "cat" or "rat." "Missy, only a minute ago you said that you didn't take one of those polite little spaniels that Obi offered you because you loved me so; and now — to think of it — a strange dog coming! I'll go out in the snow and

have one more fight with Tiger to get even about
the duck leg, and then I don't care — what —
becomes — of — me ! " and Waddles crept toward
the door with drooping head and tail, all his
fierceness having vanished.

" Come back, you poor dear," called Anne, "you
haven't heard but half ! " Then, as he did not
move very quickly, she half lifted, half dragged,
him back to the foxskin.

" Now look me straight in the face, Waddles,
for you've got two of the very worst of the Puk-
Wudjies living in your head, — Sus-Picion and
Jea-Lousy. Father says, ' Did-not-Think ' and
' Did-not-Mean-To ' don't *begin* to make as much
trouble as they do.

" In the first place, the new dog is not for me, it
is for Tommy. It is only a bit of a four-months-
old puppy dog that will like to run and play.
Father wants him to grow up with Tommy, so that
they will love each other as we do. Then you see,
you and I can stay together all the time as we
used to. This dog's mother lives at the Horse
Farm, and is one of Miss Jule's very best big
St. Bernards — the big strong kind that, in the
cold country where they come from, can dig
out people that are buried in the snow. As for
being strange, why, you know that all Miss Jule's

animals are as friendly as they can be. So now, give me a nice little kiss on the ear, and as a great treat you shall sleep on my bed in a nest made of the afghan. Come, jump up, I hear mother on the stairs and she won't kiss us good-night, you know, unless we are quite in bed."

"The Winds of Night, the Winds of Night; let us in for we are cold," wailed the voices outside the window, where the sleety snow coated the panes.

"Is that you, Kabibonokka?" whispered Anne, as she drew the eider-down quilt up to her chin. "What business has the north wind here when it ought to be spring? Mother has bought all her flower seeds and Obi would have made the hot-bed for them yesterday if you hadn't brought this snow back to bury everything. How do things get so mixed? What made you come back? Last week I saw a bee in the violet frame. I wonder if he expected to find the Flower Market open, and what became of the message he was carrying? Perhaps it froze! Do you think a message could freeze, Kabibonokka? And I wonder what has become of Heart of Nature now that all his garden is dead and buried. Perhaps he has gone, to sleep the winter sleep, like the Woodchuck."

"Heart of Nature never sleeps, and work in his garden never ceases," answered a Voice from beside the hearthstone. "I have been abroad all day working to protect my own and soon I go out again. The Plan directs the seasons and marks their courses, but rebellious forces strive and wrestle for the mastery and make delay and havoc.

"A vagrant voice called Kabibonokka from the north. Quickly I bade the snows descend and shield the earth from his rude breath. To-morrow, if he leaves, Shawondasee will come and help me gather up the snow again. Meanwhile I whisper to the Coon, 'Keep close in your tree hole.' To Crow and Jay, 'Stay well within the cedars lest your eyeballs freeze.' To Quail and Grouse, surrounded in the stubble, 'Dive in the snow blanket, lest you perish.' To the Eel beneath the ice, 'Begin your journey down the river to your spring sea chambers before the ice gates lift.' As to the grass and plants and trees, snow dulls their ears, they hear nothing, and their sap lies cold and still and safe."

"I'm so glad you've come back!" cried Anne, sitting up in bed and clasping her hands. "You don't come to see me often, now that Tommy is about so much and I have to stay indoors and do my lessons. How is that, dear Heart of Nature, for there are so many *whys* that need answers that I'm sure I've forgotten half of them?"

"Anne, do you remember the password in the land of the Three Hearts?"

"Brotherhood!" said Anne, promptly.

"Yes, brotherhood — an equal sharing. You must listen to each of the Three Hearts if you would understand the Plan. I have but given Heart of Man his turn."

"Of course, lessons and books and people mean Heart of Man, but, dear Tree Man, please tell me *why* do things ever mix up and Winter and Spring interfere, and some animals eat others, and all that? Why does the Plan allow it, and where are all the things that you are never sure whether you have seen or only dreamed?"

"The Plan fixes its laws of birth, growth, and death, the beginning and the end; between these heat and cold, wind, water, tempest and calm, all contend for mastery, and when House People speak of haphazard and mysterious cross-purposes, you know they mean —"

"Wabeno, the Magician!" cried a shrill voice in the chimney. "Wabeno, the Magician!" echoed a calmer voice at the keyhole. Anne rubbed her eyes and looked about very much puzzled. She had not quite caught Heart of Nature's meaning, perhaps because she was sleepy, but those voices, surely they belonged to Kabibo-nokka and Mudjekeewis. What could the North and West Winds be doing there at the same time?

She slipped out upon the foxskin rug to listen, pulling the down quilt after her.

"Who is Wabeno, the Magician, and where does he live?" she whispered. "Does he belong to the Brotherhood of Beasts, or what? Creep into the chimney, Winds of Night; for though I may not let you in the window, you can come quite near, for the fire is low."

"Do you speak, Kabibonokka, while I get my breath," said Mudjekeewis, panting. "Ah! the distance I have come to-day from heat and sand and summer to this snow, simply because Wabeno gave his signal."

Anne was going to speak impatiently, and then stopped herself, for Kabibonokka said: "Before man walked the earth, nothing asked *why* about anything. What came, came; what went, went all unquestioned. When the Red Brothers ar-rived (the first men we ever met in these lands), 'why' was the very first word they said. For many things they could find no reasons, because they did not understand the Three Hearts and their language; so every strange thing that befell, they laid to Wabeno, the Magician.

"He was born in Wabun Annung, the Morning Star, or so they said, and of the race of Wenona, whom the Robins and Bluebirds loved so well. A warrior was he, young and strong and beautiful, yet no one had clearly seen his face, for a leafy mask half hid it. He had no wigwam, any tree trunk was his home. He carried no bow or spear, and Kaw-kaw, the far-seeing Raven, perched on his brow for a head-dress, its eyes shooting lightning bolts. Thunder boomed from his magic drum if he struck it fiercely, but at a gentle touch it yielded a note like the feathered drumming of the Ruffed Grouse, and he sang a call that all must answer.

"'Hear my drum, hear my drum, you who dwell across the earth! Hear my drum! I am Wabeno! This is my work!'

"Then following, sometimes in leash and sometimes free, came his faithful Wagoose, the Dream Fox, with his shadowy pack and his book of wondrous fading pictures.

"When the Red Brothers heard Wabeno and his train, they closed their eyes tightly, for only the mind's eye may see him unblinded; while to sleep-closed eyes alone will the Dream Fox show his picture-book, and lead the sleepers long journeys through strange countries all in a minute.

"Two days ago I, Kabibonokka, was travelling northward with Wabasso, the White Rabbit, and between us we led Winter, who walked with lingering tread. Suddenly I heard a signal to return, and I came, calling among the trees to the Winds of Night to learn who had work for us; but there was no work, and so we wrought mischief, and troubled Heart of Nature, who dropped the snow to keep me from his garden. Who, then, could have called us but Wabeno?"

"And I," cried Mudjekeewis, "I was lingering in the southwest country, where the cactus walls the sand-heaps, and the century plant already shows the buds of its April flowers. I heard a signal and I came, only to find it Winter. Who called me but Wabeno?"

"Winds of Night, idle Winds of Night, I have work for you, though you came at another's bidding," called Heart of Nature. "Go up and tear the veils from the stars and polish them bright, and help the young moon to find her pathway down the western sky; pluck the dead branches from the tree tops, scatter the last clinging seeds; then cease, for I have much to plan and set in order before morning."

"Mistress," called Waddles, waking up with a whimper and finding the bed empty, "mistress, do come to sleep. I'm fairly shivering, and the wind is coming in at every crack until my hair stands on end. Don't you see the fire is nearly out? You will have a snuffle cold, and then we shall have to stay in the house for days and days!"

"What did you say, Waddlekins? Ah, yes, the fire is low and there is no more wood in the basket," said Anne, stumbling back to bed. "Why, the stars and moon are out, it must have stopped snowing! How the winds whistle and scold; if I could only understand all the things they say. Ah! how I wish the Dream Fox would show me his picture-book.

"Why, there he comes! The rug fox must have been a Dream Fox when he was alive! The picture-book — too! The poor old blind Crow up in the woods — and the Bob-whites — all — asleep — under — the — snow. I'll get Obi to take them — some — food — to-morrow, and we — will help — Heart of Nature — dig — out — his — g-a-r-d-e-n, and — begin — his — "

Footsteps crossed the hall below and came rapidly up the stairs.

"It is nothing, dear," said Anne's father to her

mother, looking in at the door. " I thought the child was at her old trick of playing Owl and looking out the window in the dark but she was only talking in her sleep."

II

What happened One very Cold Day

WADDLES usually waked up very early in the morning. After taking a complete bath, in which his tongue did duty for a sponge, and queer little sucking, sputtering noises took the place of splashing water, he would trot deliberately down stairs and out the back door to hear what news of the night the Earth had to tell him. If there was a great deal to learn, and the grass or light snow spoke of Rabbit, House Cat, or Scent Cat, everything else was forgotten; otherwise he soon returned to the kitchen, where, by looking steadily at the cook with his most wistful expression, he usually succeeded in securing at least a sample of the family breakfast.

This particular morning it was barely light when Waddles finished his toilet on the hearth rug. He looked at the frost-covered window-panes, shivered, gave a sneeze, and tip-toed across the painted floor toward the bed again. He hesitated, looked at the afghan nest at the foot, then pushing his way *under* the bedclothes cuddled down in a particularly warm spot with his nose on his mistress' shoulder, where, half an hour later, when Anne was wakened by the building of her fire, she found him.

"Why, Waddles!" she cried, "what is the matter? You know very well that you mustn't get *into* bed. Are you sick, or did the Dream Fox show you a big picture of the Miller's cat to frighten you? He showed *me* a lot of strange things about cold and ice and hungry birds, and by and by I'm going to ask Obi to go out to see if he can find any, and we will take them some food. It is Saturday, you know, so there won't be any lessons.

"I think it must be very cold," she continued, jumping up to look at a pretty little thermometer on her bureau, and flying back to bed again.

"Ugh! only 30°. I think we won't get up quite yet, Waddlekins."

"I didn't have to look at that weather stick to know that it is cold.   I could *smell* it," said Waddles, nestling down unreproved.   "I hope it's too cold for the new dog to come to-day."

"We tan't have breakfas' for ever so long, and no baths at all this morning," shouted Tommy, tearing along the hall into Anne's room, where, jumping into the middle of the bed, nearly smothering Waddles, he looked like a little goblin, in his red blanket wrapper with his pointed hood and his pointed red felt slippers.

"Do you know *why* we tan't have our baths, sister?" he said, pulling her eyes wide open with his icy little fingers.

"Well," speaking with suppressed excitement, "the water pipes are all fwozen down in the kitchen, and father says they may burst and make leaks.   Then you know the plumber will have to come and *maybe* he will give me some lead and let me melt it in his firepot to make bullets for my bean shooter.   Father doesn't seem to like plumbers, but I fink they're lots of fun.

"Then we tan't have breakfas' yet, 'cause the milk's frozen too.   I wonder if it froze before it was milked or after.   Which do you think it was?   Oh, Anne, you are doing to sleep again; *please* tell me which way the milk froze, because if it froze before it was milked, I should think it must make the poor Bossies drefful cold."

Anne had to laugh in spite of feeling a little cross with Tommy for teasing.

"Why, the milk froze after it was milked, of course. The cows are too warm to let it freeze before, and if it did how could Obi and Baldy have milked it?"

"I didn't know," said Tommy, unabashed by facts, "'cause some things freeze softer than others. I'm going to see how fwozen milk looks and then I'm going to make my bed into a bear's den with the blankets. Come and be the little rabbit, Waddles, and I'll be the big bear and jump out and eat you;" but Waddles declined emphatically, by leaving his comfortable place and retreating under the bed.

"Bad Waddles, you won't do anyfing I want," pouted Tommy, going away. "You're only a stuffed flannel dog, anyway, and I shan't invite you to play with me any more!"

"Now you see how it is, missy," said Waddles from under the bed. "I'm very glad you've taken me back, and I really think I'm even willing for the new dog to come."

"No, sir, you needn't come in again," said Anne, preparing to get up. "When it's cold it's

extra hard to get up for good if you keep coming back again. We mustn't be monkeys in the
kettle, Waddlekins."

"We are not monkeys, missy," said Waddles,
scornfully. "Monkeys are those queer animals
that do not look like any of the Beast Brothers.
They wear clothes like House People and have
long tails like rats. The man that came up here
last summer with that box of noises, that he turned
on with a handle, had a monkey to steal things for
him. That monkey climbed up to your mother's
window and took her nice shiny thimble off the
table, while she was getting cookies for him. I
barked to call you, but the monkey jumped
down on my back and bit my ear; then I nipped
the man's pants, and he went away very quick."

"To be sure, mother's thimble was lost the very
day the hand-organ man was here," said Anne,
pausing; "but the kettle monkey was different
and mother used to tell me, when I was a little
girl and slept by her in a crib, that I acted just
like him.

"You see this monkey had lived in a very
warm land, where he could play out all the year
without wearing clothes, just as you do. One day
a man caught him and took him away from his
friends and brought him where it was very cold.

As there was not time that night to make Mr. Monkey a coat, his master put a blanket over him in a box in the kitchen.

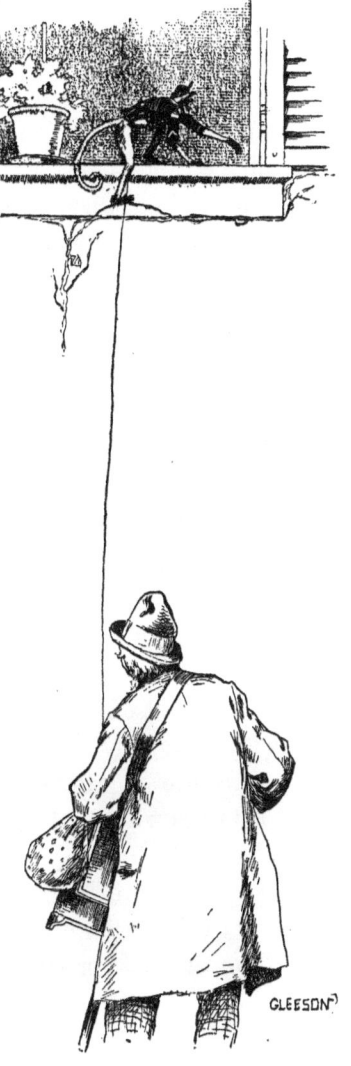

" In the morning the cook came down stairs, made the fire, put the kettle on and went away. Very soon the monkey got out of the basket and began to look about for something to eat, but he couldn't find anything, and soon began to shiver dreadfully. Then he went over toward the fire and climbed up on top of the big teakettle, which was only a little bit warm.

" He took the lid off and looked in, for monkeys are very impolite animals, that always touch everything they see; next he put one paw in the water, finding it very warm and comfortable.

" 'I will get into the kettle and then I shall soon be warm all over,' he said to himself. He was. In a minute he felt too hot, especially in his feet that were down on the bottom of the kettle. He jumped out, but the room felt so cold that he jumped in again; but he couldn't stay long, so he kept hopping in and out until, if the cook had not come and put him back in his blanket, he would have been boiled to death. So when I hopped in and out of bed on cold mornings, mother used to say, 'Foolish little monkey, come out of the kettle.' "

The fire was burning nicely by this time, so that Anne could dress comfortably, and the little silver line in the thermometer was going slowly upward, but the water in the pitcher that stood near the window was still frozen hard.

"I wonder what the use of cold is, anyway," she said, as she warmed a towel and rubbed some of the frost off the window so that she could look out. "It only spoils everything, and kills Heart of Nature's big garden as well as our little one. I don't see why the Hearts allowed the cold in the Plan; this is the very coldest day there has ever been, I'm sure."

"Cold and I work together to-day," said a voice from the melting frost on the panes, which Anne knew belonged to Heart of Nature. "No garden is made ready without ploughing and digging, and Cold with his children Frost and Ice were among the first ploughmen in my garden, Anne.

"Heat and Cold were the two first labourers that Heart of God chose to work out his Plan, far back in the bygone ages, when the Earth was but a new-born thing and I was alone with Heart of God."

"Oh please, dear Heart of Nature, tell me about when the Earth was young, and what the Cold and Heat did to it, and which is the oldest, the Earth or the Moon."

"There is no way for House People to learn the Earth's story but from the Earth herself — she alone can tell it rightly. Cold also will himself show you how he and his children plough my fields. Go to the old barn by the wood edge, — the barn where Ko-ko-ko-ho lodges on winter nights, and ask the great icicles that hang from the roof to tell you their story.

"And as for the rest, you must ask the Moon about that, for she follows the Earth through the sky garden year in and out."

"Sky garden? Please, I thought gardens had to be places dug in the earth, where things are planted."

"Nature's garden is everywhere, — in earth, sea,

and sky; in all these places her gardeners are toiling equally to carry on the Plan.''

"Mistress," said Waddles, growing impatient at the way in which Anne was slowly brushing her hair and looking out of the window, "won't you please tie the ribbon on your braid quick and come down stairs? Even if the milk is frozen my nose tells me that there is delicious bacon being cooked with eggs, and you know we *always* have buckwheat cakes in winter on Saturday mornings."

Obi worked at Happy Hall altogether now; that is, he lodged at Baldwin's cottage across the road, went to school all but the last spring term, and worked about the place during the summer and between times for Anne's father. Baldwin was the man who took care of the horse and cows, and did the harder work. The children were both very fond of him and called him Baldy for a pet name out of fondness, and not because he had very little hair. No one seemed to know about his hair, for he wore his hat in the barn and outdoors, summer and winter.

Baldwin had been trained by Miss Jule, down at the Horse Farm, and consequently was very fond of animals. But as you have not perhaps met Miss Jule, I will tell you about her.

Her father, who was always called the Squire, owned one of the largest grass farms in the county, and raised the finest cattle and most beautiful horses ever seen. In fact, people came from miles away to buy them. When he died, people asked Miss Jule what she should do with the farm.

" Run it myself," she said, shutting her lips together tight to show that she would not argue.

" It will run away with you and all your money besides," said one grumpy old farmer, who had expected to be hired as manager.

" You will see," said Miss Jule; and they saw, but not what they expected.

The horses throve. No one broke the colts to harness or saddle but Miss Jule herself, and there was not a docked tail or a cruel check-rein to be seen among them. As for dogs, Miss Jule kept big dogs and little dogs, and even had a sort of hospital where all the unfortunate animals in the neighborhood came to be mended or cured, according to their various ailments. Cats, Miss Jule did not keep, because she loved birds, and then she said, "Of what use are cats if you can have a good ratting-terrier?"

Martin boxes stood on a pole in the barn-yard, all the nearby trees had Wren boxes on them, and she hung out horse hair where the Chipping Sparrows could find it to line their nests; also strings for the Baltimore Oriole, and always kept a big earthenware pan full of water under a particular lilac bush in the garden for a birds' public bath-tub.

You may wonder why so much is said about Miss Jule; but you must be introduced to some of Anne's friends. Miss Jule was such a particular friend and such a delightful person, who understood people's feelings so well that the children often took little animals and treasures for her to keep, that they did not think would be quite welcome at home.

That morning Baldwin, Obi, two of the select-
men, and some hands from the Horse Farm were
very busy breaking out the roads. The snow
had drifted badly, being very deep in some
places, while others were bare, and the sleet of
the early evening had covered the snow with a
crust, and the trees with diamonds that glittered
in the sun.

Immediately after breakfast who should come
riding up to the side door at Happy Hall but
Miss Jule, mounted on Brown Kate, a very sure-
footed mare, who picked her way daintily and
seemed to enjoy the novel sport as thoroughly as
her mistress.

Miss Jule was a very funny figure on horse-
back, for she was quite tall and not very young,
and she wore a fur coat and cap and very big
blue spectacles to keep the snow glare from her
eyes. But the fourfoots and all of the young
twofoots would never have noticed it if she had
looked twice as queerly.

Anne dashed out when she saw Miss Jule,
and then flew back crying, " Oh, father-mother,
may I go down to the Horse Farm ? Miss Jule has
come for me. She says that she has saved some
birds that were nearly frozen yesterday, and that
she thinks there are a lot of Quail in the snow

in the brush lot, and she wants Obi to come and get them out from under the crust before they freeze and starve.

"She says I can ride behind her on Brown Kate, and when we come home this afternoon the roads will be cleared and I can bring Tommy's new dog with me. Yes? I may go? Waddlekins dear, you *must* stay at home; you would simply break through the crust and smother, your legs are so short. Please stay with Tommy to-day, and then to-morrow the new dog will be here and you and I will begin all over again."

*   *   *   *   *   *   *   *

It was difficult to understand how it could be so cold when the sun shone so brightly. The little icicles hanging from the spruces shivered and cracked as the North Wind dashed around the corner of the house, whispering in Anne's ear, " What fun we winds are having ; see where we have piled the snow quite over the back gate ; but we have been kind enough to sweep a place bare in the garden where you always plant the early peas. Our frolic is almost over. The sun is getting too strong for Peboan, it blinds him, so he has dropped his last load of snow, and to-morrow he will be marching northward again with Wabasso, the White Rabbit."

" I wonder if they call this month March, because it's the time that Winter has to march off," said Anne, laughing to herself at the idea.

" I think not, though, for I've read in my Roman History that it was named after Mars, the God of War, because it was such a quarrelsome kind of a month."

" Here and there, where we winds travel, the months have different names," said Kabibonokka. " Over in the West country some of the Red Brothers still call this month the Moon of Snow Blindness, because there the snow always lingers late, and at this season the sun shines on it with a brightness that burns the eyes out."

" That's what it is doing to my eyes now, so if you please, North Wind, I'll pull my veil down, and please don't whisper in my ears, for it makes them very cold and they might freeze and break off, like the icicles yonder. Don't pull my hat so, Kabibonokka ; let go my cape, sir, it's very rude of you." But the North Wind only gave a long whistle and swept down the road, snatching off Obi's cap and sifting a rift of loose snow around his neck.

There was a great wood fire in the sitting room

down at the Horse Farm, before which Anne
warmed herself, and after Obi came down Miss
Jule gave them bowls of hot milk with slices of
crisp toast to break in it. Then they started to
make their way back of the hayricks over to the
old barn, where Miss Jule said she had put her
cripples. Anne carried a salt bag of "bird hash,"
as Miss Jule called it, and Obi carried another
bag full of buckwheat over his shoulder to spread
about for the Quail.

"This is lucky," thought Anne, "for while
we are feeding the birds, I can ask the big icicles
how they plough the ground and help Heart of
Nature in his garden."   .

"Why, Obi," she exclaimed ten minutes later,
"how this place has changed ! There used to
be big holes in the barn roof and now it is all
thatched over with straw, there is hay piled round
the ground and queer little holes made here and
there, like those in the pigeon house. Oh !
there's hay inside and all sorts of perches,
something like our chicken roost."

"Miss Jule had it fixed this way," said Obi,
dropping his bag and beating his hands to warm
them, "so that the birds and things that stay
about here all winter could creep in and out of
the wind, and she keeps mixed seeds there, too,

for the birds. The Quail would have been all right if they hadn't strayed off to the upper fields and then couldn't get back. She makes the men leave loose stacks of corn stalks here and there in the fields too, so maybe the Quail are safe hidden in some of them. You'd better go in out of the wind and wait while I go up and look."

Anne went into the barn and began to peep about. It was the same place where she had met Ko-ko-ko-ho the day that he took her to see the Bad One. She had often wondered what had become of the Great Horned Owl and, without knowing it, she said aloud, — " I do wonder if Ko-ko-ko-ho is alive; if he is, he must be rather old for a bird."

" Alive, House Child, but in very poor health, and nearly starved too," said a shrill voice, and with a flop and a lurch Ko-ko-ko-ho himself stood before her. His feathers were ruffled, while one wing did not close properly, giving him a lop-sided appearance.

" Why, how did you come here? I thought you didn't like barns, — or perhaps you have given up stealing chickens and pigeons, and people are not hunting for you any more."

" No, I met my misfortune in trying to get one of Miss Jule's pigeons two nights ago. We had finished our home, with an old Crow's nest for

D

a cellar, in the top of a great tree in the swamp, (we left the ledge because, after the Bad One died, too many people came there), and my mate was beginning to sit on two beautiful white eggs. I promised to bring her something good for supper.   All of a sudden the terrible things that you can feel, but not see, — the Winds of Night, — caught me in their arms, and, though I fought my best, I, who am the King of feathered fighters, — they dashed me against a tree and I dropped to the ground, in the barn-yard itself, with one wing lamed.

"Next morning, I thought Miss Jule would either have me killed or put me in a hateful cage, which is much worse than death to any of the wild-born brothers.   But they put me in a bag and brought me here and left me lumps of meat to eat.   My wing is better, but I have bad news from home. This morning, Chi-kaug, the Skunk, who lives near our swamp, came up looking for food and told me that our eggs are frozen, and my mate has gone away seeking me; for when she gave her long 'come-home' cry last night, — a call that echoes through the woods and makes even House People shiver, — I did not answer.   Those spiteful Winds of Night must have caught the message and carried it the other way on purpose."

" Why did you make a nest so early?   It was very silly, I think."

" Oh, we always do, though I don't know why; you must ask Wabeno, the Magician."

" Have you brought *us* any food?" lisped a White-vested Junco, coming shyly from a corner of the hay.   " There is a flock of us in there and some White-throats too, and Grackles and a Jay; but we are a bit afraid of that Owl, even if he is sick, and we dared not come out."

Anne opened the bag of food.   On the top were some pieces of raw meat which she threw to Ko-ko-ko-ho, while the rest of the bag was filled with acorns, cracked corn, oats, and bread-crumbs, and at the very bottom was a beef bone and a bit of suet.

" Here's plenty for all of you.   Now you wicked old Owl, do you see that crack in the floor?   Mind and be very careful to keep your own side of it, and don't even *look* at these other birds."

" This corn suits me exactly," said Tchin-dees, the Jay, politely.

" How nice these seeds are," murmured the Juncos and White-throats; " we must save that bone for Ma'ma, the big gold-winged Woodpecker, — she has scant eating nowadays, — and the Chicka-dees shall have the suet as soon as they come in."

"I wonder if my mate will *ever* find me again?" muttered Ko-ko-ko-ho, pausing as he swallowed his last piece of meat.

"Ask Wabeno, the Magician," whispered Kabibonokka, rushing through the door, and ruffling the Owl's feathers until they stood on end.

"Come out, Anne," he whispered in her ear, "and see the sign of Peboan's departure. Watch the ice bolts that lock the water into snow, slowly unloose, and see the big icicles slip away to water again."

"Yes, but before they melt I must ask those icicles to tell me how Cold, Frost, and Ice work in Nature's garden," thought Anne.

The weather was growing warmer. The Winds had stopped their pranks and were only rustling in the roof thatch. The ice crust on the snow was melting with a little crackling noise.

"Are you the icicles that Heart of Nature told me about?" said Anne to a great pointed mass that hung almost over the door.

"Yes, we are, if you are the House Child who wears the Magic Spectacles. What can we do for you?"

"Tell me about Cold and what it is good for, and please begin at the very beginning."

"Well, little Anne, the beginning is more mill-

ions of years away than you can count; but if it
had not been for me there might not have been
any earth, or it would have to have been made
differently. When Heart of God made the Plan,
the only thing he took to work with was a bit of
hot air from the Sun's breath, that he whirled
about like a fiery ball. Then he made me, Cold,
and told me to touch this ball and help to make
it solid. By degrees I cooled it on the outside to
a rocky crust. Then Water came next and covered all the earth and it grew cooler still. But
for a long time only seaweeds and shapeless
animals lived in the water; it was too hot for any
other life. Then through long ages, Heat and
Water and I worked out the Plan to shape the
earth for man.

"Heat boiling up within the earth cracked the
rock crust and piled up mountains. Again I
thrust my fingers into the rock cracks and split
them into bits, that Wind and Water could grind
to dust and scatter far and wide to cover the
rocks with soil that plants and trees might find
roothold.

"All this was in the days of the Earth's fashioning. Here, in your country, each of these time-
less days brought a new form of life. Seaweeds
and shells at first, then insects, frogs, lizards, fishes,

reptiles, birds. Giant beast brothers roamed about in tropical forests that lay in places now covered half the year with ice and snow.

"Still man had not appeared, the earth was not yet ready; every form of beast was of a higher order than the one before, the air was purer, great palmlike trees gave shade, but there were no people.

"Then was I called again. I touched the earth, who, swerving northward in its course, began to grow cold in parts where it was once warm. The tropic forests disappeared, and ice and snow were kings on this cold day."

"Please, was it as cold as yesterday, and how long did it last?"

"It was so cold, Anne, that every living thing died on the places the ice covered. I pushed my fingers deep into the rocks, tore them asunder, and sent the fragments rolling thousands of miles away to lands they knew not. My icy streams dragged along great boulders that under the mass of ice ploughed hard rocks into soft earth.

"'Stop!' said the Plan; 'now disappear and let me see your work.'

"So I retreated to far-off mountain tops, where we lie between the peaks to rest. New fruits sprang from the new soil, new trees, we had enriched the ground so that good grains might grow — wheat, oats, and corn — instead of marsh weeds. The earth was ready then for Heart of Man."

"Can you tell me whether water is juicy rock, or ice is rocky juice?" continued Anne, still puzzled; and without waiting for an answer, "And how can you work in Nature's garden now that it is all done and men live in it?"

"Is a garden ever finished, little Anne? Every fall your ground is dug and ploughed and fresh soil added to feed the plants. So every winter I go down to the water in the ground and touch it and it freezes hard. Then when spring comes again, and I call back the frost, the ice swelling as it melts splits the earth apart, ploughs into the soil and leavens it. Look in your garden soon and you will see buried stones pushed up and the earth all cracked and rent. Thus rocks are worn to make new soil, and valleys are filled and mountains planed away. Until the earth stops going round, so will the ploughing and planting go on in Nature's garden."

"When the water that froze in my pitcher thaws, will it crack the pitcher?"

"Surely."

" Why does ice swell when it melts ? " persisted Anne.

"Ask Wabeno, the Magician," shouted Kabibonokka, knocking off the biggest icicle as he disappeared over the hill down which Obi was coming slowly, carrying something carefully under his arms.

"Did you find any Quail?" called Anne, as soon as he was within hearing distance.

" They are all right, only hungry," Obi answered. " They went into the stacks of corn stalks — such things make fine shelter; but this poor bird is nearly dead. I found him most frozen to the crust." So saying, he uncovered a fine Ruffed Grouse that he was shielding carefully with the empty grain bag. It did not move, though you could tell by the expression of its beautiful eyes that it was alive.

" There is something the matter with its legs," said Anne; "one seems to be bent, and its claws are frozen stiff. I think we had better take it down to Miss Jule as quick as we can." So they hurried off, walking on the tops of the stone fences whenever they could, to save time.

" Miss Jule, may we have some warm water to put this poor bird's feet in ? They are all frozen," said Anne, as soon as they were inside the house.

"Not hot water, girlie, snow," said Miss Jule, promptly opening the window and securing a handful. "Give the bird to me; no, I won't hurt it — now turn it on its back, gently, so, and watch me rub its poor little claws." Then she began very carefully to rub each claw with snow.

After five minutes or so one claw began to grow softer and curl up, then the other. Next she pried open the bird's beak and gave it a few drops of warm water.

"Now we will put it in a basket out in the pantry, with some food near-by, and it will soon pick up," she said cheerfully.

"Please, why didn't you put its feet in hot water and set it by the fire?" asked Anne.

"Well, you see when flesh is frozen it is all hard and drawn up, and if it gets hot and thaws too suddenly, it will swell up until it almost bursts; so it is better to keep it cool and rub the cold out little by little."

"Yes," thought Anne, "the same as when the frost comes out of the ground it swells up and makes cracks in it, and the water swells up in the pitcher; only I don't believe that little bit of water could crack my pitcher, for it wasn't but half full."

After a one o'clock dinner, Anne went down to
the stables to see the horses and be introduced to
the new dog, and Obi searched among the har-
nesses for a chain or strap to lead him home
with.

"Here he is, Anne," called Miss Jule, as up
trotted a clumsy bundle of buff and white woolly
hair supported on four legs that wabbled with the
weight, each leg ending in a paw that weighed a
pound.

"Is that — a — puppy?" gasped Anne, as the
great thing jumped up, tried to lick her face, then
rolled over on the ground and gnawed one of her
rubber boots.

"Yes, and a very fine one, too, for four months
old; when he is grown he will stand thirty-four
inches at the shoulder."

"What is his name, Miss Jule, and what is the
matter with his feet? Have they been frozen too
and swelled up?"

"His name is Mat, but I think Lumberlegs
would be more suitable at present. His feet are
quite right, only his body will have to grow to
catch up with them, just as a colt has to grow up
to its long legs," said Miss Jule, laughing.

"Lumberlegs is a splendid name for him; but
somehow I thought a puppy would be rather little

at first," said Anne, with a sigh. "I'm afraid Waddles will be simply *shocked* when he sees him, and if he chose to fight, Waddles would be *nowhere*."

On the walk home Anne kept telling Lumberlegs what he must do, and begged him to be *very* polite to Waddles. He, however, spent most of the time in running around Obi and twisting himself up in the chain, until, when they were in sight of the house, Anne had made up her mind to take him to the barn for the night; but there sat Waddles on the steps looking anxiously down the road.

"Mind what I tell you now," said Anne to Lumberlegs, as Obi unsnapped the chain from his collar. Waddles stood immovable, with a most scornful expression and his head and tail erect.

Wasted words! Lumberlegs made a bound, crouched a moment, and then with one dab of his paw rolled Waddles down the steps, all the while grinning and wagging his tail as if it was the best joke in the world.

Anne started to pick up Waddles and comfort him, telling Obi, who was laughing heartily, "To take that horrid brute to the barn and tie him up."

Much to her surprise, however, Waddles picked himself up without growling, whispering, "Mistress, as he's a stranger I think you might excuse him; I couldn't have done that better myself, and, if we get to be friends, I think I see the finish of the Miller's cat."

So Obi took Lumberlegs in to be introduced to Tommy; while Anne, on running up stairs to see if anything had happened to her water pitcher, found it cracked in two.

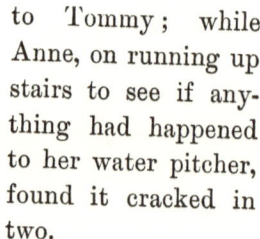

III

Dr. ᎠᎾᏋ

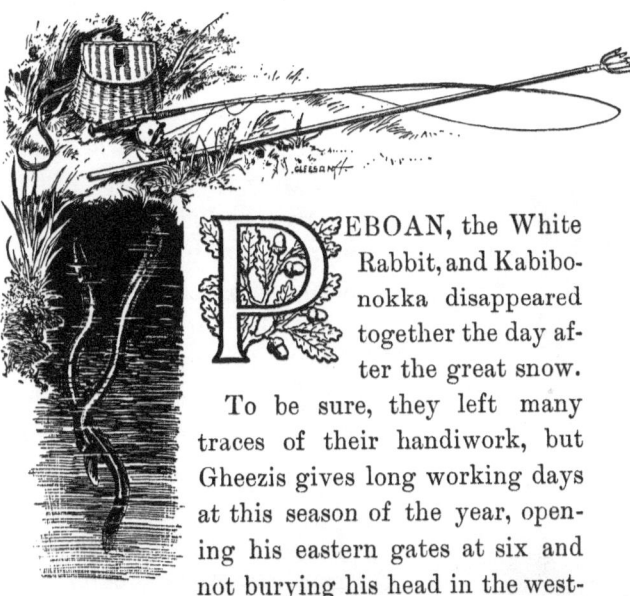

EBOAN, the White Rabbit, and Kabibonokka disappeared together the day after the great snow.

To be sure, they left many traces of their handiwork, but Gheezis gives long working days at this season of the year, opening his eastern gates at six and not burying his head in the western cloud pillows for twelve hours. Nothing is so annoying to snow as to have the Sun smile ; it is the one thing that it cannot endure, and just now the Sun fairly laughed with merriment and called the South Wind to carry his warm breath

into corners that he could not reach alone.   All
day long these two toiled together, worrying the
snow until it turned and fled, taking any way of
escape it could find.   Some of it changed to
water and ran away as fast as it could downhill to hide in the first friendly brook or pond.
Some of it sank deep into the ground, the rest
turned into mist and lifted itself into the air.
At night, when the Sun and the South
Wind grew weary, Mudjekeewis came
and swept the vapours away, or, if
they were too thick and heavy,
clinging fast to his broom,
Keewaydin came to help
with his purifying breath.
So it happened that in a
very few days there
was nothing to tell
of the great storm
but little patches
of white on the
north side of fences,
and in sheltered hol-
lows, broken tree limbs,
beaten   down   bushes,   and
streams that roared and threat-
ened to leap over their banks.

Early one afternoon, as soon as lessons and dinner were over, Anne, wearing long rubber boots, went off through the orchard and up the hill toward the old oak trees where she had first met Heart of Nature and heard the grass grow. It was her favourite outdoor playroom, cool in summer, sheltered from the wind in all but the bitterest winter weather, and dry on an early spring day like this when all the meadows and river woods were shoe deep and soggy with mud.

Anne sat down upon an old log, the remains of an oak, blown down many years before, and looked about.

"Not a scrap of a leaf yet," she said, sighing; "not even a real nice grass blade to answer questions, though Obi says there are Pussy-willows over by the mill pond. I wonder what has become of Rattle and Stripe-back, the Chipmunk? My, what a to-do the Crows are making over in the river woods! I think I'll try to wade over there as there is no one here to talk to. I wonder what has become of Waddles? I couldn't find him anywhere."

" *We* are here, House Child," said a clear crisp voice, "we are always here; and though the other trees, that give deep shade and wear leaf cloaks in summer, are bare, we are ever-green."

"You dear little Christmas tree, I had almost forgotten you," cried Anne, looking around; "and the tiny pines, too — why, how they have grown! They are taller than you, yet they are a couple of years younger. Why is that?"

"They are White Pines, and though we belong to their family, they seem to grow faster than we Spruces. You see they wear longer wands, with fewer side branches; while we make shorter growth and our leaves are much thicker, so that we give better winter shelter for the birds."

"Leaves! I didn't know that Evergreens had leaves. I thought those green prickles that grow all over you were called needles. Yes, I'm very sure anyway that father says ' pine needles.'"

"Do you know what a leaf is, and what its work is in my garden?" asked a voice from the great oak tree.

"Oh, Heart of Nature, you are back in your very own tree again. Now I'm *sure* spring has come and everything will be right," cried Anne, clapping her hands in delight. "Yes, I know about leaves, that is — a — little. They are what the tree breathes with, — sort of like lungs, you know."

"Yes, they help the tree to breathe and they

supply it with its food of air and sunlight, while under the earth the roots are busy sucking up more solid food, and sending it up in sap for the leaves. While root and leaf work in perfect brotherhood, all goes well, for each is useless without the other.

"In autumn when I call the sap backward, and bid it sleep in the roots while Kabibonokka reigns, what happens to the leaves?"

"They are through working and they dry up and drop off," said Anne, promptly; "and close beside the place where they hung, and sometimes quite under it, there is a tiny little point of a bud quite ready to unroll and be a leaf or a twig next spring. But, dear Heart of Nature, the Evergreen needles don't unroll or fall off or change colour or do any of these things, so they *can't* be leaves."

"Where did the soft brown Pine needles come from that you and Tommy raked up last autumn, to make a carpet for your play wigwam on the other side of the house?"

"They must have fallen off the big old Pines, I — suppose," faltered Anne; "but I never have noticed them come down, and the trees didn't look a bit bare without them anyway."

"The needles are as much leaves as those of an Oak. Look at this little Spruce, that you call a

E

Christmas tree," said Heart of Nature. "You
see that the needles on the end sprays that grew
last year are set closely together. Look at the
next joint of the branch that marks the previous
year's growth; they are not quite so thickly set.
Go back one joint farther and you see the needles
are scanty. One joint still farther and there are
no needles, the main stem is bare, though little
side twigs of newer growth still wear their green
feathers. So, Anne, you see by this that the little
leaf needles may cling for three whole seasons,
and as only a third part of them fall away at any
one time, the trees seem truly *ever-green.*"

"It is very wonderful," sighed Anne; "I
don't see how there *can* be so many kinds of
leaves when they all do the same sort of work."

"The Plan arranged it all," said Heart of Nature, "and then every plant as well as animal
works according to its kind. Do you remember
when the little Oak left the acorn lunch basket,
how it stretched up two hands, while the Pine
stretched out six slender claws? The differences
of things are from the very seed."

Mudjekeewis came slowly up the hill and
whispered to Heart of Nature, then they two
hastened through the woods together, leaving
Anne to talk to the little Evergreens.

"One thing I know, it is very hard to tell you needle trees apart," said Anne after a while. "I wish your leaves were not so much alike. I know a Hemlock, of course, because it waves its branches about so, and the Pines have long needles and the Spruces stumpy ones. If you only had nice flowers and fruit, it would help one so much !"

"Oh," cried the Pines and Spruce together, "our leaves are as different as oak leaves are from nettles. We have the most *beautiful* hardy fruit beside, that stays on so long that you can look at it all you wish. We are *surprised* at you, Anne, when you wear the Magic Spectacles, too."

"The Magic Spectacles are to see the rare strange sights in Whyland," said Anne, provoked at having overlooked something that was under her nose, and yet not liking to own it.

"In Whyland the talk I would teach you is of the Nearby," whispered Heart of Nature, passing down the slope again and using the very words with which he had first spoken to Tommy-Anne.

"Please tell me about your family," said Anne, turning hurriedly to the little Pines. "That is, I should like to know about as many of you as

grow nearby enough for Obi and me to see," she added.

"There are eight of us hereabouts," said the Pine. "Seven grow wild, where the wind, the Squirrels, the Jays, or our parents have dropped the seeds. The eighth lives in the big hedge at the north side of your garden, where Heart of Man planted many of them in a close row to keep the wind off, for its home woods are farther north than here.

"The Pine is the Homestead Family of us all, though we are gathered in different households as cousins are among House People.

"I am the White Pine. You see I wear fine long silky soft needles, five in a bunch. I can grow to be a hundred and fifty feet in height if I am let alone; but my white wood is valuable, and so I rarely live my life out. In late spring the grown-up Pines hang on the upper branch tips the feathery catkins that are the flower in our family. Then follows the cone, our fruit, for between its divisions the seed grows and drops away before the cone itself falls. These cones, a bit longer than your middle finger, are often smeared with pine gum, and House People gather them up to make bright fires in autumn."

"Of course, I always have some to make my 'go-to-bed' fire blaze up. White Pine, *five soft needles* in a bunch, middling long sticky cones," Anne repeated, as if learning a lesson.

"There are Red or Norway Pines in the Miller's woods," continued the little tree; "they have reddish bark and they only grow to be half as tall as we do, and they only have *two* stiff needles in each bunch; their cones grow in bunches, too, and are smooth and not half as long as ours are.

"Then the Pitch Pines over on Wild Cat

GLEESON

Mountain have
rough bark and
cones and three
stiff hard needles in a bunch ; their
blood makes turpentine, and they are
useful trees. So if you will do a little
thinking, you may easily tell us apart."

"*My* brothers are quite as easy to
know," put in the Christmas tree, who
was itself a White Spruce. "Our pale-
pointed leaves are set on singly, not in pairs,
and are only half an inch long or thereabouts. Our drooping cones are slender and
a couple of inches long, falling the first winter ; while my brother, the Black Spruce, wears
shorter cones that stand up and cling to the trees
for several years.

"The Hemlock Spruce, our graceful dancing
cousin, has flat, round-ended needles, sweeping
branches, and little loose cones that you would
hardly notice."

"You said that our garden hedge was one of

your family; but it doesn't have any needles or cones, only sort of flat twigs," said Anne.

"There again is a difference in the Plan," whispered Heart of Nature. "The Arbor Vitæ of the hedge has neither what you call leaves nor needles, but flattened scales that do its work quite as well. The reason that you do not see the cones is because your trees are kept trimmed back like bushes. The pointed-topped Red Cedars, with the fragrant heart wood, growing on the stony hill have these same scaly leaves and no cones, but instead, bluish berries that winter birds love. That flat straggling Dwarf Cedar, or Juniper bush over yonder on the ground, wears these same leafy scales and purple berries."

"It *sounds* very easy," said Anne, who had been trying to keep count of the different Evergreens on her fingers; "but I think I had better take up a collection of these needles and twigs and cones and take them home and put labels on them, the way mother does on the ferns and flowers in her herbarium. I wonder where Waddles is?" she added.

"Going down the river road with Obi," said Rattle's eldest son, who had the fall before moved into the family oak and had quite recently set up squirrel housekeeping for himself. "And, do you

know," he continued, "the great lumbering House
Fourfoot that came from the Horse Farm is with
Waddles and stays with him all the time. Yesterday they were up here trying to dig me out
and — " But he had no one to listen, for Anne
was going across lots to the road as fast as her
rubber boots would allow.

"Obi," she called as soon as she was within hearing distance, "Obi, wait — a — minute. Where
are you going with that queer looking pitchfork
and the fishing pole?" Anne dropped down on the
broad stone fence by the road to rest, for the soft
ground and her boots made running very tiresome.

"That isn't a pitchfork, it's an Eel spear, and I'm
going to the river for Eels," said Obi, pausing.
"Some of the biggest ones go down the river now,
just when the ice has broken. If they're hungry,
I can hook some, and then I'll try spearing in the
mud for the fellows that haven't come out of their
winter holes yet."

"I wish I could go too. Will you wait while I
go and ask father-mother? Please do, and I'll
take Lumberlegs back; we don't want him, and
anyway he belongs to Tommy, who has to stay indoors to-day because he was croupy last night."

"Your father said you might go; I asked him
in case I met you. I shut Lumberlegs into the

barn, but a minute ago he came galloping down the road. You see we brought him up from the Horse Farm, and so he thinks that he belongs to us."

Waddles said nothing but walked to and fro with a careless, jaunty wag of his tail, first sniffing the air, then the ground. No one noticed that he winked knowingly at Lumberlegs, who immediately made a puddle of himself in the middle of the road.

"Go home," ordered Anne, pointing back toward the house.

Lumberlegs only flattened himself still more, wagging his tail and sprinkling Anne with mud.

"*Do* make him go home, Obi," she begged; "he will splash round in the water and spoil your fishing."

Obi took a firm hold of the broad collar and braced his feet, but merciful Miss Jule had made the collar so loose that it slipped over the dog's head, tumbling Obi over backward, while Lumberlegs never budged.

"Waddles," ordered Anne, "either make that dog go home or see that he stays away from the river; *we* can't waste any more time on him. He doesn't understand one word we say, and though he is big, he is so fat and soft that I don't like to whip him."

"Yes, missy," replied Waddles, meekly, falling behind and whispering something to Lumberlegs, who grinned and immediately got on his feet, gave his companion an admiring lick and ambled beside him, until the turn in the road, where the pair crawled under some bars and splashed across the low fields toward the mill-pond.

"Say, say! they're up to mischief," cried Tchin-dees, the Jay.

"Keo-keo, hunting is hunting, so mind your own affairs and don't tell tales! I never meddle unless I'm hungry," cried Zoah, the Red-tailed Hawk, as he sailed to and fro, making magic circles in the sky, with scarcely a wing flap. Then he flew to the top of a tall tree in the river woods, where he had nested for many springs.

Notwithstanding, Tchin-dees kept on calling as he slipped through the trees, "Beware, Wazhusk, the Muskrat; take the water path back to your winter lodge.

Two House Fourfoots are on the hunting path, — one is the little Fourfoot with long ears; but the other, though newer born, is of a greater bigness than the Gray Wolves that Kaw Ondaig's great-grandmother used to know.

"Fly up from the mill-pond, Wawa, and go on your journey; you have rested quite long enough for a Wild Goose. Chi-kaug, get back under the stone fence; this mighty House Fourfoot is young, and more valorous than discreet; he does not yet even respect a Scent Cat, *though that day will come.*"

Meanwhile Anne and Obi continued down the road toward the river, and they could hear Aspetuck roaring and scolding as he rushed along, instead of whispering gently as he did in summer-time.

"Is the ice gone, and isn't it very early for Eels?" said Anne. "You know only a week or so ago we walked across the pond, above the dam, on the ice."

"It all went down of a lump two days back," said Obi. "If you want to catch the nice, fresh tasting river Eels you must be sharp at it after the ice goes, or they will have gone down, too, and the pond Eels, though some of them are big, taste more muddy."

"Why do Eels go down stream in the spring? Do all kinds of fish go down, too? Are Eels fishes or snakes, anyway?" questioned Anne;

while Obi, who was rather slow of speech, waited until they reached the bridge before answering.

It was well that the bridge was good and strong or it would have floated away that day, as many another had done before.

"I guess you had better stay up here," said Obi, presently, "while I work up stream a little and find a pool where the water is slack, or I might spear a few Eels by the falls up near the dam. If you come you'll get in over your boots, as sure as water's wet. Besides, you can see all right from here, up and down."

"But you didn't tell me why Eels go down, and if they are snakes or fish," reminded Anne.

"They're fish, I'm sure of that much," said Obi, "though I guess they are as near snakes as can be without getting into the Snake Family with both feet. I don't know *why* the big ones go down the river in spring, but they *do;* or why fish, that is *some* kinds of fish like Shad, come up the river right after the Eels have gone down. Shad don't get quite as far up as this though; they come where the river gets broad, down nearer salt water. Baldy says he always used to set nets for them along in April, for they don't bite much.

"See! Look up there in that little slack place under the old willow root. I saw an Eel jump

clean up on land and slide back again ; I'm sure
as luck that a big Pickerel was after him ! There
goes another ! My, the water in that side flume-
way is all stripy with them ! "

Obi stopped to bait a pair of hooks, his fingers
trembling with excitement, and then strode off.

" Mayn't I try to catch just one ?" pleaded Anne.

" I'd let you in a minute if it was anything but
Eels, but they are awfully snappy things, and they
squirm so you'd most likely get your fingers
hooked, and that's poor fun. Suppose I had to
cut the hook out ; you wouldn't like it a bit."

Anne amused herself by walking up and down the
bridge for a few minutes, and then kneeling, rested
her chin on the middle rail and looked into the water.

" You don't seem a bit like yourself, old Aspetuck," she said.

" I don't *feel* like myself either," answered the
river, stopping and swirling around the bridge
pier to gain time to answer. " This is the season
when I am bothered to death by all the water
tramps from the hills that rush down and insist that
I shall lead them to the sea. I'm really worked to
death, and I'm all in a whirl, as you see."

" But why do you bother with these tramps ? "
said Anne ; " why don't you tell them to stay
where they belong ? "

"Heart of Nature says that I must show them the way each spring, so that the land may become dry and be fit for the crops to grow. There, I must be off again."

"Please stop long enough to tell me why Eels go down the river and Shad come up in spring," begged Anne; but Aspetuck continued whirling by without speaking, except to scold and drive the water tramps, now bidding them stay in the proper channel and not keep snatching pieces from the banks, then hurrying them along.

"We can tell you about the Eels and the Shad, too, if you will listen carefully, for our voices are small; we must whisper and cannot roar like Aspetuck; we may only sing on spring and summer nights."

"Who are you? I can hear you, but I see nothing," said Anne, looking toward the wet bank, where a little line of foam showed rainbow-hued bubbles, as the sunbeams played on it.

"We are the Nee-ba-naw-baigs of the Red Brothers, the Water Spirits, children of Pau-pauk-kee-wis, the storm fool. No one may *see* us who lives above the water. We serve Wabeno, the Magician, and do his bidding in all the waterways."

"Do you always live in the water and always move like Aspetuck?"

"We travel here and there, singing our songs to all who listen, but our home is in the Village in the Pond."

"The Village in the Pond! I didn't know that there was anything in the pond but some fish and Eels and Water Lilies," exclaimed Anne, in surprise.

"Ah, you are very young yet, and you cannot travel all through Nature's garden even in the bunch of years that House People call life — so it is not strange that you do not know. But, as Heart of Nature has lent you the Magic Glasses, and you understand our language, you shall *see* this village if you wish. When the first white lily blooms the first day on the mill-pond, come to the landing and enter the boat that is always fastened there. Then you shall see this village, with its streets and houses, trees, gardens, and the birds that skim its air. Remember, when the first Water Lily blooms."

"Oh, how splendid! I won't forget," cried Anne; "but about the Eels and Shad. I suppose the Eels are hatched in the pond, and as soon as they are grown up they want to go out swimming and see the world."

"Oh no, House Child. The Eels are born down in the deep salt-water chambers, where the seas and rivers swirl and make eddies with the shock of meeting. In the Goose Moon and in the Planting Moon the tiny Eels swarm up the rivers. Some are of the smallness of a horse's hair and some like osier wands."

"Please, what is the Goose Moon and the Planting Moon?"

"The Goose Moon is the name the Red Brothers gave to the month of April, when the great Wild Geese flocks fly northward; and the Planting Moon is May, when the Red Men planted their corn, Mondamin the *Zea Maize*, that it might yield good harvest e'er the Moon of Falling Leaves."

"Where do the baby Eels go, and what do they eat?"

"Everywhere and everything. 'Go up,' whispers Heart of Nature, 'always up; fill the lonely ponds and silent watercourses.' The Eels obey, and sometimes gliding snakelike overland they enter land-locked ponds and springs. Sometimes they slip up the straight sides of rocks that hold back mill-ponds, and so enter them. Nothing can stop them in the spring when Heart of Nature speaks.

"Three years it takes a new-born Eel to fully grow. Then when the ice lies thick, or when it breaks up in the Moon of Snow Blindness, Heart of Nature calls the full-grown Eels that he chooses to be parents, saying, 'It is full time: go down to the sea nurseries; tarry not, but go.'

"Then the chosen ones depart, for many Eels, though fully grown, remain in ponds and lakes, and wax exceeding fat and old in idleness."

"Do the parent Eels come back again with their children?"

"No, never. When they enter the sea chambers they are forgotten of all, save Heart of Nature."

"But what becomes of them? Maybe they turn into salt-water Eels," persisted Anne.

"If you would learn what goes on in those deep sea chambers, ask Wabeno, the Magician; for no man knows, not even the wisest, if these hold nests or seaweed cradles."

"I wonder why some things are always secrets," mused Anne.

"There are two worlds, — the known and the unknown," whispered Heart of Nature, sweeping across the lowlands with Keewaydin, who was collecting and driving before him the sluggish, unhealthful vapors. "The eyes of the seen may not fathom all the lessons of the unseen, lest they grow too far-sighted and too keen, and

F

scorn the near-by things. If one mortal was allowed to go into this wonder world and then return, he would be so wise he could outwit his fellow-men, and thus the password *Brotherhood* would be destroyed. Those who wear the Magic Spectacles may always see the farthest; and if they use them well, as they grow old the glasses clarify and change, until their wearers may see even the first and greatest Heart."

The Water Spirits stopped singing for a minute, and the rainbow foam hid in the bridge shelter and grew pale.

Obi hallooed, and Anne looked up to where he stood pointing to two fine Eels that lay squirming on the bank.

"A minute ago it did seem a pity to stop their spring excursion; but if they are going to disappear as soon as they get down to the sea chambers, we might just as well have them for supper as not," argued Anne to herself.

"You wished to know why the Shad comes *up* the rivers in spring," continued the Water Spirits.

"Yes, and why he has so many loose, useless kind of bones," added Anne.

"Heart of Nature and the Plan know a reason for his fashioning; but we may only tell you what the Red Brothers say about his coming.

"Long ago, — so long that many of the great beasts of that time have been forgotten, save for their earth-hidden bones, — long, long ago, when even the first Red Men were but children living houseless and clothesless in Nature's wild garden, hunger came among these people living by the sea-ending rivers at the end of winter, and they besought Gitche Manito, the Great Spirit, to give them more food.

"They were gathered under some great pine trees by a river bank, at the season when warm rains had swelled the stream, when back in the woodland they heard the beating of Wabeno's drum.

"It came nearer and nearer; then they heard the pattering of Wagoose's feet among the leaves. Then the shadow of the Magician passed by them to the water and rested on a sandbar amid stream.

"'Watch,' said his voice, 'watch while I make a fish.' Then Wabeno chose a forked twig for the spine and, stooping, seized a handful of pine needles, which he fastened to it for ribs. Then shaped he the outside cleverly of clay until a large plump fish was there. Calling Wagoose, he bade him take it by the tail and lay it in a shallow, at the first beat of his drum.

"Then the Red Brothers heard the beating and

a voice said, 'This is my gift, my brothers, — a fat spring fish. Every Goose Moon and Planting Moon, when the sun warms the shallows through, this fish and all her race shall run upward from the sea to seek the fresh waters of her birthplace. There shall the eggs be laid, and then again, before ice locks chain the river waters, all of the tribe shall seek the warm sea chambers and there remain unseen, unharmed, until the warm spring currents bear to them anew my message, — Give you good fishing, brothers.'

"So the Shad go up the rivers every spring, and lay their eggs, seeking their birthplaces even as the birds who turn from tropic countries to the haunts where they were nested. And they still carry in their sweet flesh the tiny bones that once were pine needles."

"I wonder if that's a *really truly*," thought Anne, and then said aloud, "I can believe the pine needle part; is the rest true?"

"Ah," laughed the Water Spirits, "the Shad *truly* come up the river every spring to lay their eggs in the fresh shallows, and *truly* they go away before ice chills the water, and *truly* their bones are as pine needles; but what they do between the coming and going no one knows. As to the rest of the Shad's making, ask Wabeno; perchance he will bid Wagoose show you the very picture of it in his book, for there it lies."

" Anne ! Halloo ! Anne ! " called Obi, " come — here ! " Anne started, and saw that Obi was looking intently at something that seemed to be in his right hand, so she trudged off, going behind the alders that skirted the river so as to keep out of the water.

" What *is* the matter ? Where did that blood come from ; did an Eel bite you? " she asked in one breath.

" What I thought might chance to you has happened to me. That last Eel fought, and I got the hook in my hand — that's all," said Obi, trying to conceal his pain; " so instead of *my* having to cut it out for you, *you* will have to get it out for me."

" Oh, Obi, won't it pull out without cutting? " said Anne, shivering.

" Nope, the little ears on the hook that are meant to catch in the fish's mouth hold on to my finger the same way. It's got to be *cut*, and the quicker it's done, the better for me ; if the hook stiffens in there, I'll have a sore hand."

" Couldn't we go down to the Doctor's ? "

" He went up the mountain road right after dinner," replied Obi, taking his knife out of his pocket with his left hand, and opening it. "If the hook was only in my left hand I could manage by myself. I didn't think you'd be so silly about a little blood. When you chopped your foot with the little axe, and stepped on the scythe, and stuck in the Miller's barbed-wire fence by the hair, and got pinched by the fodder cutter, I always helped *you*, anyway," said Obi, feeling hurt.

"I'm not a *bit* afraid of blood," said Anne, suddenly stiffening up and setting her teeth. "Which blade is the sharpest? The little one, I think. Wait until I wipe it, 'cause you know everything must be *very* clean, so as not to poison cuts and bruises, father says."

The hook was buried in the base of Obi's thumb, and it would take at least two cuts to release it, he explained.

"When I say 'now,' begin."

Anne took a firm hold and never faltered.

"Now," called Obi, shouting as if Anne were half a mile away.

Out came the hook. Obi put his thumb in his mouth while Anne dropped the knife, and sopping her handkerchief (which was fortunately quite clean) in the water, brought it back for a bandage.

Just then wheels rattled across the bridge and there was the Doctor returning from the mountain. The wound was shown and everything explained.

"Famous! three cheers for Dr. Anne! I couldn't have done it better myself."

"Won't you tie it up, please? We didn't have anything to put on it but suck and a wet handkerchief, though of course, Waddles can cure all his hurts with suck and lick and no handkerchief."

The Doctor, who was as dear and jolly an old fellow as ever wore a soft felt hat and high boots, and spent his leisure in fishing, opened the satchel that always went driving with him and took out a pot of ointment, a wad of soft, fluffy cotton, a neat little roll of bandage, and some sticking-plaster wound on a reel like tape, and in a trice Obi's hand was trig and comfortable.

"I wish I had some of those things for my very own," said Anne, wistfully; "Tommy and I seem to be scratched up *very* often."

"You shall have these as a reward for *doing* instead of *squealing*. See, I'll put them in this box, and you take them home and keep them handy. Only remember that the ointment is to keep poison out of cuts — but is not good to eat.

"Jump up on the back of the buckboard, youngsters, and I'll drive you home. I think you would both look better if your faces were washed."

Then Obi and Anne began to laugh at each other, for they were smeared like veritable Indians with war paint.

Suddenly the Doctor pulled up his horse, — "Hear the frogs peeping," he exclaimed; "a sure sign of spring, though the farmers say the frost can stop them three times before it goes away. Ever been to find these 'peeps,' Dr. Anne? No? It's the best time now, with no leaves to hide them; clever little fellows those frogs, heard much oftener than seen, for they can change colour when they wish to hide.

"Hello, what have we here? Is that Tommy's

new dog ? Whew — but his face needs washing too."

They looked toward the meadow bars and there was Waddles trotting gayly along, a trifle only of mud on his feet, while behind him wearily laboured Lumberlegs, completely pasted with slime from nose to tail, and a bite on one ear, but wearing a happy expression as he scrambled through the bars and laid a great Muskrat at Anne's feet, as she went to meet him, and then put his paw on her knee, mud and all, for a caress.

" Keo-keo — good hunting for the House Four-foots," screamed Zoah, the Hawk, sailing high over the meadow again.

" Didn't I warn you, foolish Wazhusk ? " screamed Tchin-dees.

" Lucky it wasn't a Scent Cat," laughed the Doctor. " Waddles seems to have adopted Lumberlegs and, mark my words, he'll put him up to every sort of mischief that it takes two dogs to do."

" Lumberlegs will help me clear the Wood-chucks out of the rocky pasture in time," said Waddles, solemnly, to Anne; " but as you say, missy, these young animals are a *great responsibility*, and may often cause *us* to be misjudged."

" Good-night, ' Dr. Anne,' and shake hands,"

said the real Doctor as he stopped at Happy Hall gate. " Put a fresh bandage and cotton on your patient's hand to-morrow, and if it troubles him, call me in for consultation."

Anne went blissfully into the house, hugging her precious box, while Obi led Lumberlegs to the stable to have the mud removed by the carriage hose. As for Waddles, he simply disappeared, as he did not approve of water except for drinking purposes.

IV

The Signal

THE March moon was at the full before the Pussy-willows and Alder catkins could make up their minds to believe that winter had really gone, and trust their plumes to Keewaydin's rough handling. For the clear cold Northwest Wind reigned among the gray branches, played touch-about with Mudje-keewis whenever he passed by, and blustered and scolded at such a rate that gentle Shawondasee did not even venture to whisper for days together.

A night came, however, when an hour before sunset the winds' voices had altogether ceased, a mellow glow spread over the slowly greening lowlands and bare hillsides, Red-winged Black-birds gave their juicy call from afar, Bluebirds were about the barn, many Song-Sparrows sang cheerfully from garden and roadside, while a very plump bright-breasted Robin actually spied the first delicious earthworm of the season.

"Listen, how the frogs are peeping!" said Anne to Tommy, as they walked up from the barn after a visit to some very new fluffy chickens. "Don't you want to come down in the meadows and see if we can find some of the tiny little frogs? The Doctor says they are as cute as can be."

"No, I don't care for frogs," replied Tommy, with a quiver in his voice; "I care for dogs and they — don't — like — me. Father said — he said Lumberlegs was to be my *very* own, to play with me and everything; but he isn't mine one bit — not even his name. You and Obi named him before he came, and it's a dreadful, horrid name, and he is a horrid dog, and he won't stay with me, and he's too big. To-day he walked on my new soldiers and bent all their legs, and I wish father would send him away."

By this time the tears began to peep out of the corners of a pair of very big brown eyes.

Anne knelt down by Tommy and drew him close to her, for she did not know exactly what else to do. What he said was perfectly true, for though both Waddles and Lumberlegs treated Tommy with great politeness, they would have nothing to do with him.

"Come with me and look for frogs, and to-night I'll ask father to take you where they sell little dogs and let you choose one for yourself. But I don't think we will send Lumberlegs back to Miss Jule, because he was a present, and it isn't polite to return presents; besides, Waddles has adopted him for his child and is taking great pains to train him.

"Won't that be nice to have a little dog, just as little as you please?"

"Y-e-s," hesitated Tommy, blinking back his tears; "but not such a *very* little dog either — 'bout big enough to kill rats.

"There is Baldy going down the road to the mill to bring up the feed. Please help me call him, Anne; mother said I might ride down with him and buy six banty eggs of the Miller to set under the big brown hen, and I've got the money sewed into my pocket."

"Baldy! B-a-l-d-y!" The horses stopped and
Tommy was pulled up over the tailboard and
went bumping happily down the road in the
springless box wagon, while the question of dogs
was forgotten for a time.

"Baldy won't be back for at least an hour,
so I might as well go and look for the frogs by
myself," thought Anne, whistling to Waddles,
who was taking a sun-bath under the glass of
one of the violet frames, and came out looking
very guilty.

"Now, Waddles, aren't you *ashamed* of yourself," said his mistress, severely, "after all I've
said to you about being a good example to
Lumberlegs? What if he should go and take
a nap in among the violets or new lettuce, and
then when he was scolded say, 'Why not, I saw
Waddles do it?'

"Where is Lumberlegs? You don't know?
Very well, I'll excuse you this time, and you
may come down to the old spring meadow with
me, but remember no sniffing about and baying
at Rabbits. *I'm* looking for peeping frogs, and
by the way they sound I should think there
must be thousands of them."

Waddles trotted solemnly after Anne, looking
over his shoulder rather nervously from time to

time, until they were well out of sight of the
house.

"Sphee-phee-phee-sphee!" chanted the chorus
of frogs, directly ahead of Anne, where bushes
of all kinds marked the bed of a sluggish water-
course that was entirely hidden here and there
by mats of last year's cat-tail flags.

Anne picked her way carefully, stepping on
sedge tussocks and partly decayed logs, stopping now and then to pick an especially pretty
wand of Pussy-willows. She slipped once, and
trod upon something that crushed with a crisp
noise, which was followed by a most disagreeable
odor.

"Dearie me," said Anne aloud, "I wonder if
I've trodden on a bad egg; but how did it come
here? No, it isn't an eggy smell either; it's more
like a Scent Cat."

"You have smashed one of my brothers," said a
voice choking with anger. As Anne hopped to
another tussock and looked down she saw a
curious looking plant peering up from the wet
leaf mould. A thick purple and green mottled,
pointed hood partly hid, not a queer little goblin
face, as Anne half expected, but instead enfolded
a thick fleshy spike, powdered here and there with
yellow pollen. Not a leaf was in sight, though

some tiny green rolls were piercing the ground, close to the hood, which might be leaves later on.

"I suppose you must be a plant, though I'm sure I've never seen you before," said Anne, apologetically; "but I've never been down here quite so early." Then after stopping to think a moment, she brightened up and asked: "Have you anything to do with those tufts of big green leaves that I've often found here in May, and later they have bunches of hard berries? Those plants do really look something like cabbages."

"*I* am the *flower;* those green tufts are the leaves, and the berries are the seeds. A very handsome flower I am, too, don't you think, even if you do not appreciate my perfume?"

"You — are so far down in the ground that — that — I can't see you — so very well," stammered Anne, wishing to be truthful, and at the same time polite.

"May I pick one of your family? I see that there are a great many of them about besides the one that I hurt."

"No, you may *not;* we are not to be handled and made into bouquets like common flowers; we lose our attraction when we leave home. We belong to a very exclusive and aristocratic family; it counts among its members the hothouse Calla

Lily and the giant-leaved Caladiums that House
People are proud to plant in beds upon their
lawns. Besides these there are other brothers of
the home swamps, — the pale wild Calla, the Golden
Club, and the Sweet Flag. Why, that pert young
fellow, Jack-in-the-Pulpit, is my very first cousin."

" How interesting," said Anne, trying to remember all the names; " Jack-in-the-Pulpit is a
great friend of mine. We have some lovely
Callas in the study window, too, and I can see
that your flowers are shaped something like theirs.
But the Calla leaves grow first and then the
flowers, while your flower comes up first. Why is
that ? "

" Listen, House Child. To us belongs a very
great honour. We open the Flower Market ; *we*
are the very first blossoms in it ; we give the Bees
messages to carry and something to pack in the
seed-lunch baskets even before Pussy-willow has
offered her grains of precious life dust.

" To be *first* in the Flower Market we must not
waste time in growing leaves. We prepare for our
blooming far back in the old year. In autumn,
even, our flower buds are fashioned and hidden
down beneath the ground. This purple hood is
not the flower ; the flowers are huddled on the
fleshy spike within, close to the seed-lunch

G

baskets.   Heart of Nature made the hood to keep all warm, lest Shawondasee calls out of season, and we peep out only to be rebuked by Kabibonokka.

"Heart of Nature was wise; we often peep out, lured by a warm winter day, and Peboan tramples us down.   Sometimes I have been rash, and boldly pushed up my head in February, but it was useless —one flower cannot make a market, and no Butterflies came for messages."

"About your perfume," asked Anne, hesitatingly.   "Why is that so queer — I mean so different from — from other flowers, and have you any name?".

"Our perfume truly is very rare and strong It is made so, to direct the early Bees and insects to us without loss of time.   The Red Brothers give us a lovely name, Chi-kaug Flower, and in the wild countries the big bears consider us a most delicious spring salad."

"Why, then, your plain name must be Skunk Cabbage, and you are the flower that the Milkweed Monarch told me about years ago, for Chikaug was the Red Brothers' name for Skunk. The Monarch said that you are always the very first flower to bloom."   As the Cabbage did not reply, she continued rather indiscreetly: —

" Some very early flowers have beautiful leaves and a lovely perfume, too. The Trailing Arbutus up on Wild Cat Mountain, for instance, and the dear little blue Hepaticas in my woods above the orchard."

" Humph, House Child, it does not need Magic Spectacles to see that those are last year's leaves that you are speaking of; the new leaves follow the bloom with both those flowers. The great trees like Maples, Elms, Birches, and Willows all flower before their leaves come out."

" I don't think I've noticed any real flowers on those trees — only sort of queer looking little tassels and things."

" No matter how a thing *looks*, House Child," said the Chi-kaug Flower, fiercely, " everything is really a flower that has a seed-lunch basket and precious dust to fill it with. That is the important part. Heart of Nature gave flowers pretty coloured petals and perfume, to remind the Bees and Butterflies to do their work in the Flower Market. I wish you would go away; I'm sure I hear a Bee buzzing, though those horrid little frogs make such a noise that I'm nearly deaf, and if you are here the Bee will surely overlook me."

Anne skipped over the tussocks almost as quickly as a frog might, and then called Waddles, who was standing on three legs with his tail straight out, "pointing" in the most approved fashion.

"I can hear the frogs *everywhere*, but the question is, where are they? Can you see them, Waddle-kins?"

"I *smell* them every-where, mistress; but as they hop instead of walk, their trails are mixed and crooked."

"Why not look straight in front of your nose?" piped a tiny voice, as an alder bush brushed Anne's face. There, to be sure, almost on the end, perched a wee yellowish-brown frog not more than an inch long, with bulging eyes and a quivering throat.

"Yes, here I am, though most of my brothers are down there in the water with only enough of their noses out to

GLEESON.

keep their voices from drowning," said the frog, swelling his throat like a balloon.

"Sphee-phee-phee-sphee," chirped a hundred little voices.

"I'm delighted to see you," said Anne, cordially; "are you one of Dahinda's very young children? Do you know I haven't seen or heard of that great frog since last summer; where did he spend the winter?"

"Dahinda, the Bull Frog? Oh, he stays down in the mud all winter as we do. We do not belong to his family, however; he is a common Water Frog, — a lonely sort of a fellow, — while we are Tree Frogs, — sociable little chaps, and much more graceful. We have suckers on the ends of our fingers and toes to help us to climb, so we can walk up window-panes even, without slipping. In summer we may leave the marshes and go travelling about the trees and gardens, wherever we please. Look!" and the frog held out one of his hands so that Anne could see the "suckers" that looked like hollow blisters upon the ends of his webbed fingers.

"What do you think, one member of our family that lives in a far-off hot country has such big feet that he uses them for wings, and flies."

"Really truly?" gasped Anne.

"Yes, really truly; you see, as I told you, we are very superior frogs," — and the pygmy cleared his throat and joined the chorus for a moment, merely to prove that he could.

"All the marsh things seem to be very proud of themselves," thought Anne, but she only said : —

"What is your name? I suppose you must have one."

"Yes, certainly; my name is Hyla Pickering. Hyla is the family name, but when Flowers, Beasts, and Birds are given high sounding names, the last is always put first. I have a cousin who doesn't begin to sing so early in the spring, and though he isn't nearly as handsome as I am, what do you suppose he can do?"

"Jump a hundred feet at once," guessed Anne.

"No, *he can turn any colour he pleases.* If he sits on a gray mossy stone, he can look gray and mossy; if he goes on a fresh green plant, he turns green; and if he wishes to go to sleep on a branch with a mottled bark, he can grow mottled. So his name is Hyla Change-colour."

"How wonderful !" exclaimed Anne, forgetting where she was, and nearly stepping into the water.

"Heart of Nature lets him do this so that his enemies may not see him, also that he may catch his own food unseen."

"What do frogs eat?"

"All kinds of meat and game; we like animal food."

"Meat? Game?"

"Yes, flies, insects, and such things; and the big water frogs, like Dahinda, eat little ducks and lizards, snakes, mice — almost everything. In fact, Dahinda and his tribe are sometimes cannibal frogs.

"We are more dainty, and when we come up to your garden in summer, or you hear us calling for rain in the trees on the lawn, you needn't be afraid of us and throw stones into the trees, for we only do good."

"I thought the things in the trees were Tree *Toads*. Do you belong to the Toad Family?"

"No, indeed; they are clumsy, ugly things, with short hind legs; they cannot leap as we do, and their hands and feet are not made webbed for swimming. Their skins are thick and warty and full of sour juice; some of them are fine singers though, and they are great bug catchers."

"Please, Mr. Hyla Pickering, won't you tell me *how* a tree frog can change colour?"

"Ask Wabeno, the Magician," whispered a voice from the thin mist that was rising from the ground.

There was no wind, and for a moment Anne was puzzled.

"Ask Wabeno. Heart of Nature may not tell House People all the secrets of his garden, lest they grow too wise. Go up out of the lowlands, Anne; the evening mists are only good for Frogs, Will-o'-the-Wisp, and Jack-o'-Lantern."

"Oh *please*, stop a minute, dear Heart of Nature, and tell me if Wabeno is a really truly."

"Why not ask Wabeno himself?" said the silvery voice, rippling off to start the spring planting in the garden of wood and wayside, and give the Meadow-lark the key for the first notes of his spring song.

Waddles had walked uphill toward the light woods by the old barn, stopping every few minutes to point. Anne followed him, looking carefully, as there seemed to be something of a commotion going on in among the trees. Chipmunks and Gray and Red Squirrels were chattering, Rabbits hopped and scurried everywhere. A great Crow perched on a dead hickory branch, talking in a quavering voice to some Purple Grackles and Red-winged Blackbirds, and a beautiful Ruffed Grouse stood erect upon a stump, his feet braced firmly and his wing raised.

"What can be going on?" said Anne, half

aloud. "It will be full moon to-night, I heard father say, and I wonder if there is to be a spring Forest Circus. If there is, I can't see it, because little Oo-oo, the Screech Owl, said a House Person can never go to this Circus but once."

"Mistress," whispered Waddles, "don't you see those lovely Rabbits? I haven't had a good run since before the great snow, — mayn't I take one now?" and Waddles gave a little bay of suppressed emotion.

"Hush! yes, run anywhere you like, away from here. There goes a big Rabbit downhill," said Anne, well knowing that Bunnie would have a perfectly safe start of the hound.

"What is all this about; is there to be a party here?" asked Anne of Adjidaumo, the Red Squirrel, who kept dropping hickory-nut shells on her head.

"It's the first event of the year for the Bird, Beast, and Flower Brothers," explained Adjidaumo, stopping to turn a nut in his paws as his teeth sought the best spot for gnawing.

"Yes," said Anne, eagerly; "what is it called, and what happens?"

"It's called the Gathering of the Clans, and the Ruffed Grouse gives the Spring Signal," whispered the Squirrel.

"This is the first night since the Brush Beacons burned that the Brotherhood of Beasts have all been awake and keen for hunting; and though there are few birds as yet, there are enough to make the meeting legal."

"Legal! what do you mean?"

"House Child," said Heart of Nature's voice, "do you know what day this is?"

"It's the twenty-first of March," said Anne, promptly, "and the slip on mother's Wordsworth calendar said, —

> "'Like an army defeated
> The snow hath retreated,'

and it has."

"Yes, the twenty-first of March, the Vernal Equinox. According to the Plan, on this day my earth garden locks the back door on winter and opens the front door to welcome spring. Alas, in some parts of my garden she gets but a cold greeting. Still the Wild Clans remember, and at least a Beast, a Bird, a Flower, always answer my call."

Just then there was a great fluttering among the birds. There were any number of Robins and Bluebirds, Meadow-larks and Grackles, constantly arriving, and chattering to those who had stayed about all winter. A fine pair of

Hawks held themselves rather aloof, while Little Oo-oo blinked solemnly from his home tree-hole. Bob-white ran out from the leaves, but without whistling, and Anne could see the forms of many of the Brush Beacon Beasts crouching behind rocks and trees. Small Woodpeckers tapped, Chickadees whistled, and the big Flicker laughed so loud that the Rabbits turned somersaults downhill in fright. Evidently they were all waiting for some one.

"Phee-bee,-phee-bee-a," called a faint voice. Instantly every animal was alert. "Phee-bee,-phee-bee-a," sounded again clearly overhead, and in dashed a little brown Phœbe Bird, out of breath, but otherwise quite well.

"Now by this sign the Clans declare the gardens, the woods, and the fields are ready to greet Spring. Listen to the Signal!" called the Ruffed Grouse, making a rapid, continuous drumming noise in some mysterious manner with his wings.

"How did he do that? I was looking right at him and I can't tell," said Anne, turning to Little Oo-oo, who, from not having much to say, was thought to be very wise.

"How? Ask Wabeno, the Magician, for he has lent Ruffle the very sound of his own drum."

"Why do they think so much of the Phœbe,
Oo-oo? It isn't a rare bird."

"It is an insect eater, the first fly-catcher to
leave the Winter Birdland," said Heart of
Nature. "When it comes, we know that insect
wings are humming. The Phœbe, the Chipmunk, and the Pussy-willow are my pledges to
my people; not until the Clans see these will
they believe that winter is over."

Anne edged herself along nearer to the Ruffle,
the Grouse, who, to her great surprise, seemed
to know her and began to chat pleasantly.

"I don't remember having met you before,"
Anne said.

"Oh yes, you have, but you probably did not
recognize me, because that day I was in distress;
my coat was all awry and I was lame and nearly
frozen."

"Are you the poor bird that Obi found frozen
to the snow, and that we took down to Miss
Jule? I often wondered if you felt quite right
again, and where you went."

"The very same, and if you'll come up beyond
the old barn sometime in May I will show you
my mate and family."

"Where is your mate now?"

"Oh, somewhere about, waiting to be called,

when I am ready for housekeeping. It is the rule in our family that females *never* speak until they are spoken to."

"How can you call her? I didn't know a Grouse could sing."

"I drum for her, as you heard me drum just now to proclaim it spring. We game birds love martial music better than vocal; so I play the drum, while Bob-white prefers the fife, and friend Woodcock, who I see has just arrived and is probing for worms over there near the spring, has a little instrument of his own, half fife and half flute, to which he dances."

"What became of Ko-ko-ko-ho after the storm? Did he find his wife, and did his wing grow strong again?"

"His wing was soon cured, but he is banished, and I am to announce it to the Clan to-night before the trial.

"After Crotalus, the Bad One, died, the Beast and Bird Brotherhood lived quite happily hereabout for several years. Then complaints began to pour in about Mr. and Mrs. Ko-ko-ko-ho. They took two of my children last spring, and five of Bob-white's covey. Mother Rabbit lost more children, she said, than she could count; but as she always has more than she can take care of, and tries to board them free in her neighbours' gardens, we did not care much about her complaint.

"Some time ago the Ko-ko-ko-hos grew bold, as you know, and took the Miller's pigeons; but when they finally went down and robbed Miss Jule, our friend, we said they must be banished. Then those of us who live hereabout all winter held a private council and gave Reddy Fox charge of getting the pair away.

"When Ko-ko-ko-ho was hurt, the Fox imitated his note as best he could and led Mrs. Ko-ko-ko-ho a dance, off beyond Wild Cat Mountain, for she was the ugliest one to deal with. Then, after Ko-ko-ko-ho recovered, Reddy told him where his wife had gone, and he went too. So now they live in Rufus Lynx's own woods, and if they do not earn an honest living there, Rufus Lynx has promised to execute them. And he *never breaks his word!*"

"Who is going to be tried, and what are all those Crows making such a time about down in the old cornfield?"

"The Crows are to have a hearing. Last year, at the anniversary of Cock Robin's funeral, there were many complaints lodged against them as nest robbers, and the smaller birds that build

THE CROW'S COMPLAINT

in gardens and orchard trees wish all Crows to
be banished to the wild fields beyond the mountain."

"Why don't they come up to be heard then?"
asked Anne.

"They are too cowardly; that is one reason
why the Rulers of Birdland despise them so.
They are almost the only birds who will leave
their young in times of danger. Then, too,
they sneak about and lie so. Only think, to-
day they have sent a poor old Crow, who had
one eye frozen in the storm, to plead for them,
instead of coming up in a body themselves."

"Hush! the hearing is to begin," called little
Oo-oo, circling about, as the old crow hopped
feebly to a stump and cleared his throat.

"I am Kaw Ondaig, the lame-winged Crow
from the Cedar Swamp. I have been lame-
winged for many years, but now I'm one-eyed
also. In the great storm, I was too slow to fly
into the warm shelter of the old barn like the
other birds, and besides, I feared it was a trap,
so one of my eyeballs froze, and in thawing,
burst, and I am half blind.

"You say my tribe are cowards. It is too
true, but those who are always chased always
run, so it comes by inheritance. Look at the

Rabbit Family. It is the same with them."
(At the word "Rabbit," all the bunnies dodged
into their holes.)

"You say we are cannibals. We are sometimes, but only in the nesting season, when we
crave fresh meat for our young. You say that
we are ugly, croaking things, dismal to look at.
So we are, but it is not easy to be cheerful and
pretty when a black dress is all that is allowed
us the year through.

"As for singing, we have voices and sing among
ourselves, yet others do not understand our songs.
When we think we are singing like Thrushes, it is
called croaking."

"I wonder how that can be?" queried Anne,
aloud.

"Ask Wabeno, the Magician," answered Ondaig;
"Kaw-kaw, the Raven, rides upon his shoulder
and whispers in his ear. Kaw-kaw is jealous of
us, so ask Wabeno.

"May I sing you one song in behalf of my poor
tribe before they are condemned?" continued
Ondaig.

The Clan had decided what they meant to do,
but they gave Ondaig leave to sing, out of pity
to his misfortunes.

When he finished his quavering song, some of

the birds seemed quite affected, and after a little consultation the Grouse drummed once more for order, and announced : —

" This is our decision. As Crows are cannibals and nuisances in the nesting and planting seasons, though rather harmless the rest of the year, we decree that those who wish to build nests must go to the other side of Wild Cat Mountain and stay until their cannibal season is over, while any others may remain here, if they will never even roost in a tree where there is a bird's nest ! Moreover, the penalty for remaining here after to-day is to be chased by House People, Hawks, and Kingbirds !"

Ondaig flew off to carry the decree to his tribe, who were so angry that they all flew to beating him as if he were to blame. In fact, the poor Crow would probably have lost his remaining eye if it had not been for Zoah, the Red-tailed Hawk, who swooped down and dispersed the crowd, which clattered off, leaving Kaw Ondaig and another cripple behind, as the only two who did not wish to build nests.

" Go down to Miss Jule's and she will let you live about the barns," called Anne ; so the two old bachelor Crows flopped off, and any day you may see them walking contentedly in and out of the granary at the Horse Farm.

H

The sun was almost setting when Anne remembered Waddles. He was returning from his chase with something fluffy in his mouth, which, a moment after, he laid at Anne's feet.

"That is all of the Rabbit I could bring you, missy; I didn't eat a scrap, — it ran so fast," he panted.

Anne picked up the bit of fur; it was poor Bunnie's white-lined tail.

"Oh, Waddles, for shame! how could you?" scolded Anne, stamping her foot. "It isn't fair hunting manners to bite tails off."

"I didn't bite it, missy; I only tried to persuade the

Rabbit backward out of his hole by it, and the tail moulted right off, the way the rooster's tail did, when you caught him last summer."

" Oh, Waddlekins," laughed Anne, shaking her finger at him, "you are growing young and sly again, and I don't half think you are a proper person to have adopted Lumberlegs."

As they left the wood with the setting sun behind them and turned toward Happy Hall, the great silvery moon was rolling its disk above the opposite end of the road.

" There is the moon before sunset and as large as life," said Anne; "yet it doesn't look like anything while the sun is about. I wonder — if there ever was a man-in-the-moon and if there are any people there now ? "

" Hush, don't speak to me now," said a faint voice slipping down the moonbeams. "Day is not my time for answering questions. I'm not allowed to speak while the sun is up, but if you will leave your blind up, I'm due round by your window by eight o'clock, and then I may stop a bit and chat. The night is my day, so the Red Brothers called me Dibik Gheezis, the night sun.

" Anne, oh, Anne ! " called Tommy, who was dancing excitedly about the walk at the top of the garden. His father stood looking at something near the ground with a puzzled expression, and Obi was leading Lumberlegs off toward the barn.

"What do you fink, but Lumberlegs did bury his dinner bone in the lettuce bed and then went to sleep by it to watch it, all the afternoon, and all the baby plants that aren't dug up are stwashed."

"Waddles, you must have known this," said Anne. "Go down and stay with Lumberlegs in the barn to-night."

Waddles went, but he did not stay.

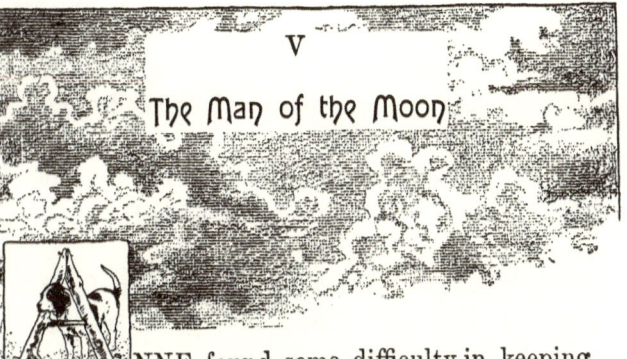

V

The Man of the Moon

ANNE found some difficulty in keeping her appointment with the moon that evening. In the first place Tommy begged that she would put him to bed and "make him a story." It took a long time to tell about the frogs and the rabbit tail, and Tommy grew so excited about the latter that he tried to make Anne promise to find the poor hurt Bunnie next day and fasten its tail on again, with some of the rubber sticking-plaster the Doctor had given her.

Then when Anne finally reached her room her mother came up for a bedtime talk, and so it was half-past eight before the lamp was put out and she pulled up the shade to let in the moonlight.

By this time the Moon had passed the farther window and was peeping in at the one nearest her bed.

"You had better go into bed and be quite comfortable," said the voice that came down the moonbeams ; "my story is rather a long one and you will be cold sitting there on the floor, for my rays cannot give you warmth as the sun's do." The voice was perfectly distinct, and yet it sounded very far off and cool, like wind that had blown over an icy mountain.

"It's very strange," thought Anne, "that I can understand what the Moon says. It isn't a near-by thing, it doesn't belong to the Flower Market or the Brotherhood of Beasts or Birds, and it certainly doesn't do any work for Heart of Nature. I wonder to what family it belongs?"

"The Winds of Night, the Winds of Night, who has work for us," whispered the familiar voices in the chimney, and, as if at their call, a flock of gray silver-edged clouds trooped past the moon, casting shadows on the floor.

"Mudjekeewis, is that you? You who go everywhere and fly far above the earth when you drive your cloud horses, have you ever been to the Moon? Perhaps you keep your chariots there."

"I never go so far from this earth garden, House Child ; round and round we winds go, over oceans and plains, over mountain tops that are almost buried in the sky ; but the Plan directs that we never leave the earth altogether, lest we lose ourselves in the great unknown, that House People call space."

"What are you and the other winds made of, Mudjekeewis ? I can feel your touch and see the work you have done, and yet I have never really seen you yourselves."

"We winds are merely the air in a hurry, — the air that is the breath of the warm-hearted earth and clings about her so that in their turn the Brotherhoods of Flower, Bird, and Beast may breathe it, and so live. When this breath of life is quiet, it is called air. House People say, ' Open the window and let in the air ; ' but when the air is restless, in a hurry, and rushes along, they say, ' The wind is blowing.' Look up at those clouds that graze like sheep far off in the sky pasture. See, ice crystals hang to their fleece ; it is the North Wind that drives them along."

"House Child," interrupted the Moon, "do not give ear to the idle words of the winds, for they have no beginning and no end ; when one brother sleeps the other wakens. The day of Dibik

Gheezis, the Night Sun, is brief, and Weeng, the Sleep Spirit, is ever wrestling with him for possession of it.   Ask what you wish to know quickly, lest Weeng touches your eyelids with his fingers."

"I'd like very much to know exactly what you are, and — and — and all the whys — everything about you — and if there are any people living on you?"

"If you wish to know who I am, it is easily told — more easily than what I was, for that is a mystery.   I am a thing of the past, a back number.   A desolate, worn-out, cold-hearted sort of an earth, destitute of everything.   I am out of heat, water, air, and people.

"I'm not even *the* Moon, as people on your Earth call me, but only *a* moon dancing attendance on my little earth as many other moons escort their earths here in Skyland, in the endless race around the Sun.   I have always been accustomed to playing second fiddle to the Earth, so of course I'm used to it; but I do think I deserve to have a better fate than to have wash day named after me."

"Wash day !   How?"

"Moonday, or Monday, as you House People will spell it, taking advantage of my helpless condition not only to name a sloppy day for me, but then to leave a letter out."

" Do you belong to a Brotherhood or Guild, or are you all alone by yourself ? "

" Nothing is by or for itself, and there is no loneliness in the Plan when it is undisturbed by cross-purposes," whispered Heart of Nature. In Skyland, where the earths and moons live, there are many families, each obeying the rules of a particular household.

" This earth where I have my garden and that moon that seems so far off, as well as many other earths and moons, belong to the household of the Sun. He rules them all according to the Plan, gives them light and heat, sets them a path in which to walk about the sky. The Sun is king over them, under the Plan, and watches always, keeping his compelling eye on every member of his family, holding each to its own pathway."

Anne crept slowly toward her bed, after raising the window shade as high as it would go, and pushing back the curtains as far as possible, she fixed herself comfortably where she could look the Moon full in the face.

" Now please, Mooney dear, tell me everything you can," she said, clasping her hands above her head. " But I wish you wouldn't move so fast; I'm afraid you will go past the window before we are half through talking. Can't you ever be still?"

"That would be breaking Rule No. 1 in Skyland, which is '*keep moving.*'"

"What if you don't?"

"Then you fall up out of sight."

"Fall up! I never heard of falling up."

"It all depends upon where you are standing; up from one place is down from another."

"But," said Anne, not feeling able to argue with the Moon, "when one of you fall, *where* do you fall *to?*"

"Ask Wabeno, the Magician, for no one who has fallen through space has ever come back to give me an account of his journey," said the Moon, blinking solemnly as a procession of cloud Elephants, Camels, and Buffaloes, chased by a great Dragon, passed before its face.

"What is the next rule in Skyland?" asked Anne.

"'*Follow your leader,*'" replied the Moon, promptly. "That is why I am always running round and round the Earth and the Earth is all the time tramping round the Sun."

"Why don't you go round the Sun by yourself and let the Earth alone?"

" Moons are only second-class sort of things, you see, and they have to serve two rulers and turn three ways at once. On their own axles, round their leaders, and along with them at the same time, while the Earth only turns on its own axle and rolls along its path around the Sun."

" Axle! why, that is the bar a wagon wheel turns on! I didn't know earths and moons had axles."

" House People use another word, *axis*, and explain about its being an imaginary line."

" I suppose they call it imaginary because they can't see it; most people say that of things they can't see," said Anne, " for you know, Mooney dear, if it was a real axle there would have to be ends to it sticking out somewhere."

" And so there are ends, to be sure, though House People will say it is all stuff and nonsense! What else are the North and South Poles? "

" Of course, I never thought of that; but why doesn't some one find them, I wonder? "

" Some one is always trying to, but suppose somebody did find them, meddled or tried to dig them up and take them to a museum or sell them for relics? Suppose some one bent them and sent the earth switching off the track right into the Sun, or maybe against me, to crack my crown?

" A pretty mess there would be, to be sure!

No, when any one gets rather near to where the
north end of that axle is buried, Wabeno beats his
drum, Wabasso, the White Rabbit, leaps from
his snowy form and wakes Peboan, and quickly
they bury every bit of food.   Then Kabibonokka
rushes by, and together they go to rivet icy fetters
around all the passages to that axle's end.   So he
who really finds it must have outwitted Winter,
the Ice King, the North Wind in his own for-
tress, Famine, *and* Wabeno, the Magician."

"They aren't outwitted yet, that's very certain,"
said Anne, with a sigh of relief that there was no
immediate danger of the earth's running off the
track from a bent axle.   "Now please tell me
how you came to be a second-class affair, and if
all the stars go about as you do."

"The Sun is the only star in the particular
family of Skyland to which my earth and I belong.   The other Suns, that House People call
stars, are so far away in other sky countries that
they seem very small, though they may really
be bigger than our own Sun, I've heard it said,
and you must know one hears a great many tales
going to and fro in Skyland during a life as long
as mine."

"Do all those far-away Suns have families to
rule the same as our Sun?"

"I don't know," said the Moon, hesitating a moment; "I've never inquired and I've never looked; we may not gape and stare, for the third rule in Skyland is ' *eyes front*,' for if one of us fell out of step the whole procession might be boggled up and we would all go flying about hither and thither like those homeless gas bags of comets with the fiery tails, that make us stay-at-home bodies so nervous when they come prowling about."

" Won't you please go back to the beginning ? " prompted Anne.

" To the beginning?   To the time when this earth and the other planets were like fiery eggs given off by their Sun parent? "

" That will do, if you don't remember any further; but I'd rather you would begin with only the Sun."

" Well then, there was that great ball of light and heat that you call the Sun, and the First Heart made the Plan to have a colony of planets about it.

" Now the Sun is not all pure liquid fire, as it seems to be.   In the very inside there is a solid dark core surrounded by the blazing, burning atmosphere, that even I can't face without winking, but that you House People may not even *peep* at unless through smoked glasses."

" How do you know that the Sun isn't fire all through?"

" That is easily learned, even by House People; they see, through their telescopes, dark spots on the Sun's brightness. What are these spots but where rifts in the blazing atmosphere show the solid core.

" In the beginning of this Sun Family, to which I belong, bits of this fiery vapour whirled away from the Sun and flew into space. Some bits flew a great way and some not so far. As soon as these whiffs of hot breath left the Sun they were told the first rule, 'keep moving,' and as the hot vapour of which they were made began to spin, it took a round shape, so at first all the pieces looked like so many separate Suns.

" The Plan had a use for all of these new globes, and they were set moving and developing, each to go in its own path until it reaches the goal marked out for it. What this goal is no House Person may know, though they are always watching and spying up into the sky to find out. No one knows the Plan but the First Heart — not even Heart of Nature.

" While these new Suns were young they were very hot and gave light like their parent; but as they gradually cooled they shrank and grew more and more solid and their heat became less and their light dim, until at this day almost all of the Sun's family shine merely by the light that they catch from his own face.

"Now Moons are not children of the Sun, but grandchildren, for they are made of the hot breath of the particular earth or planet they follow. I was of the breath of that planet which is called the Earth; as I cooled, I naturally followed her, around. So it is with other Moons that follow other planets.

"It took many years for the Plan to make the Earth ready for Heart of Man to occupy. House People may not count the time from the moment when the vapours cleared away, light dawned upon a solid earth crust, and the waters rolled back, until the day when the earth was ready to yield food suitable for Heart of Man. House People have not numbers enough to reckon it, yet to us of Skyland it seems only a few short days."

"But Mooney, what was happening to you while your leader, the Earth, was being grown?"

"I grew also, but my development was swifter. You know that when potatoes are taken from hot ashes a little one will cool much quicker than a big one."

"Yes, but how do you know about potatoes?"

"I may not tell the secrets of my past. I *know*, that is enough. You must not hurry me. I was a very small planet, so I cooled quickly, and all the changes that the Earth went through until it became the garden for Heart of Man, I, too, experienced. Mountains rose on my sides, rivers ran and oceans ebbed and flowed, and people of a sort lived on me. But I went on quickly cooling until my very heart was chilled. Then I gave off no moist breath to make air and water, for I was an experiment made to test the workings of the Plan.

"Listen, House Child. As Heart of God saw that the earth garden was complete and ready to receive the new animal who was worthy to wear his image and be called Heart of Man, the last life left my cold body. As a garden the Plan needed me no longer, and I then became merely Dibik Gheezis, the Night Sun, who was thereafter to help and be a servant of the chosen Earth of all."

"Poor Mooney, I never thought that you had ever had such an interesting life, and died of such an awful chill! I don't quite see how you are very much help to the Earth, though of course it isn't your fault. And what became of the last animals that lived on you?"

THE MONTHS

THE

The Hard Moon. Jan.	Planting Moon. May.	Moon of falling leaves. Sept.
The Coon Moon Feb.	Strawbery Moon June.	Deer Moon. Oct.
Moon of Snow Blindness. Mar.	Midsummer Moon. July.	Magic Moon. Nov.
Goose Moon. April.	Cork Moon. Aug.	Snow Shoe Moon. Dec.

WABENO'S KALENDAR

" Not much use ! " cried the Moonbeams, quivering so with emotion that Anne feared for a moment that a heavy cloud was going to hide them. "Not much use! I did not believe that you could be so ignorant. How could there be an Almanac without me? How did the Indian Brothers divide their large pieces of time? "

" I think they cut notches on a time stick, one for every winter," ventured Anne, feeling rather cornered.

" Yes, they did; but each of those notches marked a year. How did they measure the next smaller divisions? "

" They — called them — why, of course, they called them Moons. The Moon of Strawberries was June, and the Planting Moon May, and July the Midsummer Moon. So I suppose our word ' month ' comes from your name too."

" Yes, it does. Listen; this is the way time from days to years is measured. The twenty-four hours it takes the Earth to turn round on its axle is a day; half of that time or thereabouts, according to season, Gheezis, the Sun, reigns, and the other half belongs to me, Dibik Gheezis, the Night Sun, the light borrower. Always one of us is shining on some part of the earth.

" The division of the months is my work. The

I

scant twenty-
eight days that
it takes me to walk
around the Earth
gives name to the
Moonth, tricked of
a letter to month.

"The time it takes the Earth to follow
its path about the Sun is called a year,
and while it does this once, I have made
my monthly circuit thirteen times. But
House People think the number thirteen
is crooked and unlucky, so they divide up
the thirteenth month and give a few days
of it to each of the other twelve, and
say that twelve months make a year. The
Red Brothers give their year thirteen,
while Wabeno makes his Kalendar with
twelve and one long month of Moons to
bind them.

"You can well see that one who gives
name to time and dates, and has
its picture in the Alma-

nacs, is very important in the affairs of Mother Earth."

"Of course, I didn't think of that sort of work. I mean that you did not help Heart of Nature's garden to grow by making heat or rain or anything of that sort."

"No — not exactly; but I make a cool and pleasant light at night for my namesake, the Moon Moth, and his kin to see their pathways to the Flower Market. I watch the Brotherhood of Beasts upon their hunting trips, and I paint magic pictures in cloud and earth and water to give delight to Heart of Man. One thing I do besides all this, — a *very* important thing, — I help make the tides both rise and fall.

"The Earth tips as she turns daily on her axle — I mean axis — and I, though cold and lifeless, have still the power of drawing water toward me, and twice a day it rushes and rolls up and twice spreads back again."

"Is it *very* important that the tides should go up and down?" asked Anne, incautiously.

"Important! If it was never high tide how could the big ships that go dancing to and fro across the water ever reach dry land? They would all stick fast in the mud. I wish you would ask more sensible questions. And if the tide was never low, how could House People dig clams?"

"I beg your pardon," said Anne, humbly. "Will you please tell me what became of some of the other bits of the Sun's breath that turned into planets? Were there many of them, and did any others but the Earth have moon children? Though perhaps they are so far away that you aren't acquainted with them."

"I've never spoken to them, or been really introduced, but runaway comets and shooting stars from other families have given me news about them. There are eight large planets, or children of the Sun, who have separate pathways in our race track. Besides these there is a bunch of little ones that I have never heard much about.

"These eight are all of different sizes, and as no two take the same path, they are all at different distances from the Sun, and of course some are quite warm and some quite cold."

"And do they all have years and months the same as we do, and can they all go round the Sun in the same time?"

"Please think a moment, House Child," said the Moon, rather tartly. "Suppose there were eight men riding bicycles around a tree in the middle of a field, and some were close to the tree and some were on the outside edge, which would get around the tree first ? "

" The one the nearest to the tree, of course."

" Very well; it is the same way with the planets. The one nearest the Sun has only eighty-eight of the Earth's days in his year, and the farthest takes one hundred and sixty-five of the Earth's years to round the course once."

" Oh dear, how very complicated ! " sighed Anne to herself ; " the whys and hows of Sky-land are much more like arithmetic lessons than the reasons why of the Bird and Beast Brother-hood.   I'm very sure I like the Earth garden best.

" Please tell me how the planets stand in the race track.   I suppose, of course, this Earth is the biggest."

" It is *not;* the Earth is among the smallest ; it only seems big because you are plump on it. I look larger to you than Jupiter, — the largest of all planets, — but that is because I am close. I'm only about two hundred and forty thousand miles away."

" Do you call that close?   *I* think it is as far away as *forever*.   How far away is the Sun then ? "

"Oh, a little matter of ninety millions or so of miles."

" Please, Mooney, how large are you yourself?"

" Nearly fifty times less than the Earth, my mother."

" Oh *dear*, it gets worse and worse. Don't tell me any more figures, but only the names of the planets and which have moons."

" Very well — listen! Mercury is the name of the smallest; he runs nearest to the Sun; he has no moon children; neither has Venus, who comes next ; she is really the beauty of Skyland. We all admire her greatly, and she seems to know it. You yourself may often see her in the west of an evening after sunset, smiling both to the setting Sun and to *me*. I do not smile my brightest at you until after the Sun is well out of sight, for no moon may shine brightly upon its earth until after the Sun has set."

" What makes sunset, please?" interrupted Anne.

"As the Earth turns on its axle, the part you are standing on turns its back on the Sun."

" Then the Sun is there all the time ?"

" Certainly; a part of the Earth turns away, goes into the shadow of itself, — that is all."

" What planet runs beyond Venus?"

" The Earth, with me for her only moon child. Beyond her comes Mars, fiery and warlike, though

small of size; he has twin moons.   Then the
bunch of planets called Asteroids crowd along
close together.   Again, beyond, comes Jupiter, the
giant, proud, haughty, followed by four fine
moons, all as large, and one much larger than I.

"Now I speak of almost the outside boundary
of our Sun's domain, and news from those points
is vague and uncertain; still I have been told that
Saturn, the next planet, is the strangest of all the
Sun's children.   Eight moons has he, and besides,
he is girt about with shifting rings and belts of
light that whirl and vary, casting shadows on his
face so that none may surely say how they are
formed, and making him look every inch a
juggler.

"The last two planets in the race lurk so far
away that they seem smaller than the stars of
other Sky families.   Uranus has four small
moons, and Neptune, the outsider, the farthest off
of all, has one solitary companion.   Though Neptune seems small as a pin's point, a shooting star
once told me that it was more than fifty times
as large as my own Earth.   News travels slowly
from the outside to the Sun's family; sight slower
yet, so much so that what I have heard is only
hearsay knowledge."

"What makes those spots all over you, dear

Mooney, that some people think look like eyes and a nose and a mouth, and so they say there is a man in the moon ? ''

" It makes me weary," replied the Moon, yawning behind a convenient little black cloud, " to think of the senseless gossip that House People will believe and the stories they make out of nothing. I suppose that is why they started that tale about my being made of cheese, and that the man ate me up once a month and then I grew again, and the Red Brothers saying that I grow sick and die each month. Not but what it is the same in Skyland. Mars is always getting in a temper and making remarks when Mercury and Venus get out of sight between the Earth and Sun. And I've seen a few sparks of shooting stars fairly set the entire sky afire with gossip. Those spots and pits on my face are the peaks of mountains, the craters of worn-out volcanoes, and the beds of empty oceans, — that is all ; but people had rather believe tricks and fables than easy true things."

" How is it that you grow large and small, and yet sometimes when you are very little I can see the faint shape of the whole of you ? "

" Think a moment, Anne. You know that I travel round the earth."

" Yes, surely."

" When I am behind the Earth the Sun's light is shut off by it, and the House People cannot see me. But as I move about, a tiny crescent emerges from the Earth's round shadow and catches the sunbeams. Then I am called the New Moon. Gradually I creep around until I am in full light; then I am called the Full Moon.

" I continue through the light until I enter the shadow on the other side, and gradually, as I go behind the Earth again, I am called the Waning Moon, until I wholly disappear. Sometimes, when I am only the slim new crescent, if the air is clear enough, sunlight is reflected from the Earth upon my shady side to show my full face, for it is always there, though in shadow; then House People say, ' The old Moon is in the new Moon's arms.' "

" So the Earth reflects sunshine on the Moon just as the Moon does on the Earth — how wonderful ! " sighed Anne, unclasping her hands from behind her head and dropping them on the counterpane.

The Moon had crossed the window and was disappearing behind the frame at the left side.

" Why, that is the same way the Earth shuts

the Sun's light off," murmured Anne, "because the Full Moon is really all outside there now."

"Good-night, Anne," whispered the Moonbeams, tiptoeing softly backward toward the window; "it is Weeng's turn now."

"Only one more question, dear Mooney," she begged, sitting up suddenly. "Please, who were the very last persons or animals that lived on you, and what became of them?"

"Wabeno, the Magician, and Wagoose, the Dream Fox," whispered Weeng close in Anne's ear as she dropped back softly among the pillows.

VI

Wħat tħe Coal Said to tħe Kindling Wood

THE Goose-egg Moon held many cold, dreary days, in spite of the fact that the Ruffed Grouse had given the Spring Signal and Hyla Pickering and his orchestra tuned up persistently every evening.

"We can't go out to find any *whys* this afternoon," said Anne to Waddles, as they stood looking disconsolately out of the study window down toward the barns. The rain was falling in sheets, beating the fuzzy catkins off the trees and burying them in the muddy walk, while every few minutes a gust of wind brought it against the window with a swish.,

"There isn't a bird or a butterfly or a flower or anything to talk to. I wish Tommy hadn't gone to town with father and mother yesterday. I 'most think I should enjoy playing 'den and bear' with him under the dinner table," continued Anne, with a sigh, "for I've done all the lessons that were marked."

"It is dull, to be sure," replied Waddles, yawning and adroitly snapping up a big fly that buzzed against the lower panes. "I wouldn't mind playing 'snatch bone' with Lumberlegs if you will whistle him up from the barns and give us a bone."

"Waddles, I'm surprised at you, when you know that it is a *mustn't be* for Lumberlegs to come into the house in wet weather. Do you remember the first time you brought him in, when Aunt Prue was visiting here, — how he shook water all over her new cape? But what sort of a game is 'snatch bone'? I don't think I've ever heard of it. Did you teach it to Lumberlegs?"

"No, missy, he taught me. You see, as I lived so many years alone with you I knew very little about dog society and the only game I knew was 'lone bone.' In that game you take a bone and growl at it, then knock it away, or up in the air with your paw, jump after it and try to catch it as it drops, shake it, bite it, and growl again.   It is very good exercise, but it's awfully dull to have to do your own growling.   'Snatch bone' is much more exciting.   You need a good strong beef or mutton bone for this game; little bones wear out too quick.   We dogs go out in a place where there is plenty of room.   Lumberlegs takes the bone, lies down, and puts his paw upon it and gives a growl as a signal to begin.   Then I wag my tail hard.

"Lumberlegs throws the bone up in the air; we both jump to catch it; the one who gets it runs around with it in his mouth as fast as he can go, and the other one tries to snatch the bone away from him.   Sometimes we both get a good hold with our teeth at the same time, and then we wrestle and tumble and grab with our paws, and the one who holds on the longest takes the bone back to his side, growls, and then we begin again. When time's up the dog that has the bone may eat it."

"It sounds as if it might be fun," mused Anne; "but don't you ever grow angry and bite?"

"That is against the rules. You may sit on the other dog if you can, but never bite. So it's really better to play when you aren't very hungry and the bone doesn't count for so much. Then it's sport; but if you are hungry and keep getting only a taste, it's provoking, and then it's only a common fight and no real sport.

"It's nice and warm in here, missy, and I think, if you don't mind, I'll curl up and take a nap, and by and by, if you have any of those cookies that I smell baking, you might wake me up;" so saying, Waddles stretched himself in front of the fire, his nose nicely fitted between his front paws.

A fire of cannel coal in a basket grate rested on the fire-dogs, instead of the usual logs; for it had been such a long cold season that the big log pile had burned away too fast,. and the woodhouse was nearly empty. Anne kneeled on the rug, opened a long box that served as a window seat, and looked in. There was not much to see, — some great lumps of coal at one end, while the rest of the box was filled with pine kindling wood, split in various lengths and sizes.

"Miss Jule said she would give me a big knife like hers, with three blades, a hoof pick, and a punch in it to make holes in leather, just as soon as I could whittle a good-looking clothespin with my old knife. I think I might as well begin now," said Anne, taking a small but stout jack-knife from her pocket.

"It would be better to have a clothespin to copy, though. I think I smell cookies too, — the crispy, gingery ones."

In a moment Anne returned with the clothespin and nearly a dozen thin, scallopy cookies on a plate, which she set carefully on the floor beside her. Next she selected a bit of wood from the open box, propped herself against it, and began to whittle very slowly and carefully.

"Cri-cri-crick!" cried the Cricket under the hearth.

"Buz-bumbl-buz," answered O-o-chug, the House Fly, beating his head recklessly against the window.

"Humph! the Voiceless Brotherhood is waking up," said the near andiron, as a tiny gray Moth, with silver-powdered wings, crept out from the edge of the hearth rug and fluttered to Anne's skirt.

"What is the Voiceless Brotherhood?" asked Anne. "I never heard of that before."

"All the insects and animals that have no voices in their throats, but speak with some other

parts of their bodies, or by signals," said th
Cricket, coming out of his crack and crossing th
hearth with a single jump.

"But surely you have a voice; you mak
almost as much noise as Hyla Pickering."

"I have a call, — for Heart of Nature gives t
every animal who needs a mate some way of call
ing her, — but no voice. My call is like the cry
a fiddle gives, — watch and listen! Look at my
upper wings, see the rough spot on their under-
sides; I draw one of these wings to and fro
across the other and the call is given; but it does
not come from my throat, for I have none, and no
lungs. Listen again, 'Cri-cri—cri-cri-crick!'"

"How strange that is!" cried Anne. "But
you must be different from birds and frogs; they
sing and call to their mates mostly in spring, but
you cry all summer long. That is, I think you
do, if you are one of the Crickets that live under
the grass."

"Yes, I'm a brown Field Cricket. I have a
summer home outdoors, but when winter comes
I creep inside, and if the house is warm it makes
me think it is spring, and I chirp up. The reason
why I chirp all summer is a great family secret;
but I don't mind telling you, because you are such
a friend of Heart of Nature.

"In our family the females not only have no voices, but no way of making any sound at all, and so we are allowed to sing to them all the season to keep their spirits up.

"We are a very revengeful family, and if any House Person kills one of our kin, Wabeno shows us the offender, and, biding our time, we work our way into his house and, with our sharp scissor jaws, cut his best clothes to strips. We are very strict, too, among ourselves, and if one of our children or our mates disobey, we immediately eat up the offender, and there is an end of the matter without discussion. Yet, if people are good to us, we not only do them no harm, but soothe them with our songs and coax them to sit and rest by the fire and see the Dream Fox's picture-book.

"I have a big cousin living in foreign countries who loves House People so well that he always lives in houses, and some people like his song and keep these Crickets in cages like song birds, — cri-cri-cri!"

"What are you, and where are you trying to go?" asked Anne of a little Moth that was striving to crawl under one of the plaits of her tartan-plaid skirt. "You are very small and not a bit pretty. Are you any relation of the Moon Moth

K

or the Milkweed Monarch or Tiger Swallow Tail
I can hardly see how you look. Do you work in
the Flower Market? If you do, I should think
you would only be able to carry messages for
tiny wide open flowers like Mignonette or Can-
dytuft."

"I'm only a very distant relation of those big
Butterflies and Moths. No, I do not work in the
Flower Market; in fact, I have a very dull time.
I dislike bright sunlight and prefer to stay in-
doors. I belong to the Wool Exchange, and am
particularly interested in the carpet business.
Please let me get out of the light and hide in
your skirt."

"Don't you let it!" buzzed the House Fly;
"if you do, that sly little thing will lay eggs in
some corner of your gown, and then when they
hatch into worms they will eat the cloth and
spin up into cocoons, and more Moths will come
out. These evil young Moths make holes in
everything woollen, and mow the fur from muffs
and capes as if they were cutting grass.

"What is worse, too, these wicked little Moths,
working slyly in the dark, lay two broods a year,
— one in spring, one in late summer, — so woe be-
tide those who give even a single Moth a hiding
place. Kill that one, Anne, with a swift pinch;

for if he holds the Wool Exchange all summer in your pretty gown, it will be fit for nothing but Rag Fair in the autumn.

"How do I know this? Despised as he is, persecuted by men and spiders, beaten out of houses and caught by the wings on sweet sticky paper, O-o-chug, the House Fly, sees a thing or two as he walks head downward on the ceiling, and I see two other Voiceless Ones in this room that ought to be put out."

"Oh, what are they?" cried Anne, starting up and looking into the shadowy corners; "I can't see a thing. There, I've pinched that Moth, and he has all turned to gray dust."

"I know you don't *see* anything; that is why the things are very dangerous. Take up the corner of the rug behind the sofa — what do you find?"

"Some mites of beetles, kind of mottled, with a wavy red line on their backs; they look something like Lady Bugs. Oh! and when I touch them they draw up their legs and play dead."

"They are *not* Lady Bugs, but father and mother Carpet Beetles. They fly about, in and out, in the summer season and feed upon plants; but when they lay their eggs they creep into floor cracks and dark crannies. In a few days, if it

is warm enough, their eggs hatch into larvæ covered with a woolly skin that looks like a shred of dark brown worsted. This is called the Buffalo Moth. How it eats and eats, moults its skin and eats even that, doing this half a dozen times and working great damage, until it is fully grown! Then it splits this skin for good, and you can see the legs and wings of what soon will be a full-grown Carpet Beetle.

"If your fine rug is riddled with holes from underneath, blame the Buffalo Moth. If a new blanket looks like a target full of small shot, blame the Buffalo Moth. Cloth, cotton, paper, fur, lace, — all are grist for its mill."

"Then I'll kill these Beetles too," said Anne,

promptly executing them with her knife. "Now, where is the other bad Voiceless One?"

"The third is the Book Louse, a partner of the Book Worm," said O-o-chug, "and even now they are eating the paste that holds the binding on those old, leather-covered books, on the high shelf, that your father says you must never touch. Tell him from me that he had better give those books a sun-bath for their health, else their backs will soon grow weakly and mayhap break."

"Missy," said Waddles, suddenly waking up, "was I right about the cookies?"

"Yes, sir, you were; but I was so busy with these voiceless things that I forgot all about them. No, don't help yourself; wait until I break your share into pieces and put it on a paper."

Waddles stretched his legs, bowed his back, and licked his lips, saying in a half-grieved voice: "You always used to let me eat out of your hand and never bothered about catching crumbs in paper. Besides, I never spill crumbs."

"I know it, Waddlekins, but it's one of your responsibilities; Lumberlegs slobbers and spills such lots of crumbs, that mother said, 'If you feed the dogs in the house, they must eat from a paper.' I guess rules are always made for the crumby people."

"Then why don't you eat off the paper too, missy? You are making crumbs," and Waddles began to pick them up daintily with the tip of his tongue.

Anne laughed and hugged him so suddenly that she tipped against the wood box, at which a lump of coal lost its balance and rolled into the kindling wood.

"Keep your distance, Smutty Nose!"

"Smutty Nose, indeed! How dare you call me that?"

"Well," said the Kindling Wood to the Coal, "who are you?"

"House People call me Coal, and sometimes when the weather is very cold, King Coal."

"They spell the real *King* Cole's name a different way," interrupted Anne.

"They couldn't very well do that," replied the black lump, "because *I* am the real King Coal; the *other* man was the usurper, so he didn't dare spell his name correctly for fear of being arrested for forgery."

"How is it that an old hard dead thing like you can burn as well as I, who was last summer one of the tallest pines on Wild Cat Mountain?"

"I don't think that is half so strange," said King Coal, brushing the dust from his face, "as the reason why either of us burn at all. Do you know why we do ?"

" I only know what the Winds of Night whisper to us on the mountain from the time we reach our six green finger-tips above the soil, until the axe stroke tells us that our tree life is ended.

"The Winds say: ' Reach out, O Pines; with both foot and hand draw food from the earth and stretch begging palms to the sky ; grasp the sunlight, hold it fast. Grow, swell your limbs, and prepare greater storehouses for the hoard of sunbeams. Warm shall they feel as you grasp them, yet they soon grow cool in the storehouse. But when Wabeno speaks or touches you with fire, back to the air shall these stored sunbeams return, and all that will remain of you will be the ashes of the storehouse walls.'

" All this is true. For twenty years I stretched out my hands and begged for sunbeams, grasping and hoarding them. To-day they throw my ribs into the grate and touch fire to them. Wabeno calls ! I blaze, and all the store of sunlight disappears into the air and leaves a pinch of ashes."

" And you pass on the magic touch ? Do not I blaze, too, when your heat touches me ?" asked King Coal. "And though I blaze longer and fiercer, is not my end the same — a heap of ashes ? "

"Certainly," said Anne, "and both sorts of ashes are grimy things, only wood ashes are good for plants and coal ashes aren't. I don't think if I were you, Kindling Wood, I should call King Coal 'Smutty Nose,' for though you are certainly cleaner in the beginning, it seems to me as if you might be relations."

"We are," said the Coal, "though it isn't to be wondered at that this newly cut pine wood should not understand the relationship, for it has taken the cleverest House People years and years to find it out. The story of it seems stranger than the wildest picture in Wagoose's book, and more wonderful than all the tricks of Wabeno, the Magician.

"There are many magic gases floating about the Earth that are not needed for the Brotherhood of Man or Beasts to breathe, — in fact, some of these vapours are very hurtful to animals. The Plan says that the Plant Brotherhood shall suck these gases from the air, digest them, and return part of them to the air again purified, while the plant keeps the hurtful part for its own food."

"Humph!" said the Kindling Wood, "I didn't know exactly how it was done; but I knew I was always sucking in and breathing out, and that the Winds of Night were always bringing and taking

vapours from my leaves.   But how, pray, did you
know all this?   Did the rock of which you are
made come from a forest?—for of course you
are a rock."

"Everything in Nature's garden belongs to one
of three great Brotherhoods,—the Animal, the
Vegetable, and the Mineral," said King Coal, "and
I have belonged to two of these,—the Vegetable
and the Mineral.   I once was a plant, a tree of a
forest thicker and greener than any that have ever
been seen by Heart of Man.   I am now a piece of
coal, a mineral claiming kin with rocks, dug deep
from the earth.   Between the beginning and the
end of my life are many steps and as many years
as the leaves in all the forests of the world.

"There is in air, be it ever so pure, a vapour,[1]
that plants need for their daily breath.   Now
listen to how this gas was caught from the air in
bygone ages and turned into coal.

"The Moon, I suppose, has told you often how
she and her master, the Earth, were once fiery
balls formed of the Earth's breath?"

"Yes," said the Kindling Wood, "the Moon
talks about little else but the past; but we trees
on the mountain never believed what she said."

"You should believe the Moon.   She tells the

---

[1] Carbonic acid gas.

truth, for she has seen whereof she tells," said King Coal. "We have known each other ever since I also stood in a mighty forest jungle."

"Did House People cut you down, did the Winds play pranks and uproot you, or did Wawa-sa-mo, the Lightning, rend you?" asked the Kindling Wood.

"House People cut me down? There was none such in my day; never did I see the face of Heart of Man until, by a deep thunderous noise, I was shaken from my earth bed. When I was of the jungle, Man and the animals nearest to him were not yet made.

"It would have seemed a strange world to a Pine tree. Gigantic Lizards and huge Frogs swam in the waters, but no birds sang among the tall rank trees, or left their tracks in the mud; none of the Beast Brothers of the woods had come.

" The plants bore no gay flowers; they were of the Flowerless Tribe, such as your ferns, mosses, and horsetails, that carry but seed-dust spores and wave no gay petal flags in the Flower Market to lure the insect messengers.

" Nature's garden was not ready for them; the solid earth crust that rose here and there above the waters was yet thin; heat and steam made the plant growth thick; the air was still heavy with the gases that plants may suck, but that may not be breathed by man.

" Heart of Nature said : ' Grow exceedingly, ye Flowerless Plants; increase and multiply beyond belief. Suck the poison from the air and purify it; the Plan says it must be so.'

" We grew and sucked and dropped our seed and leaves, and grew again, until blackening leaf and wood mould lay in deep layers, black with the carbon the living plant had sucked and stored away."

" I don't see how air could turn into smuttiness," said Anne.

" Go to the woods to-day and you will see that it is so. Rub your hand on a smooth old tree trunk, are not your fingers smutty? Look at some dead ferns that lie sodden and beaten into the mud, are they not blackening also?

" When all the growth of many years lay in a mass decaying, and the earth's crust sank a little, no more trees grew, and water began to spread layers of mud over where our jungle was, as water covers the leaf mould on a pond's bottom. Then the mass took the first step of its long journey from wood to coal land, changing at each stopping place, and in some cases lagging behind and never reaching the end of the great transformation.

" At the first stop the blackening mass was what House People call peat, a mossy, spongy sort of stuff that may be cut in blocks, and smoulders slowly as it burns. You may find this change going on in many places even to-day.

" One day the earth crust heaved, rose, and overlapped the jungle, as scum folds over on a boiling pot; so heat and weight were added to the mass, from which some gases escaped and others boiled down to make new substances. After a long wait, compressed and molten, we grew browner and more solid and became what is called *lignite*, or brown coal. This has such a sulphurous breath that it chokes House People when they burn it. After this, harder and blacker we grew, and straightway stepped from plant to rock land, or from the Vegetable to the Mineral world.

"Look at me! I am the first of the true line. House People call me Cannel Coal. Am I not glossy like jet, that is also a kinsman? When I feel the touch of your magic torch, see how quickly I give back my stored sunshine in an oily tongue of flame!

"But though I have stored much carbon there are others of my family, all older than I, who hold more. Two brothers I have, — Soft Coal that House People burn in locomotives, and Hard Coal that makes the steady kitchen fires. Two cousins also I have, the first named Black Lead, that House People know quite intimately,— using it in their pencils and making it speak their thoughts."

"To be sure," cried Anne, "I never thought of it; but lead is very like coal. What is the other cousin? I think it must be ink."

"No, the other, the rarest, the one that has made all the changes and is the farthest away from wood, is the Diamond."

"The Diamond!   That beautiful jewel in mother's ring? How *can* that be, King Coal, when all the rest of the family are sooty and can be burned, and the diamond is so clear and white and hard that mother wrote my name and Tommy's on the study window with hers?"

"Ask Wabeno how it came to be so clear and pure; but this I know, that it will burn away even as I myself, if fierce magic heat is blown upon it, and nothing be left but a pinch of ashes!

"Besides all these, many other things were boiled from us as we lay buried, for the astral oil you burn is only coal juice and our mass unearthed by Heart of Man yields priceless dyes and drugs and medicines, that were all drawn from the air through the breathing of the trees of that ancient jungle.

"So you see, friend Kindling Wood, that we are kin, though parted in age by countless years."

"Does all the coal we burn come from your jungle, and what shall we do when it is all dug out?"

"There were jungles dotted almost everywhere that the earth's crust rose above the waters. As one sank and began its trip to Coal Land, the Plan planted another on top of it again and again, until the earth's crust was filled with coal veins."

"Just like layers in a jelly cake!" cried Anne clapping her hands.

" Jelly cake, where ? " said Waddles, starting up suddenly and then looking foolish when he realized his mistake.

" This time was called the Carbon Time,"[1] continued King Coal, " because during it the carbonic acid gas from the air was sucked up by the jungles and made way with. The air then became pure, and higher animals appeared, according to the Plan, — Reptiles, Birds, Mammals, like your cows and horses, and finally came Heart of Man.

" Listen, House Child ; when this last Heart came he dug in the earth's bosom and found King Coal and gave him the magic touch that let loose the sunshine stored away in days when man was not, — he alone had a use for King Coal, who had cleared the air and made it fit to be breathed by man.

" Now put me on the grate, House Child, push under the kindlings to give the magic touch, and hear me sing the song of those old days that is pent up within me."

Anne carefully laid a few sticks on the red ashes and placed King Coal on top. The wood blazed and the lump settled, but still remained cold and black. She gave it a sharp blow with

[1] Carbonic era.

the poker, and instantly King Coal quivered and little rivulets of flame ran down his sides whispering strange words. Anne listened to catch their meaning, but they spoke swifter than the Winds' Voices, and murmured more confusedly than the leaves to the raindrops. While in the smoke that went up the chimney she saw strange scenes and shapes that vanished, until a puff of smoke driven back by the damp chimney made her choke.

"Dearie me! ouf-ker-chew! If the gas that coal breathed in to make itself was as bad as what it breathes out in unmaking, I don't wonder it took Heart of Nature a long time to pack it all away to bake in the ground and give the sky a good cleaning.

"Oh, there is the sun! How much nicer the old dear is than the grandest hearth fire! Waddles, Waddles, wake up! It has cleared off and Lumberlegs is whining outside. Come out and play 'snatch bone.' I'll get you a fine rib from yesterday's beef if you'll let me play too, and I'll only growl and run without snatching."

So Anne shut the cover of the wood box, pocketed her half-whittled clothespin, and shook the shavings into the fire, leaving the Kindling

Wood wondering how long it would have taken for it to turn into coal if it had not been split up for kindlings — a question which neither the Hearth Cricket nor O-o-chug could answer.

VII

Kayoshk', the Sea Gull

EEWAYDIN and Wabun were abroad
one April night, running a race for mastery.
Wabun, the East Wind, clad himself in vapours
and clung close to the earth, and the smell of the
sea was heavy in his garments; but Keewaydin,
the wind from the northeast heights, rose higher
and drove the clouds across the sky. Whenever
they met or overtook one another there was a
wrestling match that lashed the tree-tops, making

the pines sigh with pain, and even wrenching the joints of the great oaks until they scolded and complained.

Anne could not go to sleep for a long time that night, but she lay quite still and comfortable, wondering what all the little noises meant, until something sounded at the keyhole, murmured in the chimney, paused at the window a moment, and then slipped in at the top where the sash was lowered.

"The Winds of Night, the Winds of Night, who will give heed to us, for we have a tale to tell?"

Anne sat up in bed to listen ; the breeze touched her cheek and ruffled her hair rudely, so she quickly nestled down again, drawing the coverlet close under her chin.

"Is it you, Kabibonokka ? I thought the North Wind had gone home to stay until the next Brush Beacons burn. I hope you haven't brought Peboan with you, because the Phœbe has come, the Grouse has given the Spring Signal, and everything believes it; the Willow has waved some yellow wands, and all the other trees are hurrying to bud out. Baldy has taken the covering off the strawberries, and in a few days, as soon as he can cart up some seaweed from the shore to dig in with the manure, we are going to plant a new asparagus bed. It takes an asparagus bed ever so long to grow big, two years I think, so if you are going to freeze up the ground again it will be very inconvenient for our garden."

"Stop, take breath and listen, Anne! It is not Kabibonokka who speaks. It is I, Wabun, the Wind of open places, the Wind of the Sea, friend of Kayoshk', the Sea Gull, of Mang, the Loon, and of Wawa, the Wild Goose, — Wabun, the East Wind, who sings the Song of the Sands. To-night is my last night of mastery before the Sea also gives the Spring Sign to its people and gardens, and I return to my home in the Morning Star."

"Oh, I'm very glad that it is you, Wabun! I've been thinking of you for ever so long. Don't you remember the night that I saw the Brush Beacons burn, you promised to come back and sing me the Song of the Sea, and tell me how it counts the sands where the Plovers' eggs lie and the Sandpipers dance? I was afraid that you had forgotten all about it. Does the Sea have gardens and a Spring Signal too? And what is the Signal, Wabun?"

"Surely, the Sea has its gardens. Its Spring Signal is the call of the first northward flying

flock of Wild Geese. Hist! the cry sounds
even now afar. Wawa's shadowy troop is passing over ; I go to give them news, then I must
wait till dawn and whisper of their coming in
the ear of Day.

"Meet me to-morrow, Anne, down on the shore
where the lighthouse guards the rocks, and the

long sand finger
points out to Sea, and
Kayoshk' sings his song."

"Down on the shore ! To-morrow
I wonder how Wabun expects me to get there,"
Anne said aloud. "Perhaps he thought I could
go down with Baldy for the seaweed. I don't
suppose he remembers that it would be a dreadfully long, wet ride home, and mother would never
let me go. Twelve miles is only a mere hop for
the East Wind. To-morrow will be Thursday,
too, and I must have my lessons. I do so wish
I could hear the Gull's Song, and see some of
Wabun's bird friends, because when we go down
there in the summer they are all gone, and last
summer we didn't go anyway. I heard father-

mother say we might go this year though, because
the new lighthouse keeper is Baldy's brother, and
he isn't to live in the light in summer, but in
the cottage on the rocks. His wife used to live
with Miss Jule, so maybe we can arrange to stay
there a whole month; but that will be too late,
I'm afraid."

The door opened softly, and Anne turned, half
expecting that Wabun had come back, but it was
her father, who said, "Did I waken you? It is
only I, little Owl. The wind is blowing so strong
from the east that I was afraid it might chill you,
and I came to put up your window."

The next morning was bright and much warmer.
Oh, what a day to go to the shore. As she was
dressing, Anne saw Baldy harnessing the farm
team, fitting the high sides to the wagon, and
otherwise preparing for an early start. Yes,
there was Obi, who was going also. He knew
exactly where to find the most shells; it seemed
cruel to have to stay at home. But Anne never
thought of teasing her mother to let her go, because she knew that a ride home on damp seaweed was a "mustn't be."

However, she was so thoughtful at breakfast
that she did not hear Tommy ask her to take

" the cap off his egg " for him, and did not notice when a groom from the Horse Farm clattered up to the side door and a note was handed to her mother, who read it and handed it to her father with a little nod of approval.

" Anne," he said, " how would you like to have a holiday now instead of on Saturday, and drive down to the shore with Miss Jule? She is going to carry some things to the lightkeeper's wife, and she thought that perhaps you had never seen the beach at this season, when the Sea Gulls are there."

Sometimes when Anne's heart was too full for words, she could only clasp her hands and look what she felt, and this was one of those speechless joy times.

Tommy, however, was affected differently. He dropped the egg he was holding, which fortunately was not soft enough to do more than say " squnch," as it struck the table, clapped his hands and cried, " I don't have lessons, so of tourse *I* can go ! "

" Waddles isn't going," said Anne, preparing to soften the necessary refusal.

" Then I s'pose we'll have to do wifout him," said Tommy, looking ruefully at the egg, but thinking only of the excursion.

"Miss Jule did not ask you, dear," said his mother. "She is going in the little road wagon that only holds a passenger and a half, at best; it is a long ride, and it would make you too tired to go to the shore and back the same day."

"Oh father-mother," he begged, with sounds of tears in his voice, "mayn't Anne go down and ask please for Miss Jule to go in a bigger wagon and stay all night? Miss Jule would if Anne begged; 'most everybody does, even dogs," he added, showing that he knew his sister's gentle power.

"But, Tommy, that is because Anne does not beg for greedy things," said his mother, smiling. "Why don't you have a picnic for the dogs this morning?" she suggested; "there are some nice beef bones that they would enjoy for luncheon."

"Yes," added Anne, "and then perhaps they will play 'snatch bone' for you; it's a very nice game."

"Snatch bone! I'd like that," said Tommy, instantly interested. "How do dogs play 'snatch bone'?"

"That's their secret," said Anne; "but you take them over to the grass field and give them the bones, and after they have eaten the meat off you'll see the game."

Miss Jule and Anne set off before nine o'clock. A road that is long for a stout farm team and a springless wagon seems short for a thoroughbred horse and light road cart, so in spite of many stops to look at this and that, they soon overtook the farm team and reached the shore a full half hour before noon.

While they were yet some distance away Anne could hear the sound of the water and see the Gulls sailing to and fro. Flocks of Crows were going down over the marshes, and the Meadow-larks were calling everywhere.

I wonder why the Gulls and Ducks and Sea Birds never come to celebrate the Anniversary of Cock Robin's Funeral," said Anne half aloud ; then asked, "Miss Jule, where are all the Sea Birds that make Humpty Dumpty nests when the Brother-hood of Builders are at work in the garden ?"

Miss Jule had to think a moment in order to understand exactly what Anne meant. In talk-ing to her father, mother, and this dear friend Anne often forgot that they did not wear the Magic Spectacles, for the three always sympathized with her and seemed to know her thoughts.

Just then they left the road and turned upon the crisp pebbles of the beach, and Anne forgot everything else in the sight before her.

The tide was half low, and foamy little waves curled along the sandbar and broke upon the beach; every sand island left bare by the falling water was covered with Gulls, while others flew calling through the air, and flocks of Ducks were continually rising.

"You can stay here awhile and watch the birds," said Miss Jule, "and when you are tired come up the back of the rocks to the lighthouse. I will go in to see Myra and ask if she will make us some of her famous clam fritters for luncheon."

Anne threw herself down upon the beach under the shelter of a ridge bound together by the strong roots of sand grass. As she wore a gray ulster and cap, she seemed to disappear and become part of the shore itself.

"I was afraid that you would not come," called Wabun scurrying across the bar, driving the sand in wheels before him. "The Geese are giving the Spring Signal of the Sea, near and far, and carrying it across to inland waters; the Shad hasten up the river to lay their eggs, and the hearts of all Sea Birds beat high with the thoughts of their nesting haunts that begin to call them northward with the Winds' voices. See, the call stirs them and they are rising and flying boldly by day."

Anne looked up and saw a long line of birds passing over ; they seemed to have no tails and very long necks. Suddenly their leader gave a hoarse call and wheeled, the entire flock dropped near a marshy pond a few hundred yards back of the shore, while at the same time a flock of black, white, and gray Ducks rose from the other side of the bar and lining up after a little skirmishing flew close above the water almost due northeast. Anne kept perfectly still from sheer amazement, looking first at the sea and then at the sky. Suddenly a Gull with a pale gray coat and black wing tips flew over crying, " Wake, a-wake-wake ! " and suddenly sank to the sand close by Anne.

" I'm awake," she answered. " I couldn't possibly go to sleep here with so many ' whys ' that I want to know, swimming and flying around."

" You must be the friend of the Winds of Night, —the House Child who wears the Magic Spectacles," said the bird, " for I can understand your words and you mine. Wabun, the East Wind, bade me find you and tell you my story. I am Kayoshk', of the Red Brothers, the bird that House People call the Herring Gull."

" I am very glad to speak to you," said Anne, sitting up, as she saw that the bird was not afraid.

"I've never even seen any of you until to-day. Where do you spend the summer, and why do you never walk with the Bird Brotherhood at the Anniversary of Cock Robin's Funeral?"

"Cock Robin! I never heard of him," said the Gull; "he must have been a Land Bird, while we, Children of the Sea, have different voices, haunts, and habits. The only anniversary we celebrate is the 'Death of the Labrador Duck.'"

"You've never heard of Cock Robin, and I've never heard of the Labrador Duck, so we're even. Were you very dear friends, and did you live near it? Was it a pretty Duck, or good to eat, and why did it die?"

"One question at a time, if you please. I think I must tell you my story, if you wish to know so much about our world.

"We Sea Birds come chiefly from the far north, where the North and East Winds rock our cradles. We are of many families, whose names even you could not remember, — Auks, Puffins, Petrels, Loons, Grebes, Sea Ducks, Terns, and many others besides. Though we are of different tribes, one thing unites us — the love of the water."

"Auks!" cried Anne, joyfully; "then you must know 'His Grace, the Great Auk,' who ran away

on a bicycle from the Smithsonian Institute to
come to the Forest Circus. Only he was very
dry and dusty, and said that he was so rare and
had been dead so long that he was worth hundreds of dollars."

"You don't tell me that you've really seen one
of those preposterous birds," said Kayoshk', very
much interested. "Now, though I'm a Sea Bird,
I've only heard of them, for they've all been
dead these fifty years and more; but their first
cousins, the Razor-billed Auks, that live near
us in the north, and come down the coast visiting
with us every winter, are always bragging about
these big relations of theirs, and I never really
believed before that there ever were such things.
Did the Great Auk that you saw tell you what
became of him?"

"He didn't say himself, because you know,
as he was stuffed, he didn't talk much; but
Ko-ko-ko-ho, the big Horned Owl, said His Grace
died because he sat still in one place so long that
he lost the use of his wings, and people came and
caught him. I remember, too, that one of the
Puk-Wudjies made fun of him, and he got very
angry."

"*People came and caught him,*" repeated the
Gull, sadly; "that is the reason for the ending

of so many Bird families. That is the reason
why we Water Birds, who must live in the open,
and trust our eggs to the care of the sun
and sky, grow more and more wild and
shy, and huddle closer and closer to the
rock ledges and lonely island coves of the
far north, where we vainly hope people
may not come and catch us. Few of us
mariners may seek the shelter of trees for
our nests; our family sometimes does so,
but many others place their hopes in wind
and water.

"The first thing that I remember was
when I was running about a sandy beach
at the foot of a ledge of rocks. The tide
floated up nice jelly food, which I ate
ravenously. Many other young
birds, like myself, were

walking about, feeding, or taking short flying and swimming lessons in company with their elders, while everywhere on the sand, in shallow nests of seaweeds and grass, were mottled gray and brown eggs from which more Gulls would hatch in due time.

"It was a pleasant life we led in those days. I remember how I admired my parents in their beautiful light gray summer coats, with black markings on the wing tips, lovely, soft white breasts, and fine yellow bills, and I wondered why I had to wear such a mixed-up gray and brown pinafore. But I learned before winter came, and my parents put on their streaked travelling hoods, that I should not wear the pearly gray and white costume until I was fully grown."

"Then," interrupted Anne, "I suppose those dark Gulls over on the shoals are young birds. I thought they were the females, because you see, Kayoshk', a great many females among land birds do not wear as pretty feathers as their mates."

"It is so with many of the Ducks," he replied; "but with us long-winged swimmers the males and females dress alike.

"As I was saying, we had gay times and good feeding that season. Well I remember the morning in autumn, the first time I made a long flight with the flock out to the fishing grounds. The fog shut down suddenly when we were nearly there, and we sank to rest on the water, waiting for the mist to rise. Presently it lifted a little, the sun shining softly through it. There were boats on every side and men pulling in nets heavy with fish. I was afraid, but all the other Gulls arose, and calling joyfully, began to feast upon the scraps of fish that floated past. Many times have I followed the boats in the fishing ground, and in the wake of ships; but never since have I tasted food like the fish of that first festival.

"When autumn came we moved from our summer home

At the Fishing Grounds

and travelled about in flocks wherever the feeding was good, gradually going southward until we reached this beach, where my parents had spent several winters. Then I met many of the other Sea Bird Brothers travelling in the same direction, and often when fog came suddenly we slept in parties, floating on the water, so many of us being together that we seemed a floating island of feathers."

"Can birds sleep afloat?" cried Anne. "I should think they would tip over and sink and be very cold besides. Isn't it dangerous?"

"Oh no, we sleep as comfortably as the Eider Duck sitting at home on her down nest, and as for cold, — why, only this last winter I have watched the Sea Ducks rise from a night's sleep splashing merrily almost among caked ice. Dangerous! it is not the water and the cold that offer us harm, but people, always *people*."

"People! but how could people reach Ducks hidden in fog and afloat in open water?"

"By learning their sleeping haunts, creeping silently along in boats, and when the fog lifts firing ruthlessly upon the dazed flocks as they leave the water in panic. I have seen it all and so I know that what I say is true.

"But there is pleasure as well as danger in

M

our wanderings. Oh, if you only knew the joy
of flying races with our friends the Winds, on
fogless days when the sky is gray and the Sea
breathes hard!

"The Winds whistle defiance and we give it
back note for note, soaring, buffeting, and screaming for joy. You hear my tribe calling now far
and near about this bay. Are not their cries
those of the Wind in the ship's rigging and the
echo of the bos'n's whistle?

"We have heard the Spring Signal of Wawa,
the Wild Goose, and our hearts throb in response; one by one we shall start on our northward journey when Shaw Shaw, the Swallow,
leaves his tropic winter haunts and returns to
your barns."

"Do you know Shaw Shaw?" cried Anne;
"why, he is as much a land bird as Cock Robin."

"That may be, but I have met his flocks
journeying by moonlight in the sea path and often
warned him against the lighthouse windows in
his course, so we are friends. Many such friends
we have met in our wanderings; other Gulls
too, cousins of different families, sometimes join
the winter flocks.

"Ah! going back to that first season, how well
I remember one lovely Gull that flew with me;

she was of another tribe, — the Kittiwakes, — who hold themselves much higher than the Herring Gulls, building their nests in rock ledges and flying with the dash and grace of Sea Swallows.

" What a dainty creature she was, to be sure, — no larger than a Pigeon. When I met her she was wearing her winter coat of gray and white with a gray hood, and black-tipped wings. How beautiful she will be in her whiter summer headgear, I thought. I shall keep near her and ask her to be my mate when Wawa gives the Signal."

" Why didn't you ask her then ? "

"Among birds it is against the law to ask promises in autumn; we must wait until spring; but when spring came her flock had separated from ours and I could not find her. I asked every Sea Bird I met, and finally I told my story to an Old Squaw Duck who seemed to know the business of everybody from the Arctic Circle to Delaware Bay.

"'E'unk, e'unk!' she scolded, wagging her head and splashing about as she spoke. 'How can you be so foolish? Don't you know that a Kittiwake may not mate with a Herring Gull? It's impossible! Both tribes would turn you out and then you would have no home grounds and your children would be sea tramps.'

"So I said no more. On the way home I
met a very pleasant Gull who was hatched three
nests above mine on our beach; she wasn't as
graceful as Miss Kittiwake, but we had played
together on the sand as children, and we both
liked the same feeding grounds, so after we
reached home and celebrated the Anniversary of
the Labrador Duck, we mated and set up nest-
keeping."

"But you haven't told me who the Labrador
Duck was, and how it came to die."

"To be sure! It happened long before my
day, in the time of my very great-grandmother, I
believe, when there were more birds than people
along this coast, and it was safe for Gulls to nest
in almost any place they fancied.

"The Labrador Duck was a handsome bird,
who used to travel with the Gulls on their winter
journeys as far south as this beach, always being
very pleasant and sociable.

"One autumn none of these Ducks joined the
flocks. The Old Squaws scolded and said, ' Sly
things, they have stolen a march on us.' But
all that winter not one was seen; none joined
the northward flight in spring.

"The Kittywakes had not seen them, nor
Mang, the Loon, nor the wide flying Wawas. A

snow cloud, drifting from the Arctic Zone, said, 'They were not there'; the Rosy Tern, fresh from the southern gulf said, 'They were not there.' Then, as we slept floating, the Winds of Night whispered, 'They are all dead.'

"So in the morning the Gulls arose, crying with grief for their comrades as they settled round the nesting sites, and we do this every year, and every sailor knows the sound."

"What became of the Ducks? Did they sit still and lose their wings like His Grace, the Auk?"

"Ask Wabeno, the Magician, for not one of us knows, not even the oldest Old Squaw. They never sat still, and their flesh was not sweet to the taste of man; yes, you must ask Wabeno."

"Haven't you any other celebrations that aren't quite so sad?" asked Anne; "something like the Forest Circus or the Brush Beacons?"

"Not among the Sea Birds, but the Sea People have one; every summer when the Crabs cast their shells they have the Shedding Dance, and that is a very funny thing."

"Oh, where do they dance it, — on the beach?"

"In the Highways under the Sea at the spot where high and low tide meet. If you want to see the dance come here when the July moon is new and find that spot and — wait!

"But now to return to my mate. For a while everything went well; there were many nests on our shore that summer, but one day when we returned together from the feeding grounds everything was in commotion; the parent Gulls were dashing about screaming wildly, for there was not a sound egg or young Gull left on the place, and the sand was spattered with broken shells.

"'House People have been here and robbed us; we must go on again,' wailed an old Gull who had seen many summers and moved many times. 'I advise all Gulls who are young enough to change their habits to learn to build their nests in trees, like the wise Fish Hawks, for soon there will be no beaches where we may lodge safe from the eye of man.'

"Then all the Gulls began to cry louder and louder with grief at the thought of leaving the pleasant beach that was the birthplace of so many of us."

Kayoshk' paused and looked seaward rather anxiously. Anne noticed that the farm team had driven up the beach and that Baldy and Obi behind the crest were shovelling the sand from the stack of seaweed that they had gathered in the autumn, before the snow.

Suddenly Kayoshk' gave a cry and wheeled
over the water, calling, "Wake-wake-wake!"
Every Gull took wing and the Ducks disappeared
like a flash, some by diving and some by flight,
and not a minute too soon, for "Bang! bang!
bang!" echoed across the bay as a flat-bottomed
sharpie slipped round the point into the shallow
water.

"A-wake! wake! a-wake!" laughed the Herring Gulls, now safely out of reach.

Anne sat perfectly still for a few moments.
Were the sands singing a song? It seemed so.
No, it was Wabun whispering among them and
whirling the dead grasses around on their stalks
until they made sharp circles on the sand, like
the marks of a compass.

"Water and I made the sands," chanted Wabun.
"My brothers, the North and the South and the
West Winds, — we worked together. We dried
and bleached the rocks, rain crept in and wore
and tore and froze and pried and powdered them.
We blew this powder aloft, whirling it, driving
it, heaping it, scattering it, the rivers swept it
along, cut it away from the banks, and piled it
on the sea bottom, and the sea tossed it back
to land and piled the beaches, then beat against

the hard rocks until they also crumbled. Water and I made the sands and we rule them."

"That seems to be true," said Anne to herself; "the tide has piled up the sand and little stones to make the bar, and it is wearing down the reef rocks where the light-house stands, and up at home by the river the water has cut a path through the rocks, and on top it is crumbling, and father said that rock was 'weathered badly,' and of course wind is a great part of weather." Anne began to feel stiff, and when she stood up, as she was going toward Baldy and Obi, the wind blew her about, and she looked toward the light where in truth Miss Jule was signalling to her.

Then as she climbed up the rocks, thinking of Kayoshk' and wondering if she would be at the beach to see the Shedding Dance, a delightful smell came to her, mingling with the sea salt, as she neared the light. "What could it be?"

"Clam fritters!" called Miss Jule, waving her handkerchief from the doorway, while Anne laughed so heartily at this surprising answer to her thoughts that she almost slid back upon the sand.

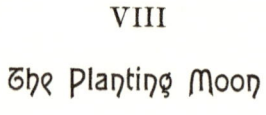

VIII

The Planting Moon

MUDJEKEEWIS and Shawonda-see finally came to stay, and signs of their housekeeping could be seen everywhere. Not that they built houses for themselves of wood and stone, or even set up wigwams, or made cave homes, like the Beast Brotherhood, for what could such errant bachelors as the South and West Winds do with homes?

No, they simply roved about, whispering the news of their good intentions in the Flower Market and through the tree-tops. Instantly the Brotherhoods heard the message. Soon Anemones nodded boldly, and shy Violets lifted their pale faces. Wake Robin awoke so suddenly and pushed so hastily through the ground that his face

170

was a purplish red and his veins stood out with the exertion. Dandelions were strewn so thickly over the rich green lawn grass that one would really think Heart of Nature must have a hole in his pocket through which golden coins dropped whenever he walked to and fro to watch his garden.

The trees hung out their green draperies, and the brightly coloured birds hearing this good news from Amoe, the Honey Bee, who carries messages swiftly and directly, came trooping back, — Tanagers, Indigo Buntings, Rose-breasts, Bobolinks, Redstarts, Warblers, and all the rest, while who should Anne discover stealing some bits of string that had blown out of the tool house, but Mr. and Mrs. B. Oriole.

Planting was the chief occupation at Happy Hall at this time, even though the Planting Moon

of the Red Brothers was May, and this was the last day of April. For weeks past Baldy and the farm horses had been continually ploughing the rich brown soil of the various fields into furrows, only to smooth it down again with the harrow. The flower beds were raked smooth and the vegetable garden already showed rows of green points where peas, lettuce, and radishes were sprouting, as well as lines in the earth where more were to be planted.

"I'm sure of one thing," said Anne to herself as she raked her own particular garden spot over for the third time, and it still looked bumpy, "Heart of Nature doesn't have half the trouble about getting his garden in order that we House People do. His ground is always ready and the winds and birds and things carry the seeds about. He doesn't have to bother with manure or straight lines — or anything.

" Deary me, I think I'll just sit down and grub with my hands,—this rake is of no use; it won't make an even mark, and if I plant my Radishes so, they will be all up and down hill. This earth is so hard I think it must be frozen underneath," and poor Anne began to beat the ground with the rake in despair of ever getting it smooth.

"Patience, patience," said a strong, gentle voice

coming from the ground. "Nothing in the wild garden of Heart of Nature or in the home garden of Heart of Man is grown without toil; in this the two Hearts work together in Brotherhood. It is because you are trying to make your garden without labour that you are failing, House Child."

Anne stopped beating the earth and looked very much ashamed; she had not thought that Heart of Nature was so near,—in fact, she had been working altogether without thinking.

"Has your bed been well dug over?" continued the voice; "has the earth been loosened and turned to the air so that it may breathe?"

Anne knew perfectly well that her father had told her that Obi might dig the bed as soon as he came from school, but she was in a hurry and had not chosen to wait, so she only answered very softly, "No, but I see Obi coming up the hill and I'll get him to do it now, so please wait a minute, dear Heart of Nature, and help me to make my rows even."

Obi came bringing a spade and a stout garden fork. In a very short time the manure was scattered and forked in, the soil turned over with the spade, forked again to mix all well, and then raked smooth.

"That looks something like," said Obi, briefly,

proceeding to do the same to Tommy's bit of ground on the opposite side of the path.

"Of course it's much nicer and even and smooth, but you don't have to dig your garden, do you, Heart of Nature?" asked Anne, doubtfully.

"I do not dig it with a spade shaped like yours, but I have ploughs that you cannot see, working summer and winter, in seed time and in harvest, in my garden. Remember, not only do I dig and plough the earth, but the Plan decrees that I must also *make the soil*."

"Make it! Why, I thought that was what the whole world is made of; that there was plenty of it, miles deep," cried Anne in amazement.

"What are those hard lumps that Obi has raked from the bed, and those gray blocks of which the fence is built?"

"Why, stones, to be sure."

"Yes, and where do they come from?"

"They are broken bits of rock. I'm sure of that, because some of the stones in the front fence exactly match the great rocks in the woods up on the hill."

"And what are rocks made of?"

"Rocks — rocks — they — oh, yes, I remember, — they are bits of earth, — hardened earth, I guess," said Anne, jumping at a conclusion, and missing.

"Listen, Anne ; though rocks are in one way the hardened crust of the molten fluid that formed the earth, they are now its skeleton, the framework that holds the seas and land together; and what you call earth or soil, in which trees and plants grow, is made of these rocks turned to powder. This is my labour, to grind the flinty rock and prepare it to yield food for man; yet you say my gardening is easy. How do I do it? By using the great password Brotherhood — alone I could do nothing.

"Heat, Cold, Wind, and Water are my aids. Heat and Cold rend and split the rocks; Wind and Water loosen the split fragments and carry them away, or beat upon them until they powder and decay, dropping into particles.

"The Flower Market works with me also, and the great trees both drop their leaves to add their rich mould to the sandy grains, and also reach their root fingers in between the stones and into rock crevices to break them further open. In this way soil is made out of stone, and is carried on continually by streams and rivers to fill bare places and make new wild gardens.

"Then, too, my ploughs are ever working in

my garden where the soil is made. You know how frost upheaves earth and stones. Have you thought how earthworms work day and night pushing and ploughing to let air into the soil's lungs, and keep it sweet and wholesome?"

As Anne stood thinking and turning over her packages of seeds with the toes of her shoes, there came a sound of galloping accompanied by a shout and a loud baying, and Tommy, Waddles, and Lumberlegs came cantering across the grass from the barn, barely escaped tumbling into the nicely raked bed, and falling in a heap in the walk, made for a minute a whirlpool, consisting of a white and a brown dog, little boy blue, a water-pot, a rake, and a salt bag full of seed papers.

"Waddles! Lumberlegs! down, down close!" ordered Anne.

Waddles obeyed at once, and Lumberlegs as soon as he saw the bed of fresh earth, for he associated such a bed with the one whipping of his short life. This was a very hopeful sign, as an ability to put two and two together and remember the result will often save young animals of all sorts from being punished.

"I was afraid you'd begin to plant before I came," panted Tommy, picking himself up, "and then your garden would grow firstest, and you'd have things to bring to father-mother before I had anyfin." (Tommy seldom used baby words, but he had not yet mastered *t*, and a few other letters.)

" Say, Anne, if your fings gwrow first, may I take them to father-mother *wif* you?"

" To be sure, but what are you going to plant? Oh, you mustn't put Squashes by your Rose-bush; they will cover it up! Why do you care for Squashes? They will crowd everything else."

" I like the nice big yellow Stwash flowers they have vely much, and bees like them too, and, Anne, I'll tell you a secret, only come close 'cause I'm sure Waddles can hear and he'd tell Lumber-legs and then he'd go down and tell Miss Jule. You know these Stwashes will be like those funny yellow, curly, goose-necked ones that Baldy had last year. Well, Mrs. Baldy put legs on two and chicken feathers for wings and tails and top-knots and nice black beans for eyes, and put them on her kitchen shelf for lovely ornaments. So I'm doin' to drow Stwashes and make two of those lovely deese for Miss Jule's birfday, so she can put them in the big room on the shelf by the music clock. Don't you fink she'll be vely glad?"

N

"I think she will like them better than anything else you could make her; she *loves* queer
funny things," said Anne, heartily, remembering
that she herself had been devoted to animals
made of vegetables a few years before, and also
thinking of the result, when she had shut up a
squash goose, a carrot pig, and two turnip Brown-
ies in a closet and forgotten them for a month.

"Not funny," insisted Tommy, looking hurt
as Anne continued to laugh, "b-e-a-utiful! How
many seeds will be 'nough to plant, do you fink?
Baldy gave me ten."

"I'll tell you what to do, Tommy; plant five
of them in a row at the back of your bed, and
we will train the vines on the fence so they won't
eat up all your garden. No! don't dig big holes;
I'll lend you this pointed clothespin planter that
Obi whittled for me. See, it makes a dear little
hole, or a straight line, whichever you like."

"Oh, I want a planter of my vely own. If I
do up to the house to det a tlothespin, will you
fix it for me wif your jack-knife? My knife is
a silly little fing and its back bends and it's only
dot a tin blade. Miss Jule's doin' to buy me a
real knife if I promise to keep it at her house
till I can whittle straight, and 'member after that
not to put it in my pocket when it's open, or run

wif it. I'm doin' to promise pretty soon, I guess; I fought I'd just wait a little and perhaps she'd buy it anyway."

Tommy brought a clothespin, which was soon pointed to his satisfaction, and the work of planting began. Anne put a row of Sweet Peas at the back of her bed, then a row of tall Zinnias, then dwarf Nasturtiums, blue Bachelor Buttons, and Mignonette, all in fairly straight rows. Around the edge she planted Radishes, sprinkling the seed very economically to make it hold out.

"There," she said, after setting the seed paper on a stick at the head of each row, "when the Radishes grow and we've eaten them, mother is going to give me some of the little plants from the hot-bed, four Geraniums for the corners, and a Heliotrope, a Fuchsia, and some Pinks for in between."

Meanwhile Tommy had planted a row of Bush Beans, and in front of them a row of mixed Peas that he had taken at random from the various packages in the tool house.

"You should put the Peas behind the Beans, for they will grow ever so much taller," prompted Anne.

"The Bean seeds are the biggest," said Tommy, stoutly. "I'm doin' to put the big seeds back-

most and end off wif dese funny Parsley ones
down by the edge."

So Anne said nothing, for, thought she, what
is the use of having a very own garden if you
can't plant it as you like. You might as well
go and look at the big garden where everything
grows and behaves as it ought.

Tommy finished his labours by planting a large
Onion at each corner of the bed, and a whole
Potato and two Carrots in the spaces between.
Then both children picked up their tools, and
bidding the dogs "come along," went down
toward the barn.

Lumberlegs seemed very much pleased at having come away from the flower beds in safety,
and expressed his joy by a vigorous wagging of
the tail, in which his hind legs took part, and in
rolling on the ground with his legs straight in
the air, looking like a very clumsy table having
a fit. He, however, considered it a very beautiful performance; it is strange what ideas of
beauty young animals have.

Waddles, feeling quite pleased at the way in
which his pupil had resisted the temptation to
roll in the beds, trotted along contentedly, never
giving Anne a hint that he saw the Miller's cat
stealing toward the chicken house. However,

just before the party reached the barn-yard gate,
Waddles gave Lumberlegs a wink and the pair
turned off around the corner.

Baldy was unhooking the horses from the big
wagon in which he had brought the toothed
harrow from the fields, while the Swallows were
flying in and out of the hay-loft windows, twittering merrily as they bespoke sites for their
May building.

"I'm goin' to drop potatoes ter-morrer in the
big lot that's just turned in," said Baldy, slowly,
as he put every strap and buckle of the harness
in place before hanging it up.

"That lot ain't been turned over this hundred
years, if ever, reckonin' by the stumps and stubs
we had to grub out o' it, and the ground's full er
arrer-heads. If you like, and the folks'll let yer,
I'd be pleased to have you come along down ter-
morrer and pick up a mess. Some of 'em's mighty
cur'us, and I reckon you'll like 'em for play toys."

"Arrows, a field full! How did they come
there, and what do they look like?" said Anne.

"Arrows, lots of arrows!" cried Tommy,
hopping up and down in excitement. "Oh, how
fine! I'll bring my bow along and shoot all day.
Won't it be fun, Anne, to have all the arrows you
want wifout stopping to pick 'em up."

"They're reg'lar Injun arrer tops," explained Baldy, as soon as he could be heard, "made er stone. There was a great battle once here about, a couple er hundred years ago, so they say, and these arrers are the leavin's, I guess. Maybe you'll find a axe-head or a spear; I found a couple o' fine ones once, down in the lot where we have the fodder corn."

"Have you got them at your house, and can we go down and see them?" begged Anne.

"Will you dive me the axe to help you cut trees wif?" coaxed Tommy.

"You couldn't have cut butter with it," said Baldy, laughing; "besides, I gave them to a man that wanted to put them in a museum fer relics."

"Only think," sighed Anne, clasping her hands earnestly, "we grow relics right here, at Happy Hall, and we never knew it. We'll come to-morrow very early, Baldy, and bring big baskets to put the arrows in."

The next day was Saturday, and May Day into the bargain. Saturdays had a great way of coming when Tommy and Anne had something they wished particularly to do. Oh, what a day it was! The air was sweet with the breath of Cherry blossoms and the dark purple double Violets were in bloom in a sunny border. The Chi-kaug flowers were withering and giving place to their fat seed-lunch baskets, while their cousins, the Jacks-in-the-Pulpits, were returning to their stands along old fences and wood edges. All the spring sounds and signs were in full force, B. Oriole bugled as of old — only a few bird notes were lacking.

"It is wonderful how everything has caught up," said Anne to herself as she walked slowly toward the "big lot." "The day of the great snow I thought it couldn't be summer for months and months, and now look!" and she spread her arms as if she would like to give everything, including the sky, a hearty hug.

"The Plan says that my garden must be ready for its summer work of growth, no matter what mishaps fall in the between seasons," said Heart of Nature, speaking from an old gnarled Willow, – a wand of which brushed Anne's face as she held it gently to look at its fresh green leaves.

"So in the making of this garden all these mishaps are arranged for. Though I must do double work and weave the leaf fabrics both night and day, the Flower Market is open, and Amoe, the Honey Bee, is happy, while in due time Gitche-ah-mo, the Bumble Bee, shall have his usual spring feast of clover.

"AND NOW LOOK"

" The fern wool is ready spun to line the nests of Penaisee, the Humming-Bird, and Sweet, the Yellow Warbler. Already the lunch baskets of Pear and Apple are swelling in the bud, and Heart of God and Heart of Man rejoice with me and see that it is good."

"Please, dear Heart of Nature," said

Anne, softly, " are there any Magic Spectacles you
can give me so that I can see Heart of God too ?
I'm getting used to you, and since Tommy came
I understand about Heart of Man much better;
but the other, I know *He Is*, for I can see what
he does, and know that the other Hearts could
not have made the Plan ; but I can never see him
any more than I can the Winds of Night."

" The human eyes that shall see that vision
clearly," replied Heart of Nature, slowly, " must
see through crystals of a wondrous fashioning —
things to be earned, not given. Some day, dear
House Child, I will tell you what these crystals
are ; the *seeing* them lies with yourself and Heart
of God."

Anne still fingered the wand of Willow, and as
she looked at it her wonder grew anew. " Why,"
she cried, " this Willow was in bud before the
great snow, and after it was over I looked at it
and all the buds were frozen, and after a while
they wizzled up. Where did all these leaves
come from please, dear Heart of Nature ? Was
it Wabeno, the Magician, who mixed up the
Winds and made all the trouble ? Was he sorry
for the mischief he had made and so came and
cured the trees ? "

"No, this work is mine and very simple, too, for the Plan arranged it all. Wabeno only does the conjuring tricks that have no reasons in them to be explained. He is the answer to unanswerable questions.

"Look at that twig of Willow, or better yet, the branch of the next tree, the sugar Maple. One leaf bud has spread into a perfect leaf, but round the leaf stem where it grasps the branch you may see some little roughnesses that cover other very small buds. These are the 'Waiting Buds,' and in them lies my power to have my garden fit for the Flower Market, and my trees ready to unfurl their draperies to shield the birds, regardless of old Peboan and prowling Kabibonokka.

"A bud comes out too soon and withers from frosty weather. At my bidding a 'Waiting Bud' takes its place and unfolds. Once, twice, or thrice even these patient 'Waiting Buds' may save the tree."

"How wonderful," whispered Anne, stroking the little buds as cautiously as if they were fairies ready to spring out at the slightest touch. "But what becomes of these 'Waiting Buds' if the first one is not frozen, but keeps on growing?"

" Different things in different trees.   Sometimes the buds give up their strength to the one
that grows, and disappear.   Sometimes they grow
out sideways into new twigs.   Sometimes they
may wait under the bark for years even, until an
accident may kill or break the limb top and then
they make haste to grow into new branches.
Thus nothing is wasted, nothing lost in my wild
garden."

" Do all plants have 'Waiting Buds'?   The
Peonies die down to the ground every fall, so
they have no branches; where are their 'Waiting
Buds'?"

" The 'Waiting Buds' of shrubs and trees are
on their branches; but those of herbs and grasses
lie below ground at the root tops, where the spring
growth starts forth.

" Ah, I must go and quiet Mudjekeewis and
Shawondasee; they are too sportive and forget
the cherries are in blossom, — they will scatter
the precious dust before the seed-lunch baskets
are filled, and then the seed germs will starve,
and there will be no cherries on the trees," and
as Heart of Nature vanished, the rustling in
the tree-tops ceased, and every leaf hung still.

" How many things there are to think of, if
you have to manage a garden that covers the

whole earth, as Heart of Nature's does," said
Anne, as she went on to the field, where Baldy
and Obi were filling baskets with the potatoes
they had cut up for planting, or dropping, as it
is called in field language.

Tommy returned from a hasty run about the
lot, dragging his bow along the ground, and
almost crying. "I tan't find an arrow anywhere, not even one. Do you fink somebody
can have stoled them in the night, Baldy?
Miss Jule says it is 'most time for the Gypsies
that sell horses to come along and camp, and that
they'd take anyfing, even the Miller's cat if they
tould tatch him."

"There's an arrer-head, I reckon, right by your
foot," said Baldy, pointing to a glistening bit of
flint lying on top of the fresh earth.

"That!" exclaimed Anne, picking it up; "why
an arrow is a long, thin stick with a sharp point,
and this is only a little bit of a thing that looks
more like a jackstone."

"Yer didn't think whole wooden arrers could
stay buried in the ground a couple er hundred
years without rottin', did yer? These here are
arrer-*heads*, that the Injuns fastened somehow on
the end er their arrer sticks. Mighty curious
things tew, not a pair er them alike, — some

little, and some so big, — folks claim the Injuns
used the big uns for spears."

"Phoof! they're no dood to me to shoot wif my
bow," said Tommy, casting that article on the
heap of uncut potatoes. "I'd rather do wif Obi
and drop potatoes than pick up any of those
things, 'cept enough for jackstones.

"Can I have a bag of potato pieces to hang
round my neck, please, Baldy?"

Being soon equipped the Potato procession
started, Obi dropping the "eyes," and Baldy hoe-
ing the earth over them. Anne, however, began
to hunt for arrow-heads, as the strangeness of
their shapes and colours interested her greatly.

After searching carefully for nearly an hour,
she had found a double handful of the three-
cornered stones, which she took under the tree
on the field edge to sort, for the sun was really
quite hot, and the warm breath was rising from
the steaming earth.

As she walked along, looking at the bits of
stone she carried in her apron, she stumbled over
the heap of whole Potatoes, and sent some of
them bouncing off into the field.

"I wish you would be more careful," said one
particularly large, smooth Potato that had rolled
into a furrow. "Pick me up, and put me back

with the others, or I may be overlooked in the planting."

"I think you might say please," answered Anne, first securing her arrow-heads safely in her apron pocket, and then picking up the Potato.

"You didn't say please, or anything, when you upset me out of the heap; you just kicked me," replied the Potato rather crossly.

"I did *not* kick," said Anne, hastily; "I stumbled. Girls must never kick anything."

"It might seem a stumble to you; but it felt like a kick to me. Potatoes have feelings, I assure you, and come of a very proud and important race."

"It seems to me that almost everything I've met this spring comes of a grand family," said Anne to herself. "There was the Chi-kaug flower that was first cousin to the Calla, and the Tree Frog who had a relative that flew with his feet, and another that could turn any colour he liked. I wonder if plants and animals have societies and call themselves daughters and sons of things.

"What family do you belong to?" asked Anne, abruptly, still holding the Potato in her hand and looking at the shallow dimples in it from which buds seemed about to sprout.

"Perhaps you have a name, too, and are related to the Rose-bushes; I heard Baldy say something about early Rose Potatoes."

"Early Rose is my aunt on my mother's side of the family," replied the Potato, with condescension. "She usually grows over in the south lot that is always used for an early crop. I am the White Elephant, a most superior late variety, and you will find my pedigree and testimonials of my character in all seed catalogues of any importance."

Anne immediately laid the Potato on the very top of the heap in a position suitable to its dignity, which act of deference seemed to please it so much that it grew quite talkative.

"I do not belong to the Rose Family. Roses, of course, are all very well in their places, but, hem, — I do not wish to seem vain, eight members of my family are so important that they have been for many years officers in the Flower Market, being in charge of the different booths."

"I suppose you are related to Turnips and Carrots and Beets," interrupted Anne, "because we eat the roots of those things the same as we eat you."

"You are entirely wrong, though your mistake is quite a natural one," answered the White Elephant, loftily; "I belong to the Potato Family.

This is a household that people both love and
fear, for some of its members have poisonous
juices and give a sleep that lasts too long.

"House People eat my underground tubers, it
is true, but they are not real roots like those
of the Beat, Carrot, and Turnip.   Nevertheless, I
am chief of the Edible Root Booth — what vegetable so important as I?   What vegetable can be
cooked and served in so many ways?   Is there
not mourning in the land if the Potato crop fails?
Though, alas, I regret to say, we do have many
ills that both spoil our complexions and give us
watery hearts.

"In the booth next to the Fruit Stall
you will find my two pet cousins from
South America, — the Tomato and the
Egg Plant.   House People eat their
fruity seed vessels; but if they should
eat the green balls that are my
seed-lunch baskets, they would
soon be very, very ill indeed.

" The Pepper presiding at the Pickle Booth is my second cousin, while over in the Drug Department you may find three more of our family, not

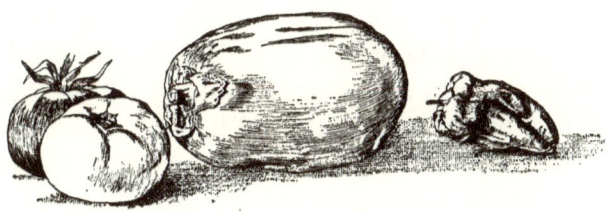

beautiful to look at and wearing poison labels on their foreheads. These brothers are Belladonna, Henbane, and Stramonium.

" Another of us, the Horse Nettle, has been expelled from the Flower Market as a vagabond weed, a mere tramp, and the Climbing Nightshade, with violet purple flowers and the smooth red berries, that House Children must *not* eat, lives with the flowers of waste grounds.

" This is a goodly showing for any family, but there is one other plant, the chief of all, even really more popular the world around, I think, than I am. He has a booth all to himself, though from his bloom he might be with the flowers. Will you believe it, House Men as well as the Red Brothers buy more from this booth than from all the lovely Flower Booths together. Yet

o

they cannot eat the wares it offers, for they do not nourish; and though they may be burned, they will not give men warmth.

"Hush! I must whisper, even when I think of this weird brother, for he is the chosen one above all others in the Market by Wabeno, the Magician, who has gifted him with the Magic Leaves that filled the peace pipe of the Red Brothers. Through the smoke that comes from these leaves, Wagoose, the Dream Fox, may show his pictures even by daylight.

"Men love this smoke, they know not why. From a speck of seed, like dust, this stalwart plant of mystic leaf springs in a season, and its name is Jack Nicotine Tobacco."

"Ah, then cigars and all those sort of things come from your family, too. Now I understand why Baldy sits outside his door in the evening and blows pipe smoke up and looks at it. I suppose he sees things. I've often asked him why he liked to do it, and he says, 'Don't know why I do.' I believe the reason he can't tell is that Wabeno won't let him.

"I want to know more whys about yourself," continued Anne. "You say your tubers are good and your seeds bad, and yet they are both from the same plant; how can that possibly be?"

"Ask Wabeno, the Magician; I do not know," said the White Elephant.

"But if your seed was planted, would the potatoes that grow be good or poisonous?"

"Perfectly good."

"Then why do we plant the potatoes in the ground instead of seeds, and why do we cut them up before we plant them?"

"I think you wish to know a great many whys all at once. To begin with, House People plant the roots because the plants will grow quicker and come up stronger at once, instead of first being weak seedlings.

"Why we are cut up is a different matter. Our tubers are branches that budded underground, and having no light to guide them they swelled into lumps instead of growing out long. Now these lumps have buds in them the same as if they were real branches. See! those little pits that are called 'eyes' in me are the buds. House People cut the tuber into bits, leaving two or three 'eyes' in each one to make new plants, as your mother cuts her Geraniums into lengths, with two or three bud joints, to make new slips."

"How wonderful!" exclaimed Anne; "and that is why some of the old potatoes, if they are left in the root cellar until the weather grows warm,

begin to sprout and try to make new plants out
of themselves.   Did the Red Brothers grow
potatoes?"

"They knew us well, for we live in the wild
garden, from South America to the far western
country; but they used us for magic, not for food.

"They called us Opin, and an arrow-head here
in the field told me only this morning that
Wabeno uses our eyes to see with when he
wishes to work some magic underground."

The planting party returned for more Potatoes,
and the big White Elephant was the very first
one taken from the heap.   Anne felt rather badly
as Baldy's sharp knife began to slice, but the
Potato seemed delighted and called from the bottom of the basket:—

"Only think, I am such a fine Potato that it
will take four hills to hold me, and possibly I may
be nearly a peck of White Elephants in the fall.
I'm so glad to be out here seeing life, instead of
shut up in the root cellar for mice to nibble.   It's
a jolly field, too, where I'm to be planted, for I
shall hear so many fine stories from the arrow-
heads; stories of battles and brave doings, and I
may meet some of my wild relatives on the field
edge."

Anne spread her treasures in her lap. The arrow-heads were of several sizes, some were glistening white, others quite black, and one had a beautiful greenish lustre.

"I wish I knew how these were made and how long they have been here," she sighed; "but, of course, one mustn't expect stones to speak like the Plant and Beast Brothers."

"A stone may speak to her who wears the Magic Spectacles, when that stone is of the tribe of Bek-wuk, the Arrow," replied a voice, sweeping low over the field with Shawondasee, and pausing close to Anne.

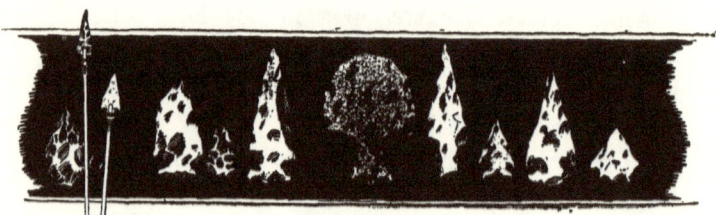

IX

The Story of Bek-wuk, the Arrow

"IT was long ago that I first saw light — far back before the days when Wenona left her father to go to her mother in the Morning Star. I was a bit of flint rock that for ages had been in the Earth's smelting furnace and afterward imprisoned in a granite cliff, the same cliff from which Wenona took her flight.

"In those days the Red Brothers of the north roved wild, both east and west, from ocean to ocean, with the Deer and Buffalo. They had neither gun nor sword, knife nor iron, horse nor cow. Their garden was the wild Flower Market, their drink pure water. These were the days of true hunting, before the Stone Giants came, and in the very last of these good days was I made."

198

"If they had no knives nor guns, how could they kill anything when they went hunting; and if they had no horses, how could they go, and who were the Stone Giants?" interrupted Anne, taking up a glistening white arrow-head, the most shapely of all, from among those in her lap, for it was upon this one the voice rested.

"Slowly, go slowly, House Child, and listen patiently if you would hear my story. We of the past who have grown slowly with the Earth's growth must take our own way and time of telling.

"As I was saying, I was of a layer of white flint rock embedded in the granite of Wenona's cliff. For ages after I had hardened from a molten mass I lay there, cold and silent. You may perhaps find such stuff as I making white lines in some broken rock hereabouts."

"Ah, yes," said Anne, "I know a place between here and Wild Cat Mountain that we call the Dark Woods. A place where I may never go alone because the rocks are high like a wall, and Aspetuck runs so quickly between them that father says it has cut a pathway for itself. In those high rocks there are stripes of shiny, sharp flint, just like you — not exactly straight stripes like those on a flag, but wiggley ones, like a crumpled-up jelly cake. You look almost as if you were made of that very same rock."

The Arrow-head seemed to quiver as Anne pressed it against the palm of her hand, and asked in an eager, choking voice : —

"Does the rock wall face the rising sun? Are there old trees fringing the top? Tall trees in a long waving line, like warriors hemmed back in a last battle; then beyond these trees an open place from which the stones have all been gathered?"

"I think the cliff does face sunrise," said Anne, after hesitating a moment, "because I remember the sun lies full on it in the morning ; but I'll go and ask Obi and Baldy — they'll know because they've been up there this winter after Foxes, and I haven't been there since Crotalus, the Bad One, died," she said, starting up.

"No, do not go, House Child," begged the Arrow-head ; "let us be alone together for a time, you and I, for you tell me strange news, and I may tell you stranger yet. About the tree fringe and the cleared ground, are they there?"

"There were trees there until last year, but lumbermen have cut them down. Father says there must have been a very old wood there once, of great white oaks, — a pri-me-val forest, he

called it, — because there are some e-*nor*mous
wrecks of stumps, with trees that are pretty big
and old now, growing between them. I don't remember any open field behind the cliff; it was all
woods quite across to the Mountain."

"Of course, of course, it would be after all these
years," said the Arrow-head. "Was there a wide,
open piece of water above, before the cliffs made
the way narrow?"

"Yes, of course — the long pond. It used to
be lovely, full of Lilies and Wild Ducks, but the
lumbermen have messed it all up to make the
water turn their saw-mill."

"House Child," cried the Arrow-head, "that
was the cliff from which Wenona took her flight
with Robin Thrush and Owaissa. From its glistening rocks was I made!"

"How wonderful!" sighed Anne, fingering the
Arrow-head tenderly. "Then there were Red
Brothers here where we live! Do tell me everything you remember, and I won't interrupt you any
more, that is, — only one question, — did you ever
meet Wagoose, the Dream Fox? Did he ever
live here?"

"You say there are Foxes here now?"

"Yes, plenty of them; too many for our chickens
to be happy."

" Wherever Foxes have lived, or man lives to-day, there may Wagoose be found."

" But have you ever seen him yourself ? "

" Never ; only to those of the Brotherhood of Beasts, of which Man is the King, will Wabeno vouchsafe sight of him. Now for my life history."

" I had lain a long time in darkness, in my rocky bed, when one day I heard a tapping around and above me. I wondered about it a good deal, slight as it was, because I had heard nothing like it before. This sound went on at times for many years, and every little while a shiver would run through the rock to which I belonged.

" One day this shiver became more violent, a splitting noise followed, and then a crash. When my bones stopped aching, I saw that it was no longer dark ; blue sky was above my head. At one side stood the cliff from which I had fallen, at the other dashed the swift running river — between these two I lay.

" As soon as I learned what had happened to me, I began to look about."

" But what had happened ? Who hammered you off the other rock ? " asked Anne, forgetting that she had promised not to speak.

" The place where I slept was near the cliff's
edge. A tiny crack lay between my bed and the
great rocky mass that was scarred through and
through by just such other cracks. Into this
seam the rain had crept, drop by drop, year upon
year, feeling its way in summer, turning to ice
in winter, and pushing against the rock when it
thawed out in spring. Little by little the crack
widened to a seam; as more rain could enter
there was more ice to push, until one spring the
crisis came and my bit could no longer grasp the
cliff, and so I fell."

" I know that must be true, because now there
is a monstrous great lump of rock, bigger than
the tool house, right in the middle of the river,
that came from the top edge of the cliff. For
even though the water has worn the corners off,
it couldn't move it, and you can almost see the
place it fell from, the stripes in it match so well.
Besides, that is the way the ice cracked my water
pitcher. *Please* excuse me for interrupting, dear
little Arrow, but if you only knew how glad I am
when I quite understand something, you wouldn't
think me rude. It's a way all young animals have,
I think, for Waddles always used to interrupt,
and Tommy does, and Lumberlegs, too, so I'm
pretty sure that Heart of Nature means us to ask

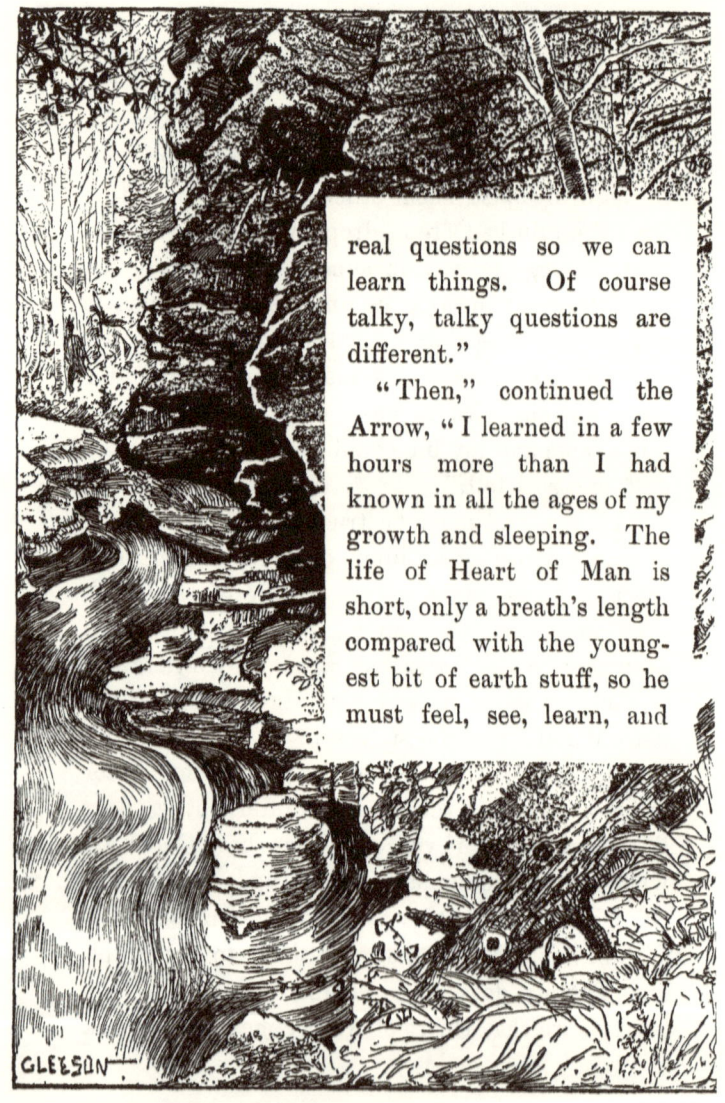

real questions so we can learn things. Of course talky, talky questions are different."

"Then," continued the Arrow, "I learned in a few hours more than I had known in all the ages of my growth and sleeping. The life of Heart of Man is short, only a breath's length compared with the youngest bit of earth stuff, so he must feel, see, learn, and act quickly to do his part in the Plan, and that day I met the Red Brothers.

" As I lay there by the river, looking up at the bare trees, so gray that I thought them made of rock like myself, and at the ice that still lodged in dark cliff crevices, I heard a sound that I soon learned was the voice of man. A dark object shot by me down the river, but swiftly as it went I saw the strange shapes in it and that they noticed me.

" The Red Brothers had been fishing for Trout and Pickerel at the head-waters far above and, as the canoe was guided into still water, the women came out from their lodges behind the wood fringe, pulled the craft ashore, and loading the fishes upon flat trays of braided rushes, carried them toward the village of wigwams. All this I did not then understand, but learned after ; yet it saves time to tell it as it was, not as it seemed to me but newly escaped from a granite prison."

" Why didn't the Red Brothers carry their own fishes home ? I don't think they were polite."

" It was their custom, even as the male and female bird both help in the nest building, or as the She-wolf, Fox, or Wild Cat toils most to feed her ravenous young.

" Two words held the rule of the Red Brothers'

household. One word belonged to man to carry out, the other to the woman, and these two words were Provide and Prepare.

" The Red Brothers did the hunting and fishing, provided the meat, the skins for tent covers and robes, and caught the fish ; the Squaws prepared the food, carried it home, prepared the skins, dried the fish. The Brothers made war ; the Squaws made ready for it. It was their law ; there was no impoliteness in it because they saw none.

" Presently three Red Brothers came along the bank where I was lying, pointing to me and many other fragments like me, some larger and some smaller. They seemed glad that we were there, and presently others came and began to gather us up in heaps, striking the larger pieces skilfully with greater stones until they fell in fragments fit to carry.

" Next day I found myself in a half-dark wigwam, covered with bark. Light came in the doorway and also through a hole left at the top that smoke, the breath of heat, might escape through it. In the doorway sat a man ; before him was a large smooth flat stone ; in his right hand he held another stone with which he chipped grains from a still smaller fragment his left hand grasped. I watched him closely, for, as he chipped, the flint

THE ARROW MAKER

fragment took a shape like that of many others lying on the ground.

" In a little time he rose, stepped into the afternoon sunlight, listened, whistled to Kaw-kaw, the Raven, who was stealing through the bare trees looking for acorns, then seated himself cross-legged again, filled a hollow at the end of a long stick with dry leaves, lighted them with fire that smouldered inside the wigwam, and straightway fire breath curled from the stick and his own nostrils, yet he himself did not burn away. Presently, when all the leaves had turned to smoke, there being no more food for the fire, it died out; he laid this stick — they call it a pipe — away, and coming into the lodge chose me from out the heap of flints and began shaping me with stinging blows.

" I was confused, as you may well believe ; first, I grew long, then was narrowed to a point, sloped sidewise to sharp edges, and finished in a grooved blunt butt. Then I was rubbed and polished by various other kinds of stones until the old man was content with my appearance, and saying mystic words, he laid me on a pile with many others like me : ' Go forth, Bek-wuk, arrow-head, thou art beautiful of thy kind,' he whispered, scarcely moving his lips; ' touch the heart of all you desire, — of the deer in the hunting, of the

foe on the war-path.   May Wabeno's keenness
be on your tip, his cunning in your shaft, and the
swiftness of Wagoose in your flight.'

"Thus was I born and made a Magic Arrow in
the tent of Kanida, the arrow maker, brother to
the warrior Kaniwa, Wenona's father."

"For many days and nights I lay in the tent,
watching what went on about me.   Other instru-
ments of killing and household vessels were my
tent mates.   Spear heads, chipped from flint like
myself, but ten times greater in length, stone axes
that would beat more readily than cut, fish hooks
wrought from bone, clay pots, wooden bowls, and
water vessels made from gourd rinds, bundles of
reeds, and feathers of the wild goose.

"Kanida would select a dozen arrow-heads
from off the pile, scan each one closely, narrowing
his eyes as he held it between them and the light;
then make ready a dozen reeds to mate them,
fastening head to shaft with horn glue and the
stout thongs of hide that the Beast Brotherhood
furnished.   Next was the shaft nicely winged
with goose quills to make an even balance.   So
were the arrows ready to go forth to live their
lives, while in and out of the lodge came and went
silent figures who bartered venison, birds, and other

food for the arrows, sometimes stopping to smoke
a pipe with Kanida, sometimes leaving quickly.

"In the lodge were arrow-heads that had seen
service and returned to be reshafted, and they
told me strange tales of war and
hunting. How they were
often rubbed with poi-
son from the fangs of
Crotalus, the Bad
One, if meant for
war arrows; and
how they had trav-
elled mighty dis-
tances in the flesh
of some slightly
wounded stag to be
made prisoners
by a strange
tribe, and final-
ly found their
way back to
Kanida's lodge
by the same chance, for the Red Brothers prized
Bek-wuk, the Arrow, above price, and never aban-
doned him carelessly.

"One day a girl came to the lodge — a child
almost, but tall and slim and very beautiful. She

P

sat upon the ground and toyed and played with
the glistening arrow-heads, plucking out those
that pleased her best, — a bit of light green jade
from distant parts, a coal black point, and — me!
A thrill went through me as I felt the soft touch
of her fingers, and solemn Kanida even smiled as
he gazed upon her, for it was Wenona — she whom
all the tribe held in part to be one of them, and
yet something far beyond.   Wenona, daughter of
Kaniwa, the Chief, whose mother had vanished to
the Morning Star.   Wenona, — whose very name
signified a quivering ray of light, — the maid, who
saw in dreams things that should happen afar off.

"This day Wenona was playful and sad by
turns, and Kanida often glanced at her anxiously;
finally he laid his flints aside, and filling his pipe
began to smoke silently, as if inviting her confidence.   As the day lengthened, pulling the shadows after it, she, crouching at the arrow maker's
feet, began to speak, at first in short sentences, as
if she read a story dimly through the smoke.

"'They are coming, they will soon be here!
The Stone Giants, people from a far-off tribe, with
faces of a strange, dead colour.   First will our
people send out good brave arrows against them,
but stone to stone the Giants shall hurl them back
with broken shafts, while they shall be uninjured.

"'Again, and many times again, shall our people try to overthrow these stone men by all trick and subtlety of war, but vainly; for in their hands the Giants carry in leash Ishkodah, the Comet with the fiery tail, with which to blind and kill the Red Brothers from without, while in a seeming friendly cup they hold out burning water

to kill them with unquenched thirst. The Stone Giants come! I hear their earth tread even now!' she whispered shivering.

"'How and whence know you this, my daughter?' questioned Kanida, with a troubled look.

" Wenona looked up, laughing gayly, her mood changing suddenly.

"'Whence know I it? Everything whispers it as gossip. Apuk-wa, the Bulrush, told it to me, and when I doubted, Annemeekee, the Thunder, said that it was so. Kayoshk', the Sea Gull, told me that he had himself seen the Stone Giants crossing a mighty river in great canoes that sank not in spite of the vast weight, and when I doubted, Wabun, the East Wind, told me it was so, for he and Kabibonokka had followed these canoes, striving to upset them, but could not.

"'More than this — draw close, Kanida, for I may but whisper — Wabeno, the Magician, told me, only the night last gone, that the Stone Giants, against whom your swiftest arrows should fall as harmless as leaves on sand, were nearing us, and presently Wagoose showed me all the pictures of their deeds to come in his magic book. Then — listen and pity, Kanida — I, forgetting, did the forbidden thing, unveiled my eyes and looked Wabeno full in the face, exchanging glance for glance. This thing my mother did before me, and thus, knowing too much, she disappeared, and after one more snow I too must join her in Wabun-Annung, the Morning Star.'

"Stillness fell on the wigwam; Wenona stole away. Kaw-kaw, the Raven, called thrice to Mang, the Loon, and we knew that Wabeno and the Dream Fox were hovering near. Kanida sat musing until his pipe went out, and his lodge fire

also died; on arousing he had to kindle it anew
by rubbing two dry bits of wood together until
their heat broke out into flames."

"Why didn't he borrow some matches if he
hadn't any?" asked Anne, without thinking; then,
answering herself, "Of course he couldn't.   If
there were no guns or knives or powder or horses
or anything, there weren't any matches, and anyway I remember that it says in my history that
not so dreadfully long ago even House People
used to have to make fire by striking iron and flint
together."

"In spite of Wenona's words," continued Bek-
wuk, "the morning came and no Stone Giants
appeared, for we Arrows had thought they were to
come at once.

"It soon was the Planting Moon, and all the
women of the tribe were busy in the clearing,
planting Mondamin, Maize, and the flat seeds of
Askuta-squash, the Gourd, whose body yielded
food and whose rind made household vessels.
Everywhere there was feasting, dancing, singing,
and magic walking around the field at night to
bless the crops.   Mai-mai, the Woodcock, left his
writing in the muddy places, and Wazhusk, the
Muskrat, forsook his winter lodge in the shallow

pond. The leaves hung out on every tree, and Bemah-gut, the Grapevine, perfumed the air with her flowers. `

"Wenona laughed and sang all that summer through, and I, Bek-wuk, took many a journey from the bow of Sacoit, a young warrior who had bought me. But I always returned in safety to him, for he shot true and lost no arrows.

"Oh, the joy of flying when the bowstring twangs! Did Swallow dart, I darted more swiftly! Did a Wild Duck speed by, I overtook it! Did a Deer bound through the woodland, lightly as a cloud shadow, I bounded after him and yet was there to meet him!

"With the harvest came yet more feasting and singing. Wenona joined the other women in stripping the ears of Maize from out the husks, and I, peeping from Sacoit's quiver, was watching her.

"As she parted the husks a blood red ear of Maize was left between her fingers. This rare red ear is a love token with the Red Brothers, and swift as I fly I could not outspeed the glance that sped between Sacoit and Wenona. The warriors nodded approvingly, and the women laughed and jostled; but from that moment she, who had looked Wabeno in the face unflinchingly, grew

pale and paler, for well she knew she must not
love a mortal; she must go unwed to her mother
in the Morning Star, and in her heart she yearned
to stay near Sacoit.

"With early spring strange messengers came to
the village, bringing news from far-off tribes, and
the words 'Stone Giants' were often heard. One
day a messenger came in quite spent with running,
and rested in Sacoit's lodge, and as he told his
story drew it also in picture writing on the skin
top of a drum, — a picture of Red Brothers shooting at strange men whose bodies were concealed
all but the face, and as the arrows touched them
they flew backward.

"The Sachems held long counsels, and the
women made the warriors ready to go forth.

"Soon there was great confusion, — warriors
came and went, returning no more. I learned
that, as Wenona had said, strange people, some
with stone bodies, had come and seized the Red
Man's land, people against whom we Arrows
wrecked ourselves vainly, people of fair words
who yet carried Ishkodah, the Comet, for a
weapon. I longed to see them, but I seemed
forgotten.

"One day Sacoit dashed to his lodge, seized me,
and carried me to the council rock where many

chiefs assembled.   On the way we passed Wenona,
and Sacoit signed to her that she should touch my
point; thus, for the second time, I felt the magic
of her fingers.   There on the rock lay an empty
skin of a gigantic Bad One; in it were crammed
some arrows, and I was placed with them.   Soon
Sacoit left for a long journey, carrying the snake
skin full of arrows with him.

"Many days we travelled, resting but never
sleeping, until we were close upon a clearing such
as I had never seen among Red Brothers.   There
were no wigwams like theirs, but strange, square
lodges built of the trunks of trees laid crosswise,
with traplike openings in them, and strange beasts
were walled in pits and pens.

" As I gazed from out the skin of Crotalus, my
eyes saw a Stone Giant walking toward one of
these lodges.   The picture writing said truly, his
body was covered all but the face, and as he
walked slowly and heavily the covering that he
wore glistened in the light, and I knew it could
not be stone."

"It must have been armour — steel armour,"
interrupted Anne.   " You know, Bek-wuk, when
the Pilgrim Fathers first came over to settle in
this country it was so long ago that some of them
wore kind of steel coats and hats to protect them

in war, and if the Red Brothers had never seen
any before I don't wonder they thought them
made of stone.   But please go on — what did
Sacoit do with the arrows?"

"When it grew dark he slipped between the
trees and going to the lodge entered the largest
trap-hole.   I thought he would surely be caught,
but he was fearless.   In the lodge were many
Stone Giants sitting about a long flat board raised
from the ground, but they did not sit upon skins
spread on the earth like warriors, but were raised
high above it."

"Of course, soldiers would sit on chairs and
benches," said Anne.

"They had no spears or bows and arrows with
them, but beside each rested a strange stick in
which, I soon learned, they held Ishkodah, the
fire-tailed Comet.

"When Sacoit entered he threw the skin of
Crotalus before the one that seemed the chief of
these Stone Giants ; then he began to talk in sign
language, and wrath shone from his face and from
the faces of the others.   Only Sacoit, the Messenger, was silent and immovable.

"All night long they argued, and at dawn they
gave the messenger food which he did not touch,
and the chief Giant, emptying the arrows from the

snake skin, put in it hard round balls and hurled it at Sacoit, with loud words of defiance.

"I had dropped far from the other arrows, and in passing out Sacoit seized and concealed me, whom Wenona had touched, so I went back with him to bear a bitter message to his tribe. When we returned, we found Wenona had gone."

"Then war began ; our warriors poured down and harried the Stone Giants, and many that were with them were not of stone, and we arrows could pierce them, and flames from our dry sticks devoured their lodges.

"What it was all about I knew not; but I saw balls, such as Sacoit bore home, fly from the sticks the Stone Giants carried and kill our young men more quickly than I could kill a wild fowl. Food was scarce, for there was scant time for hunting, and maids, women, and children stayed close within the village upon the cliff top.

"One evening Kaw-kaw came flapping noiseless to the village,—an ominous sight indeed,—and Ko-ko-ko-ho exchanged greetings with him and flew into the forest, followed by all the colony of birds of field and tree.

"Apuk-wa, the Bulrush, whispered, 'They come, the Stone Giants come,—Wabun tells it !

Listen ! Annemeekee, the Thunder, proclaims it !
Creep to the east under the dark's mantle ;
attack, Red Brothers ; it is your only hope ! '

"So the warriors crossed the river and crept
downward many miles, and there, when Wawa-
sa-mo, the Lightning, played its pranks, they at-
tacked the camp of the half-sleepy foe. Up and
down, in and out of the trees they fought, but the
bullets overmatched poor Bek-wuk's tribe, and all
the earth was strewn with crippled arrows. The
Red Brothers kindled a line of fire, thinking to sur-
round the Stone Giants by it, but were themselves
cut off. Kaniwa was slain, and Kanida, and then
Sacoit, after shooting me, his very last arrow.

"Of the women and children, some were made
prisoners and some escaped to other tribes, but
from that day to this no Red Brothers have had
their lodges on the cliff. And I have lain buried
all these years, unhandled by maiden fingers from
the time Wenona touched me until to-day, when
you, of the Stone Giants' line, have picked me up."

"You poor darling Bek-wuk, I'm going to keep
you always and have a gold loop put in you and
hang you around my neck. To think that all this
happened in our field ! But why did the soldiers and Red Brothers fight ? Which was really

wrong? I can never quite seem to find out exactly, except that both wanted the land, and the strongest got it."

"How should I know? I am but an Arrowhead. I have only seen a glimpse here and there, and those Red Brothers cannot tell, for they have all gone after Wenona, while the children of the Stone Giants flourish. Who was right and who was wrong? Ask Wabeno, the Magician."

A shout from the farther side of the field called Anne's attention from the bits of stone in her lap, and she dropped them into her pocket again, with the exception of Bek-wuk, which she held carefully in her hand.

"Anne, A-n-n-e, where a-r-e you?" called Tommy, who was floundering in and out between the furrows as fast as his short legs would carry him.

"I didn't fink you were under the twee all this time; Baldy said you'd done home. Baldy and Obi 've done home to dinner tause it's twelve o'clock, and I went up to the house for some bwead and 'lasses, tause mother lets me have some if I work out all the morning *vely hard;* and what do you fink, but Lumberlegs went off wif Waddles yesterday, but he didn't come back

wif him last night.   He's tome back now and his
face is all stratched to pieces and one eye won't
open.   Baldy says—he says Waddles took him
away to fight the Miller's cat."

"Poor Lumberlegs !   I must go up and try to
cure his poor face," sighed Anne.   "I don't see
how Waddles can be so wicked, for he came home
himself last night and never said a word about it."

"Oh, I've tured Lumberlegs all nice," said
Tommy, gleefully, "and put him in the wood
house to go asleep; he was vely, vely tired."

"How did you cure him ?   Would he let you
wash his face ? "

"No, I didn't wash it; I just sticked all
the stratches up and the hurt eye wif the nice
spool of sticky plaster the Doctor dave you, and I
rubbed some of the white butter out of your china
box on to the places between."

"Tommy !   Do you mean to say that you've
taken all the ointment, and the lovely rubber
sticking-plaster that the Doctor gave me, and
smeared it all over that dog ?   Don't you know
it didn't belong to you in the first place, and that
it's very wrong to put sticking-plaster on to dirty
wounds that haven't been washed, because it makes
the sickness all grow inside and be poison ? " said
Anne very crossly, for her.

"You said—the fings in your box—was—for —accidents—and an—accident—hap-pened to Lumber-legs—and I didn't mean to—poison him—" and Tommy began to sob, for he loved Anne dearly, and really never intentionally bothered her or meddled with her things.

"Now don't cry but come up and help me get some warm water and wash the plaster off," said Anne, patting him and hurrying off toward the house. "You meant well, but being a doctor is very important work, because I heard father say once the distance between kill and cure is less than a mile—though I don't exactly know why our doctor laughed so when father said it."

Lumberlegs was indeed a funny sight. When Anne opened the wood-house door he crawled out, tired and footsore, with his face smeared with ointment, mixed with the molasses from Tommy's fingers, and rags of sticking-plaster, which he had vainly tried to rub off, hanging to his ears.

While Tommy had gone for some warm water, Waddles sauntered in, giving his chum a friendly little lick on the nose as he passed.

"How did this happen, sir?" asked Anne, sternly.

"Well, you see, missy, the Miller's cat took three of Tommy's white banties, and I promised

their hatch-mother, the fat brown Hen, that we
would teach him a lesson. So yesterday when we
were speaking to Tiger about it, and telling him
what we would do to him if he ever came over
our side of the river again, he jumped right
down on Lumberlegs' head and clawed and spit.
Then Lumberlegs ran away and shook Tiger off,
but he would follow Tiger on down to the mill.
I said he'd better come home, but he preferred to
wait and watch out there all night."

"Where is Tiger now?" asked Anne, laughing
in spite of herself.

"I don't know exactly, — that is, I'm not *quite*
sure," said Waddles, hesitatingly.

"Did Baldy tell you what had become of
Tiger?" said Anne to Tommy, as he returned
with the water.

"Baldy didn't know *zactly*, but he said Tiger
was where he wouldn't eat any more Banties and
Pigeons, so I dess he's a long way off, tause Tiger
tould jump and climb 'most everywhere."

"I think the Chippie Sparrow in the Snowball
bush is very glad," said Waddles to Anne, "because Tiger winked at her yesterday and said,
'I'll let you off to-day so you can hatch those eggs,
and next week when I come around there'll be
five of you for my luncheon instead of one!'"

That evening as Anne stood at the back gate looking down over the fields toward the far-away river, woods, and mountain, she thought of all Bek-wuk had said and of the Red Brothers who had vanished so long ago, and she took the Arrow-head from her pocket and held it toward the setting sun.

"To think that a bit of stone should have seen so much," she whispered; "it makes all my arithmetic and spelling lessons seem such very little things."

"Anne, Anne!" cried Tommy rushing up the road, breathlessly, "the Gypsies have been here and nobody knew it until they runned away again. They stoled a horse somewhere else and the people it belonged to are chasing for them — and they left a poor hungry miser'ble Bobtailed Horse up in Miss Jule's old barn by the woods, and she and Baldy are going up to see it — and Baldy says they've left a wild dog up there, too, that'll have to be shooted maybe; it's a Widow Dog with some poor little puppies that have no father, and it's vely tross and wild. Wouldn't you just love to see a tross wild Widow Dog? I would, but Miss Jule wouldn't let me go. You come and beg her wif me, won't you?"

X

The Widow Dog

ANNE knew very well that if Miss Jule said no she meant it. So instead of going down to the Horse Farm with Tommy to beg for a peep at the wild sad Widow Dog, and the Bobtailed Horse, she coaxed him home with the promise that Baldy would tell them all about the affair in the morning.

"Besides, Tommy," said Anne, "you know that though Miss Jule doesn't like to be teased she may change her mind by to-morrow if she sees a good reason, and then no will turn into yes without any begging."

Meanwhile Miss Jule and Baldy were making

their way to the old barn on the wood edge. A grass-grown lane led to this barn from the highway ; but it had not been in use for many years, and bushes and ferns grew where the wheel tracks had been.

To-day, however, the undergrowth was trampled down, whisps of hay festooned the bushes, and fresh horse tracks could be seen everywhere.

" They must have lit out in a pretty considerable sort of a hurry — look a here ! " said Baldy, picking up a good halter. " Land alive ! if here ain't one o' them new horse sheets that they've jest got in down at the harness shop," he continued, lifting a heap of checked linen that had lodged on a chestnut stump. " See, they wuz drivin' careless and the for'ard wheel hit the stump and slewed this stuff off. I should jedge by the signs that they must a left airly yesterday mornin', and a good job, too ! Mighty strange how they crep' in here unbeknown ! "

" Don't dilly-dally around here picking up stuff that can't run away, when there's a horse and a dog up there that, according to your reckoning, have had no food or drink since yesterday morning," said Miss Jule, striding along without giving a glance at the blanket that Baldy was stopping to shake out and fold.

"Yes, bring it along, we may need it to put over the horse when we lead it down to the farm. Ah, it hears our voices and whinnies."

"You surely aren't goin' to take an old, broken-down tramp horse, with glanders likely enough, down to the farm. If it wuz fit for anything them gypsy thieves wouldn't a left it behind," objected Baldy, stoutly.

But Miss Jule did not answer; she had reached the door by this time, and standing aside threw it wide open to let in the light. A low growl came from one corner, a joyful whinny from the other.

"Do mind yourself, miss," implored Baldy. "I had orter brought a gun!"

"Gun!" snorted Miss Jule, contemptuously; "I never saw an animal yet that I thought was as dangerous as a twopenny pop-gun. Take that old pail and get some water. The horse has a few whisps of weed hay left, but must be choked with thirst."

Baldy trotted obediently off to the brook, and Miss Jule turned her attention to the corner from which the growl came. Two blazing blood-shot eyes were all she saw at first, then as she became accustomed to the dim light the growl took shape. There, chained to a post, was a large brindled bull dog, and huddled beside her, in a dusky heap, were three puppies a month or more old.

Chained, with no food or water for two days, and a family dependent upon her, it was no wonder that this poor Widow Dog looked gaunt and wild-eyed. Besides, as Miss Jule knew, a bull dog at best is not apt to be very amicable to the general public, and when a female fears that her pups may be harmed, watch out !

Miss Jule had at first intended to unchain the dog, but seeing good reasons she changed her mind, as Anne had said she sometimes did. Instead, she unrolled a paper parcel that she had brought, took from it some scraps of food and a bottle, and then looked about for some sort of a dish. She discovered a rusty tin pan that had been used to hold food for the birds the previous winter. Into this she poured a little milk from the bottle and went out of the barn.

At the sight of the food the dog stopped growling, raised her head, sniffed eagerly, and began to tremble.

Miss Jule returned with a stick she had cut, put the pan of milk on the floor, then pushed it very carefully within reach of the dog, who crawled forward, showing that something was the matter with her right front paw. Before she could get even a taste of the milk, the pups had scrambled into the dish and gobbled it up.

This time Miss Jule ventured to refill the dish where it was, and as the mother took a comfortable drink the pups ran out on the floor and began to sniff at the food scraps, and rolled over and over, trying to play and make friends. Instantly their mother sprang to the length of her chain and growled savagely, but Miss Jule spoke cheerfully to her, pushed some meat within her reach, and began to pet the pups, showing that she did not mean to hurt them.

Baldy came back and the horse was given water, a few swallows at a time, until he had had as much as was good for him.

" Lead him outdoors," said Miss Jule, " and let me see what sort of an animal he is."

Baldy obeyed, and uneven hoof steps crossed the floor and stumbled over the door-sill to the grass, which the horse began to crop eagerly.

" Humph! lame for'ard, quarter crack, and shoes off both hind feet," ejaculated Miss Jule, as she walked about, surveying him on all sides. " Worn out, — no particular disease, a bone spavin in that for'ard joint, corns in the hoofs from bad shoeing, — just worn out and discouraged, that's all. Very good frame, though, good bone, very good bone;

let's see your teeth, old
man. There then, not so
bad. I don't believe you're
more than eighteen; we'll
fix you up and you'll have
some good times yet. A
nice rest, with your shoes
off, in a soft pasture — how would that suit, eh? "

The horse rubbed his head against Miss Jule's
sleeve, and seemed to thank her with a quiver of
its soft wrinkled nose; presently she started so
suddenly that he drew his head back as if fearing
a blow.

"Baldwin," she cried, "look at that tail! Was
there ever anything so hopeless? Yet there are

fools who insist that docking, cruelty aside, is
beautiful."

The horse's tail had been docked as short as
possible, the hair having been mostly rubbed off
by an ill-fitting harness, or else shed through lack
of care; a bare stump took the place of the fringy
ornament Nature gives even the most lowly born
of horses.

"Something will have to be done about that
tail," continued Miss Jule to herself; "I've never
had a docked-tailed horse on the farm, nor the
Squire either. Yes, something will have to be
done, though I don't know just what.

"Baldwin, look here!" she exclaimed again in
a few moments, "do you see that strange white
star blaze on his face? That is like the blaze on
old Fencer, the big black mare the Squire used to
keep when I was a bit of a schoolgirl, and I've
never seen the mark on any other stock. I believe
this is one of her foals. If it's so, I can prove it
by the stud sale book. You dear old beast, do
you know, maybe, you're coming home again? Do
you think you will remember the stables and the
brook? You'll find everything just the same,
except the Squire isn't there, and you'll have to
put up with me instead.

"To think of it, you may have belonged to the

farm in the old days!" and Miss Jule, the strong-minded woman, whom no horse-dealer in the county could outwit, put her head on the rough neck of the wretched old horse and hugged him, as if she were no older than Anne herself.

"Yes, it's likely to be one of Fencer's foals; but what's the good of him? Do your best, you can't fix him up to bring but a few dollars, and what with doctorin' the spavin and shoein' and feedin', he'll cost you ten dollars to the start. Now my advice'll be to — jes' — shoot —"

"Baldwin, when I *ask* advice you may give it; lead this horse down to the farm and put him in the hay barn with the work team. I will follow with the dogs," said Miss Jule, pointing down the lane and with a look in her eye that explained why she could train colts without ever using a whip.

"Now, old dog, you feel better. Good milk and meat, wasn't it? Do you think you're pleasant enough to be unchained and walk down to my house? Yes, you do? Wagging your tail is a good sign, but how shall we move the pups? Suppose I carry two, and we let the other one walk to keep you company. Yes, you understand, don't you?

"Ah, your poor paw!" she exclaimed as the

Bull Dog, on being unchained, began to limp
along ; "some brute has given you a hateful kick;
but we'll fix that all right, for the bone isn't
broken. A bath and some liniment, a new collar,
a clean straw bed, and you won't know yourself,"
she continued gayly. "Not that you are pretty
and you're not young, but you've got good points
for your breed, and what else can be expected of
anybody ?

"Do you happen to remember your name ? Is
it Bruiser ? Buster ? Betty ? Brindle ?" But as
the dog seemed equally indifferent with each of
these names Miss Jule was forced to think that
she either had no name or else had been called by
a great many. At any rate the poor creature was
convinced of the kindness of the intentions regard-
ing her pups and the procession started, Miss Jule
shortening her vigorous steps to suit both the
puppy, who walked with a sidewise kittenish gait,
and the Widow, who hobbled.

"I don't know what I shall do with these beasts,
I'm sure," said Miss Jule to no one in particular,
as she walked along.

"Something will turn up, I suppose ; meanwhile I must keep them out of the way of Tommy.
He would be sure to meddle with the pups, and
then the Widow would chew him up. Perhaps

one of the pups might make a good chum for him,
though; they are of a faithful breed. No, that
would never do; they wouldn't countenance a
brindled Bull Dog up at Happy Hall.

"Heigho! here we are at home. I can't have
a strange dog about with other animals unless it's
had a bath, and as I don't think any of the stable-
men will fancy the job, and would probably use
the hose and chill the poor thing, I'll do it myself.

"Baldwin," she called, as she spied that useful
man going up toward his own house with his hat
pulled farther down over his ears than usual,
"Baldwin, I wish you'd keep your eye on Tommy
and see, for a few days, that he doesn't come down
here when I'm away and try to make friends with
that Bull Dog."

"Yes, mum, I'll mind Tommy. But suppose
the Gypsies lays claims to their property some day
when you've got it all reg'lated."

"Lay claim!" cried Miss Jule; "I'll have them
arrested for stealing the halter and blanket and
breaking into my barn and trespassing on my
land. Lay claim, indeed!"

So Baldy offered no more objections, but giving
his hat an extra pull hurried up the road.

A patient study of her father's books satisfied
Miss Jule that the old horse was no other than

Fox, the eldest son of the Squire's famous mare
Fencer, broken to saddle in his fourth year and
sold to a well-known rider. All the dates fitted
together, and so Fox found himself treated with
the respect due to a long-lost friend — something,
by the way, that he did not quite understand.

"I wish we knew who docked his tail, and
what he has been doing all these years," said
Anne when Miss Jule told her the story a week
later; "it would be so interesting to know just
how a horse feels about things," — then adding
to herself, "maybe he'll tell me some day when
we are alone, — horse talk ought to be real easy
to understand after frog and toad and arrow lan-
guages.

"Miss Jule, I don't think you need worry any
more about Tommy's wanting to see the Bull Dog,
because he hasn't even spoken about her since that
very first day, and he's ever so busy nowadays
going with the plough and Baldy, and he and Lumberlegs seem to be getting along better together."

*　　*　　*　　*　　*　　*

A few days after this something very strange
happened. Tommy was lost. His mother and
the maids hunted every nook and corner of the
house from the cellar to the attic, where he often

went to feed a pair of Red Squirrels who lodged under the eaves.

His father searched the barns and outbuildings and, finally, sick at heart, peered down the old open well in the pasture. Anne had not seen her brother, for she had been doing her usual morning lessons in the study. Baldy, who was bringing the work horses in for their noonday meal, said, "He stayed with me a piece, along back in the mornin', and then said he was hungry and I reckoned he went up home."

The cook furnished the latest news, saying that Tommy had come in about ten o'clock and asked for some pieces, to feed the dogs she supposed. "But he were very perticular, mum — he wanted bread and butter *and* meat to make 'samwiches,' he said, and I did be tellin' him butter was wasteful fer dogs, and he'd have to put up with lard, mum, which he did."

This gave the family new hope, that is, until Waddles and Lumberlegs were found below the garden watching a Woodchuck hole, but no Tommy.

"Perhaps Miss Jule may have come home and he has seen her go by on the way from the station and followed her," suggested Anne.

"She is home, fer certin," said Baldy, "and it won't do no harm to go see."

By this time the little village had been ransacked, — store, postoffice, and all, — with no results ; and a party, consisting of Anne, her father, and mother in the buckboard, with Baldy and Waddles following, went to the Horse Farm.

Disappointment again. Miss Jule had seen nothing of Tommy, neither had any of the grooms or stable-men, with whom he was a great pet.

While the older people were holding a consultation Anne walked sadly about the barns, Waddles following, running to and fro and sniffing here and there with a mysterious look in his face.

" Missy," he whispered, as soon as they were out of sight of the others, stopping before one of the smaller barns, " missy, I don't like to tell tales, because you say it's a mean trick, but my nose says Tommy's in here."

" Tommy in here ! Why, Waddles, how can that be ? This is where the Bull Dog lives and it's locked up and Miss Jule keeps the key. You must have a cold and so your smell is crooked."

" No, missy, Tommy is in here, and the ground says he didn't go in by the door. You'd better ask the people to look, only don't mention me in the matter. I'm no spoil-sport," said Waddles, loftily, holding his tail at an extra angle.

" This isn't telling tales," cried Anne, stooping

to hug him. "It's what father calls 'imparting necessary information'; and oh, Waddles, don't you see it is *very* necessary for us to stop mother's face from growing whiter and whiter — and nothing will except finding Tommy."

Waddles stood on guard, very well pleased with himself, while Anne flew back saying, with an effort not to appear excited, " Miss Jule, would you mind looking in the little barn where the Bull Dog lives ? "

" Bless me, child, what for ? " cried Miss Jule, looking quite startled as an idea struck her, and then adding, "of course I will look, but it's useless, for the key is kept on my desk and I've cautioned the men about leaving the door open after feeding her. That dog has been restless and tugging at her chain for the last two days, the men say ; but the pups are weaned and I suppose, of course, she doesn't care so much for them, and wants to get away."

All the same, Miss Jule sent for the key very quickly and they hastened to the barn, crowding together as the door was opened, so that Anne had to spring inside to keep from falling.

Miss Jule, who was the nearest, stifled the cry that rose to her lips, and put out her hand with a gesture to command silence. There, seated on a pile of straw, was Tommy, one pup on his knees, the others playing between his feet, while the great Bull Dog was nestled close to him, looking up with a gaze of deep affection, and now and then licking the end of his nose and chin very gently.

On seeing the group of people at the door, who were too much surprised at first to speak, Tommy put the puppy

down very carefully and ran toward them, seeming a little bewildered that they were so quiet, and then discovering that his mother, to whom he went first, had tears in her eyes.

"Oh, Tommy, how could you be so naughty as to run away and frighten us all so? Suppose that dog had torn you to pieces!" was all she said, hiding her face in his dimpled neck.

"But, mother, I wasn't naughty; I didn't run away; I only comed down here to feed the Widow Dog her bweakfast. You never told me not to come down, and I've comed five or seven days, I dess, and you never said I was lost before."

"However did you get in?" asked Miss Jule.

"Frough the little window over Fox's feed box," said Tommy, frankly, pointing to a narrow sash by the hay-rack in the box-stall.

"You came in through that slit!" exclaimed his father in astonishment.

"Yes, father, it *was* vely tight, but I camed the narrow way of me and pulled like mouses comes between boards, only it did stwash the samwiches. Fox didn't understand about me at first and he nibbled at me, but I splained to him, and he said 'all right.'"

"Why didn't you ask Miss Jule to let you see

the dog properly, instead of creeping in the window?"

"I was doing to ask to-morrow, but you see Miss Jule's been away. I did ask the men and they said they didn't have the key," said Tommy, being really so perfectly innocent of any idea of wrong-doing that scolding was out of place. Then he returned to the corner and casting himself on the straw whispered something in the alert ears and put his chubby face close to the brindled one. In a moment he had unsnapped the chain and was leading the Bull Dog to Miss Jule.

"See how good she is. I've named her Lily and she knows when I say it, — 'Up, Lily!'" and to every one's astonishment the tail wagged in response and she put her front paws on Tommy's sleeve.

"What a queer name for such an ugly, crooked-faced dog," said Anne.

"She isn't ugly, she's *bootiful*, and her face isn't trooked, it's only a little wee bit bent, and I *love* bent-faced dogs, and I've 'dopted her, same as Waddles has Lumberlegs, to be my vely own!" Then as the possibility of losing her struck him, he gasped : —

"You'll buy her for me, won't you, father?

R

Anne, you'll beg father to buy her; you promised you'd ask father to buy me a nice little dog that I'd like — don't you 'member you did ever so long back?"

" But this isn't a little dog; she's bigger than Waddles, and maybe Miss Jule won't sell her," said Anne.

" I don't care if she's big or little, she's just the right size. Oh, you will sell her, Miss Jule, won't you, for my red bank and my wheelbarrow and my white mice? I haven't shooked the bank since Christmas, and the white mice are vely nice pets; they keep growing more and more 'most every night. You'll sell me Lily, won't you, for all that?"

" No," said Miss Jule, " I won't sell her," — Tommy's father and mother looked relieved, — " but I'll give her to you." They looked amazed, and his mother said, " Really, Julia, do you think it safe? How about the other dogs?"

" Safe! Tommy will be as safe as if he had an escort of mounted police with him. When a child and a Bull Dog fall in love with each other at first sight, it's for life. As to the other dogs — there are rules in dogland. Waddles and Lumberlegs were at Happy Hall first; the Widow will understand this and mind her own business *so long as they keep away from her food and Tommy!*"

"To think that this is our baby who has tamed that brindled brute," sighed Tommy's mother as they followed Lily and her master back to Happy Hall.

"One good thing, my dear, you need worry no more about the child being stolen by Gypsies," said Tommy's father, smiling indulgently as he looked at the sturdy little legs and the face beaming with joy, adding, "Ah, the blessed confidence of young animals!"

    *   *   *   *   *   *

Anne and Waddles were invited to lunch with Miss Jule and so remained behind. While her hostess went to give some orders, Anne slipped back to the barn to see Fox.

He was looking brighter and better already, his spavin, which is a sort of sprain, had been blistered, his hoofs trimmed and the old shoe nails removed, his fetlocks and mane clipped, and he was having special food to make him shed his ragged, uncurried winter coat. Still, somehow, he didn't look quite happy.

Anne sauntered up and down the barn pulling whisps of straw from the rack and wondering to herself about Tommy and the Widow Dog.

"Why didn't she bite him at first before she knew that Tommy was going to love her?" Anne said half aloud; "for even Miss Jule, who isn't afraid of anything, seemed a little bit scary."

"There is a messenger that travels with real love, whether it goes among men or beasts, and prevents it from being misunderstood," said Heart of Nature's voice, wafting along with the fragrant breath of the hay. "This messenger's name is Confidence. House Child, when Love speaks to you in any of his many shapes, be sure that Confidence is with him. If he is not, then do not listen; it is only a trick of Wabeno, the Magician, a shadow picture from Wagoose's book."

"I don't quite understand how this messenger looks, dear Heart of Nature," said Anne, rather puzzled.

"When the poor dog looked into Tommy's face she saw there love and confidence. When you look in your mother's eyes, you see love and confidence; when she in turn looks in your father's, she sees love and confidence there."

"Ah, yes," said Anne, smiling; "yes, I remember, I know that look, I've seen it."

*   *   *   *   *   *

Fox whinnied, and Anne climbed up and perched on the side of his stall.

"I wish you would tell me about all the places you've been in and who chopped your tail off," she said, settling herself for a chat. "I do *so* want to know what horses like and what they don't, then when I have a horse of my very own next year I can be good to it. Maybe you think I can't understand what you say, but I'm Anne that used to be Tommy-

Anne and I wear the Magic Spectacles, Fox dear."

"You understand? Oh, then please tell me at once and end my suspense, is Miss Jule curing me to keep me herself or am I to be sold and have to move on again? If you only knew how tired

I am of moving on; I've hardly stayed in the same place six months at a time since I was twelve years old."

"She's going to *keep* you, you funny old dear," said Anne, brushing off some very sticky flies that were tickling his ears.

"Ah," sighed Fox, but this time it was a glad sigh, "I haven't been so happy since the day I left my first master, twelve years ago."

"Do tell me all about it, only you must stop chewing and talk rather quick, because it's nearly time for luncheon."

"When I left here it was shortly after my fourth birthday, and though I say it myself, I was a beauty. My mother, Fencer, was a famous hunter, and I had her broad chest, strong haunches, and straight limbs.

"'How finely Fox carries his ears and tail,' said the Squire, my master, and I did.

"Colonel Trevor's head groom bought me and I was led away clad in a beautiful checked blanket that covered me all but the eyes, and I took a long ride on the steam cars. When I arrived at my journey's end, I was led before the Colonel.

"'Good bone, good action, too much tail, — dock it,' was all he said. I didn't know what he meant, for I had never heard the word at the Horse

Farm. I soon learned. Not only was the hair of my beautiful tail cut away, but a part of the bone with it, leaving a miserable bleeding stump.

" The pain and soreness was bad enough, but when it was over and I took my place as a saddle horse and saw my shadow for the first time, I nearly died of mortification. However, as all the horses of my set had docked tails, I soon became used to it, — young animals like to be in the fashion, you know, — and even began to think it stylish. That is, until fly time, then I nearly went mad, and the groom being stupid mistook the cause of my restlessness, laid it to temper, and put the rein a loop lower in the curb bit.

" Still I enjoyed myself very well for a couple of years. Good grooming, good food, plenty of exercise. Then the Colonel died, and I was sold to a lady who wanted a 'stylish, well-bred horse for both saddle and dog cart.' At least she thought she did, but really she never knew exactly what she did want or where she was going. She didn't know a thing about Horse People and believed every fairy tale that the groom told her.

" She would ride me every day for a week, sitting all lop-sided, until I felt myself growing three-cornered. · The next week she would drive me in the cart, jerking me around corners, and changing her mind so often about the road that my mouth grew sore at first, then as hard as iron.

"The next week I would be left in the stable until too much food and lack of exercise gave me colic, and I had to be led up and down the road for hours and my stomach rubbed with a broom handle.

"I lived with this mistress for three years, and, though I was never abused, I lost my good temper and ruined my digestion. Then my troubles began.

"I was at an age then to take my place as a good steady family horse. I would have appreciated a home in a family without style, but who would talk to me and consider me as one of themselves. There is nothing that middle-aged horses enjoy more than an occasional apple or carrot mixed with intelligent conversation. At nine a horse prefers 'Get up, Fox, whoa, Fox!' to a cut of the whip and a jerk.

"Alas! my docked tail, which had been considered quite the thing in my youth, was now an object of ridicule. People came and looked at me, nice, pleasant-faced people with whom I longed to go, but one would say: 'Yes, a nice face, but that tail would be out of place in our surrey.' 'A good horse, and a cheap one, but I've always set my face against a docked tail, and I don't wish the children to grow used to one.' 'A good-boned critter, but with that tail he ain't no airthly use to haul truck to market or ter stand at Meetin' in fly time.' So one after another passed me by, and a grocer finally bought me to drag his wagon.

"The work was hard and the stable not very comfortable, but they always put a blanket over me in cold or wet weather, which was something my first two owners never remembered. All went well for three years more until one sad day, well I remember it, hot and muggy, when a great stinging horse-fly fastened himself to one of my flanks, quite out of reach of my mouth. The tail that Heart of Nature gave me to use in such emergencies being gone, there was nothing left for me to do but run, to try to shake the creature off.

"I ran, the wagon overturned and hurt a little girl and wrecked some costly goods. No one tried to find the cause — they simply sold me.

"Then I moved on, always from worse to worse. In the time between then and now I've dragged an ambulance, an ice wagon, a butcher cart, a truck, a milk wagon all through the freezing early winter mornings, besides doing so many other things it would take a day to tell of them.

"Finally, the worst of all came! I was harnessed to a cheap express cart to run with trunks over the smooth, icy pavements of a city. House People that have trunks to be moved seem late and always in a hurry, and we poor horses are whipped if we cannot make up the time they've lost.

"This was last winter; I struggled to do my best, but one day I fell on the cruel pavement, lamed myself, and could hurry no more. For two months I lived on musty hay in a filthy stable, then a man bought me for ten dollars, and with a string of other cripples like myself started out through the country.

"'Maybe we'll work him off on some farmer,' he said to his partner, punching my poor ribs and giving a sly laugh; 'if not, he's good for bones, eh?'

"You know the rest, and it is very good to think that I'm going to stay here now. I was afraid Miss Jule might dislike me and sell me again because of my poor tail, for I can see by my shadow all the hair has moulted now. I thought she might be ashamed to see me anywhere about the farm. You see that all my misfortunes, first and last, happened because my tail was docked."

"I'll never own a dock-tailed horse, never!" said Anne, pounding her fist upon her knees emphatically, — "that is, I mean, I'll never let my horse's tail be docked. Good-bye now, Fox, for there's the luncheon bell."

*   *   *   *   *   *

Later in the day Anne ran into the barn and putting her lips close to Fox's nearest ear whispered : —

"I've heard a great secret! Miss Jule has promised to send you to pasture for all the hot weather, and then in the fall she's going to let me ride on you all by myself every day. Not fast, you know, but so that I can learn, for she says you are of a reliable stock, and that a big old horse is better for a child to ride than a cranky little pony."

"Did she say anything about my tail?" asked Fox, anxiously.

"Yes, that is the biggest part of the surprise yet! Miss Jule asked the harness maker, and he's going to fix a tail to the crupper strap and your stump for you to wear when you go out, so you will *look* all right, though he says it won't wag as well as if it grew on."

Fox gave a whinny of joy, and Miss Jule coming in said, "What are you doing, giving him oats? Be careful, we must feed him scantily yet awhile."

"I wasn't feeding him, I was telling him about his new tail," replied Anne, forgetting herself.

"How do you manage to make him understand you?" asked Miss Jule, laughing.

"Ask Wabeno, the Magician," said Anne, almost without thinking.

"What strange little animals children are," sighed Miss Jule, as she nearly stepped on one of the pups. "Now I must find homes for these — there is always something to bother about."

"At any rate Widow Dog and the Bob-tailed Horse are both happy, dear Miss Jule," said Anne.

XI

Amog, the Honey Bee

DOG council was being held behind the barn at Happy Hall. There had been quite a quarrel about an old kennel that once belonged to Waddles. He had not used this kennel for years, but he was angry because Obi had mended it and put fresh straw in it for the Widow; for it had been decided that neither Lumberlegs nor Lily were to sleep in the big house.

Waddles was sitting in the doorway of the kennel merely to keep Lily out. Lily looked dangerous and red in the eyes, while poor Lumberlegs being frightened had trotted down to the Horse Farm and called his mother, the Duchess, who was respected in all serious matters as one of the wisest dogs in the country, besides being a splendid fighter who seldom fought.

Waddles and the Widow stood glowering at each other, muttering disagreeable words, while the Duchess had a very serious look upon her face and was giving them some good advice that they did not like.

"I was here first, and this was my very own house," said Waddles, as if that settled the matter.

"Very true," replied the Duchess, "that, of course, gives you the right to choose your own bed and make the dog rules of the place; but it is no reason why you should think that you are the only dog in the world. You have been chosen to sleep indoors and be a House Fourfoot; you are Anne's pet, but there are other dogs that are quite as pretty and clever."

"Lumberlegs is good looking and clever at hunting, but what is the Widow good for anyway?" said Waddles, rudely.

"I was made to take hold and keep hold," said Lily, speaking very quietly but looking angry. "My ancestors were trained to hold fierce bulls by the nose without flinching."

"I think you are more like a frog than a dog," said Waddles, provokingly, "and there aren't any wild bulls here for you to hold besides."

"What are you good for yourself, if I may ask, Mr. Waddles?"

"I, what am I good for? Everything, to be sure. In the first place I'm a House Fourfoot and sleep indoors, which is a very important position to hold. Then I can put my nose to the ground and tell who has been by, and where they are going. Besides, I can track Rabbits as straight as a die, and I sing such a fierce song as I run that they grow confused and forget where they live."

"Oh, so you are a Rabbit Hound and earn your living that way. I didn't know you had a regular trade," said Lily, apologetically.

"I haven't, exactly," said Waddles, hesitating, "because the master here only goes Rabbit hunting a few times in the winter."

"What were you made for, Lumberlegs?" asked Lily, suddenly.

"Our family have wide feet that spread and do not sink in snow or soft ground. We were made to live in a cold country and to find people who were lost in the snow and dig them out, and take the news of them to our masters," said the Duchess, answering for her son.

"I shouldn't think you could do much at your trade about here, then," said Lily, cocking one ear wisely.

"This is very silly talk," said the Duchess. "Dogs that live on a place like this do not always work at their trades; they are guests and friends of the House People, and they should earn their livings by watching out that nothing goes wrong on the farm, and should keep from fighting among themselves.

"No one can tell when my son Lumberlegs will have a chance to use his broad feet, or Lily her strong grip, or Waddles his keen nose, for the benefit of the family. Take my advice, Waddles, you watch out for Anne; and you, Lily, take good care of Tommy; and, Lumberlegs, do you look big and wise and learn to bark deep down in your throat and take good care of everything.

"Also mind your own business, especially at meal times, and don't even sniff and look at each other's plates, and be very particular when you bury bones to mark the place, so that you will not dig up some one else's cache and find that a harmless beef bone has turned into a 'bone of contention';" so saying, the Duchess turned about and marched home, leaving the trio looking very foolish.

This was the reason why that morning, when Tommy whistled for Lily to come and stay with him in the play room, because he had a queer rash on his face and couldn't go out, no Lily was to be found. Anne also looked vainly for Waddles as she started with Baldy in the hay wagon to go to the far-away swamp lots and bring home some pea brush that had been cut the fall before, and snowed under before it could be brought down.

It was a beautiful drive along the wood road ; all the trees were in leaf, and the air was full of the quaint little wing songs of insects as well as of bird music.

" Where are you going ? " hummed Amoe, the Honey Bee, darting from a fragrant wild grape-vine and flying close to Anne's face. " These are busy days for me, I can tell you ; voices calling from every corner of the Flower Market at once ; messages to carry from flower to flower and vege-tables to provide for the babies at home."

" I'm going to the hemlock woods between the swamp lots and the river, to look for wild flowers, while Baldy loads up his pea brush. Are there any pretty flowers or nice Beast Brothers up there Amoe ? I've never been there quite at this season, for do you know, Amoe, it will be June to-morrow ! "

8

"Flowers? — yes, plenty of them. I must go there myself this morning, so I'll keep beside you and chat as we go. Beast Brothers? — yes, there are some Fox puppies, only their mother is too clever to let you find them; and Whip, the great black snake from our pond marsh, has gone there and set up housekeeping. The Red-winged Blackbirds, Woodpeckers, Thrushes, and Quail were getting up a petition yesterday to beg that he might be made to move away.

"The difficulty was that they did not know to whom to send the petition. The Ko-ko-ko-hos might have had some influence with Whip; but they have moved away. Rufus Lynx has had so much trouble up at the mountain that he dare not come down. Reddy Fox has all he can do to feed his children with spring chickens and keep out of the hands of the farmers, and there doesn't seem to be any one to rid the poor birds of their terrible neighbour."

"Is Whip a very big snake, and does he bite? I thought that now the Bad One had died, there were no dangerous snakes left."

"Big! Whip measures six feet from tail tip to nose. He doesn't wear poison fangs; he *hugs* things to death."

"That is the way Lac and Lactina did, but they

were useful snakes that ate field mice and such things."

" Whip would be useful in a country where there is plenty of everything, but in a place like this he makes havoc. Every morning when I go abroad I see him gliding along, peering here and there, first in the low bushes, then going like lightning up some tree, every bump in his black body meaning an egg or a young bird. Yesterday I saw him coil about a full-grown Rabbit, give it a hug, and then swallow the quivering thing."

" I wish we could meet Whip to-day ; I'm sure Baldy could kill him, for he's got a brush hook and a pitch-fork," said Anne.

" Do you think he would ? Then I'll go swiftly and tell the Bird Brothers to watch for Whip and give us news of where he lies in wait. A moment only and I will meet you at the bars where one road goes down to the brush lots and the other skirts the woods. Be sure to wait for me by the white Dogwood tree."

* * * * * *

When they reached the bars Anne did as Amoe told her, and Baldy went downhill to collect his load, after cautioning her not to stray away too far.

" How many different kinds of flowers and seed pods there are," she said, as she looked from the Dogwood overhead to some rank growing little plants at her feet. These had straight little stems with swelled joints from which strange narrow green leaves stuck out like the spokes of an umbrella ; the dew was still glistening on them, making them look like some beautiful bit of enamel work covered with diamonds. The Ground Pine made a mat that reached as far as she could see up the hill, and close to her feet a splendid fern was slowly unfolding its fronds.

" I wonder how all these things keep alive that don't seem to have any flowers," she said aloud.

" There are many plants in my garden that have the precious life dust, even if they have no showy, bright flower petals to call attention to the fact, and have no need of insect messengers," said Heart of Nature, speaking from a bed of pale green Maidenhair Ferns that trembled in the breeze on the bank above Anne's head.

" These flowerless plants of my garden, instead of the heart of blossoms, use tiny spores for their seed-lunch baskets. The rusty spots on the under side of the fern frond are precious seed dust. The little forks that you will see later on the Ground

Pine are full of it, and the conelike spike on the top of that Horsetail holds the vital dust."

" Horsetail ! where ? " asked Anne, peering about.

" That slim plant that glitters with dew and looks like a young Pine."

" Oh, how sharp it is ! " cried Anne, as she picked one ; " it's sharper than grass or wheat stems."

" Of course I'm sharp, for I suck up hard rock dust from the ground to make me strong, just as wheat and rye do," said a talkative Horsetail.

" If those grains did not eat rock, their slender stems could never hold their heavy heads up, and when you see a weak, floppy field of grain you may know it didn't have enough rock dust to eat when it was young and so had weak bones. I've got so much sand in me that people used to pick bunches of my family and tie them into sort of brooms to scour tins with ; so we've got the nickname of Scouring Rushes. I can

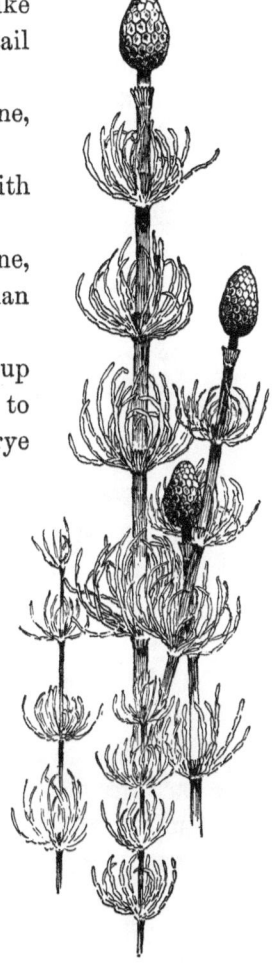

tell you something about us that is queerer yet; I heard it from a bit of granite rock that rolled downhill and stopped here awhile until some one carted it off to help make a gate-post. I belong to the same family of plants, that used to live millions of years ago, that sucked all the sunshine and fire gas out of the air and packed it away to turn into coal. My ancestors grew hundreds of times bigger and thicker and better than we do now (but, then, everybody's ancestors always did that), and we used, in those days, to associate with Ferns and Club Mosses and Ground Pines, and we've kept up the habit ever since. So you see we flowerless plants are very exclusive, keeping in a set quite by ourselves and never mixing with those bold plants in the Flower Market that are always dressing up in gay colours and gossiping and talking with the Bees."

"I'm a rather interesting sort of plant, too," said the flat-leaved Ground Pine. "Later on I grow little spikes full of magic yellow piny seed dust that, if it touches fire, blazes and snaps and sparkles more beautifully than the fireflies. It is important, very important dust too, for I've heard it said by Miou, the Catbird, who is always peeping and prying about, that House People gather up this yellow dust and use it to pack pills in."

"Do you mean that your seed dust is that flya-way powder that comes in pill boxes?" asked Anne, eagerly. "Only the other day mother was burning up some old boxes and the dust flashed and snapped like fireworks, and we wondered what it could be. Heigho! Everything in Nature's garden seems to be good for ever so many things."

"I wish you would pull up this Hog Peanut that is climbing around me; it's going to squeeze all my lovely green leaves to bits and choke me to death before the season is out," said a great tuft of Ferns; "it's very hard for a member of the Royal Family of Ferns to be smoth-ered by a mean little weed."

"These vines are very horrid things," said

GROUND PINE.

Anne, as she stooped to release the Fern; "there were some in mother's Fern bed that came with the Ferns from the woods, and we can't seem to get them out."

The Hog Peanut laughed to itself, but said nothing, while a great long-stemmed Violet a little farther down by the spring called, "I can tell you why you can't get rid of those vines, — Heart of Nature gives some of us plants two kinds of flowers, so as to be sure that we yield plenty of seed to keep up our race. One sort of flower grows and blossoms on the plant above ground, as the Hog Peanut flowers and my own purple blossoms do, the seed pods ripen and split, and the seed is scattered abroad, to grow or be lost. The other flower is a blind thing, growing from the stem under the ground. Dull and homely though it is, it has very big seed-lunch baskets, and these seeds lying close in the moist earth grow almost without knowing it, and the life of the plant is made doubly sure. I, too, bear these blind underground blossoms in late summer, and if you come and pull me you will see that I tell the truth."

"How strange," said Anne to herself; "but I wonder why such a mischievous plant as that Peanut, that no one, not even the Ferns, likes, should have two ways of making seed?"

All the Hog Peanuts on the bank and through
the wood began to titter, and one very sturdy
vine, that had wound around a bunch of Horsetails until they were prisoners, whispered, —
" Why ? Ask Wabeno, the Magician."

* * * * * *

Buzz — thud ! Amoe, the Honey Bee, had returned, and bumped his head with much force
against Anne's sleeve.

" I hope you are not hurt ; you didn't see me,
did you ? " said Anne. " Have the birds seen
Whip to-day, and has he done any mischief yet ? "

" I'm not hurt," answered Amoe, " and I saw
you quite well at a distance, but lost my reckoning when I came quite near. You see we Bees
are very far-sighted so that we may see our hives
and the flowers who need us from afar, but when
we are close to a thing, then we have to feel our
way like blind men."

" I've often noticed how you feel of flowers
when you are taking messages for them, but how
about Whip ? "

" Whip has not been out to-day ; you know it
was a cool night and the sun is not far up yet.
The Field Sparrow, the Phœbe, and the Marsh
Wren are on the watch for him ; they can slip

poison Sumac

Virginia
Creeper

poison ivy

G.

along quietly and unseen and they will bring us news as soon as Whip leaves his hole under the dead Willow in the swamp lot.

"Come up under the Hemlocks and watch me while I carry messages between some wild, shy flowers there, the stemless pink Moccasin Flowers that keep alone and apart, perching daintily on the bank as if ready to fly away if the winds but called them. They are proud flowers, too, and belong to the Royal Tribe of Orchids."

Anne began to climb a tumble-down stone fence that separated the lane road from the wood beyond and grasped at the branch of a tall shrub to steady herself.

"Don't touch that! don't!" shrieked Amoe, buzzing like a whole hive of Bees. "That is a member of the Poison Family; it is called Poison Sumach, and if you get its juice on your face and hands, or wherever else it touches, you will swell up and grow red and smart terribly."

Anne jumped down into a mass of Ferns when Amoe called, thinking at first that Whip must be somewhere near by, and sat looking up at the bush. It seemed to be harmless enough, and then she remembered that Tommy was at home with his face swelled up and red, and that the Doctor said he must have rubbed against some poisonous plant.

"I didn't think there was anything but Poison Ivy that would hurt any one hereabout, and that has three leaves in a bunch and white berries that hang down, and when it's old, you see lots of fuzzy roots all over the stems that it climbs by. The fences down at the Horse Farm are full of it. But how can I tell this poison one from the other nice Sumachs, Amoe — the ones that grow all over the mountain, and in autumn have such pretty red berries and leaves?"

"The Poison Sumachs have flower bunches that hang down like bunches of grapes and they always wear whitish berries, like the Poison Ivy. We Bees have to be very particular about this also, for if we take home the seed dust from poison flowers, we might kill some of the children of the hive. Careless nurses do this sometimes and make great trouble."

"Nurses! do Bees have nurses?"

"Certainly; we have workers in our Queen-dom; but I also am a worker and must do my work first and talk afterward. Sit down here and watch me."

Anne took her seat at the foot of a big Hemlock. As soon as her eyes became used to the confusion of light and shade, she saw that she was surrounded by troops of the prettiest plants imaginable, a nodding flower coming from every pair of green leaves.

Amoe, who had disappeared inside one of these pink flowers through a cleft in the pouch, called, "Pick this flower and peep inside and see how Heart of Nature wills that I creep in by the open door to gather the pollen dust that I need as meat for the children of the hive, then I must pass out by a narrow window that forces me to drop some of the precious pol-len dust to fill the flower's seed-lunch basket."

Anne picked the flower care-fully, and opening the pouch gently with her finger looked as Amoe bade. She was too much astonished by what she saw to speak. But Heart of Nature, lingering in the wood silence, reading her thoughts, said, " Here again in this flower you see written the word ' Brotherhood '; is it not bee for flower and flower for bee, each giving life to the other? "

Amoe crawled out again, some yellow dust sticking to the hairs on his legs, and rested on Anne's frock.

" You call that seed dust meat? I thought it was honey," said she.

" Ah, no, honey is different ; this pollen is stronger food, so we call it meat. Every flower grows it differently; to you it seems all as dust, but to our sharp insect eyes it has as many shapes as the fruits and vegetables in the gardens of House People. To the eyes of a Bee the dust of every flower has its own form. The Bee People need variety in their eating the same as others."

" You said something about a Queendom a minute ago. What did you mean? " asked Anne, as she carefully gathered some of

the wonderful flowers to carry home. "Where
is your hive? Are you one of the Miller's Bees?
He has a great many, but they seem to be always
cross, and there is such a noise in the hives it
seems as if they were always scolding."

"I'm a plain wild Bee," said Amoe, "and though
my ancestors, of course, came from some one's
hive, we have lived in the woods as free people
for a long time; I do not wear their foreign-
striped dress.

"My home tree is a hollow Sassafras. Where
it is, I will not tell, for we do not wish its lining
of rich honey to be stolen. House People have
not found our home, because the little door by
which we go in and out is the only entrance to
the Queendom.

"We call our colony a Queendom, because a
Queen is always the ruler of it. Listen, Anne:
*never in any Bee Colony has there ever been a
King!* There are male Bees, of course; but we
don't think much of them; they hang about the
hive, never help us work, and get in the way, and
sometimes in late summer, if we are very busy
storing up honey for winter, we grow vexed and
kill them off, — Drones, we call them, — because
they do nothing in nest building or honey storing,
— they haven't even a sting to their names."

"But why is that?" asked Anne. "In the Bird and Beast Brotherhoods the males work."

"Ask Wabeno, the Magician. To him alone has Heart of Nature told all the wonders of the Bee Sisters. We ourselves only know these things as they are, but not the reasons for them.

"One thing is certain, in a Queendom the female is *the* important person. With us there are two kinds of these, the Queen herself who rules the hive, lays the eggs, but does no other work, living in the throne room in the centre of the hive and not even feeding herself, and the working Bees. These last are divided into two guilds, — the Wax Workers and the Nurses.

"The Wax Workers have half a dozen little pockets around their waists to hold the cakes of wax they make until they are ready to use them to build the cells in which the eggs are laid and the honey stored. The Nurses are those who go out, as I do, to gather meat and drink for the helpless children of the hive, who live each one in a little cell by itself during the changes that turn them from a soft whitish egg to a grub, then to larvæ, and at the end of a couple of weeks to a fully grown Bee.

"Oh, how we Nurses have to toil! We know which eggs will yield Queens, Workers, and

Drones. We do not give the Drone grubs much to
eat — perhaps that is why they are so stupid. We
feed the Workers well, from the grub up; but it is
the Princess eggs that get the attention and petting,
and yield the largest Bees in the hive. The larvæ
of a Princess is not fed with common food at all,
but with rich 'royal jelly,' which we Nurses prepare by swallowing the choicest food and making
it into a sweet paste, then unswallowing it to
feed the royal line."

"Why, that is the way Pigeons and Wood
peckers do," said Anne to herself; "to think a
Bee should know so much !"

"That is nothing compared to some things we
do," said Amoe. "There can never but one
Queen rule at once in a hive. So if several young
Princesses are hatched, a guard of workers keep
them prisoners. Often the reigning Queen will
go off, followed by a throng of working Bees, to
make a new colony in another place; then one of
the Princesses is chosen for a Queen. Sometimes
a hive will have lost their Queen, and there will be
two Princesses of the same age; then the workers
hold a meeting and stand in a ring and let the
Princesses fight together until one is killed and
then they obey the other as their Queen."

"But how very cruel; couldn't they choose in

a kinder way, or let the others be called the Crown Princesses ?" asked Anne.

"Impossible! Heart of Nature knows that when the ruler is a female there must be only one at once, so that is the law among the Bee Sisters."

Amoe paused for a moment and began gathering the golden pollen from his hairy legs into little balls, which is the shape in which it must be taken to the hive.

"Others besides House People try to steal our honey, so when we are working in a hurry in late summer to fill the honeycombs, and every Worker tries to fill his bags as quickly as possible, we station sentinels at the hive door to challenge every Bee that passes and make sure that he has a right to enter. For often lazy Bees and Robber Flies, that look exactly like the Bee Sisters, will take advantage of our hurry to sneak in and steal from our store. And every one knows what happens to a Queendom when numbing frost arrives and the honeycombs are empty. Ah, how we love the sun and how we keep a-buzzing in warm weather ! "

"Isn't it very warm and stuffy in a hive ?" asked Anne. "I've seen the Miller's hives and there are no windows, only one mite of a door."

T

"No; on the con-
trary, the air is
very good; we
Bee People would soon die in bad air,
for even a little puff of smoke will kill us,
so Heart of Nature has taught us how to
keep the hive fresh. Inside the doorway are stationed the Workers who
have charge of airing the hive;
they move their wings rapidly as
if in flying, and this motion from so
many Bees drives the good air in and
around the hive and the foul air out.
The hotter the day the more need of air,
and the buzzing that you hear within
the hive is ___ the noise these

QUEEN

DRONE

Bee ventilators make at
work."

Anne sat still in speechless
amazement, and just then
Gitche-ah-mo, the Bumble
Bee, flew overhead.

"Is the big Bumble Bee one
of your Queens?"

"No, indeed; they belong to a

different branch of the family; for besides we Honey Bees the Bee Brothers number among them the Bumble Bees, that make homes in old nests; black Stone Mason Bees, that live among stone heaps; and Carpenters that bore out tunnels for their homes in old wood."

"Say, Zeay!" called Miou, the Catbird, close in Anne's ear, "Whip is out and looking in all the bushes along the edge of the brush meadow, and Mrs. Robin Thrush has this morning hatched four fine youngsters in one of the old apple trees, and she always makes such a fuss that Whip is sure to find her. There is a man down in the brush lot with a fine axe, if only we could speak his language and tell him about Whip."

"Why, that man is Baldy," said Anne; "I'll run and call him as quickly as I can, only you must tell me which way to go so that Whip won't see me, for I'm sure I don't care to meet him."

"Follow me, then," said Amoe; "a Bee always flies straight and sure, and makes a 'bee line,' you know."

Anne scrambled downhill as fast as she could, ran along the lane, crept through the bars, keeping among the bushes until she came close to Baldy, who had finished loading his brush.

"Hurry!" cried Miou, keeping close beside

her, "the Phœbe told me, in darting by, that
Whip is wound round the very limb the nest is
on and is gazing at Robin Thrush with the dreadful cold, narrow-eyed stare that means
death."

"Baldy," gasped Anne, "there
is a monstrous black Snake in that
Apple tree yonder that is going to
eat a whole Robin
family!"

"Your eyes
must be better
than mine,"
said Baldy,
looking toward
the tree, but at
the same time
seizing his
brush hook, for
he had come to
realize that
Anne could see
many things that
others could not.

Whip was so busy twittering
his tongue at the birds as he
gloated over the meal within his

reach that he did not hear the footsteps. For one anxious moment Anne looked at the nest, the parent birds with helpless, drooping wings, and the glistening black coil with head well raised. She heard the useless cries of sympathy from all the birds gathered from far and near, then the brush hook said " swish," the coil writhed and dropped, another " swish " and Whip was no longer a terror to Birdland, but a beheaded dead snake to be placed on the wagon and carried home as a trophy, though it must be said that at least four of his six feet of length protested against the whole proceeding by wriggling vigorously all the way.

" We must give the Woodpeckers an order to carve this House Child a vote of thanks on the very best birch bark," said Robin Thrush, when he had recovered his wits.

" I think it will be better if we all *sing* our thanks outside her window," said the Song-Sparrow; " I'm going to fly before her and sing from every bush on the road."

As they reached the highway Amoe, who had kept close beside Anne all the way, whispered, " The Iris by the brook are calling, and I must fly home and empty my meat basket before I can go to them ; but we shall often meet in the Flower

Market, and when anything there puzzles you, pick a blossom newly come into bloom that has received no insect messenger ; breathe on it gently and say, 'Where is Amoe, the Honey Bee ? ' and I will come to you."

*   *   *   *   *   *

Baldy stopped the horses when he reached the mill, for he had to give the Miller a message about some feed, so that Anne had a chance to slip into the garden where the hives stood. The sun shone on them brightly and the humming inside was very loud. Suddenly a big Bee darted out and off and in a moment a cloud of other Bees followed. Then the Miller's wife rushed out and called her son and they seized a box and both ran after the swarm, beating on tin pans to try to stop their flight.

"What's the matter ? " called Baldy and the Miller together. They heard the noise but could not see the cause.

" I was listening to the Working Bees fanning fresh air into the hive, when the Queen, I think it must have been, flew away and most of the others went after her to make a new Queendom," said Anne to the Miller. "But your wife need not be so worried if she can't catch them, because the Nurses will feed some more Princess eggs with royal jam, and they will hatch out ; then there will be a fight to see which one will be Queen, and everything will come out right, you know."

XII

The Village in the Pond

"BI found this sailing on the big pond behind the mill, and it is the very firstest," said Tommy, running in one morning and holding up a beautiful white Water Lily for Anne to smell.

"How can it sail, and why didn't it fall over the mill-dam and be drowned, same as Baldy said

I would if I went near the pond?" he asked, swinging the flower by its long rubber-like stem as he capered about his sister.

" The very first Water Lily ! Oh, please let me have it, Tommy ! The day that Obi stuck the hook in his finger when he was fishing for Eels, the Water Spirits promised to show me the Village in the Pond, if I went there the first day *the first Water Lily bloomed.* "

" I'm going to ask mother to let me go wiv you; *please* wait for me," shouted Tommy, dashing off; but his mother had gone out in the garden and it took him a long time to find her.

Meanwhile Anne, who was so eager about the Lily that she did not know that she had told her secret aloud or that Tommy had asked her to wait, started down the road to the river, putting on her hat as she went.

" This is the first Lily, but how can I be sure that it wasn't open yesterday ? " she said anxiously. " Growing in the water keeps them fresh until they are awfully old. I had a dish full of them once last summer, and they opened every day for nearly a week."

" Look inside the flower," said Amoe, the Honey Bee, buzzing close to her ear.

" Do you see the little yellow claws powdered

with life dust, that stand in a ring and guard
the entrance to the seed-lunch baskets? When
these little claws stand upright, then the flower
is newly opened; but when the Lily has sent all its
messages abroad and its seed-lunch baskets are
full, then these claws curve in, their colour fades,
and they close over the flower's heart tighter and
tighter each day of its life, until the morning
when it no longer opens but sinks beneath the
water to ripen the seeds and plant them securely
in the mud."

"These claws seem wide open," cried Anne,
delightedly; "please look, Amoe."

"Yes, it is a freshly blown Lily, and no Bee has
ever heard it whisper a message, and its lunch
baskets are quite empty. I'll meet you farther
down the lane; I have some business over yonder
in that field."

Anne soon reached the mill-pond and began
peeping about the edge, looking for a place where
she could see into the water, for the margin was
muddy and Alders hid the water.

"Want to see the fish jump? They are lively
this morning," called the Miller, cheerfully. He
had been taking some old wood out of the flume
and was paddling toward Anne in an old flat-
bottomed boat.

"I'm going to tie up right here to this willer, and then you can set in the boat fust rate, and not float away nor damp yer feet."

Truly, this was luck. Anne scrambled into the boat, and the Miller swung it out of the current and into the shade where, with her chin resting on the edge of the boat, she could look deep into the water. "It's very still," she whispered to herself, " and I don't see any village or people or anything except grass growing down on the bottom."

" Look again," said a chorus of rippling voices. " If the Water Spirits make a promise, they keep it. Look again, House Child. Have you put the Magic Spectacles in your pocket ? "

Anne brushed away a cobweb that had blown across her face and did as she was told. Instantly everything seemed to be in a bustle above and beneath the water. As she looked at the bottom of the pond that had always seemed like a flat floor, she saw that it was like any other bit of country. It had hills and valleys, grassy meadows, forests of tall plants, rocky peaks and muddy flats, all threaded by curious little paths along which the strangest shapes were continually passing. Some of the plants did not reach the top of the water, some had their roots in one of the valleys and their leaves floating on the water, while with some both roots and leaves floated, held up by tiny bladders arranged like so many little life preservers. The air above the water was humming with life, and the water itself seemed fairly alive with tiny creatures.

"Now I know why father says, 'Never drink pond water, no matter how thirsty you are,'" said Anne, convincingly. "It would simply be drinking bugs, even if you didn't feel them going down. I see a place for a village there under the water, and things to live in it, but where is the village itself, I wonder? I don't see any nests or holes or burrows."

The Water Spirits laughed mockingly, and began to talk all at once in confusion.

"The dwellers in the Village in the Pond do not live in common holes and nests ; most of them carry their houses about with them," said one.

"How about Wazhusk, the Muskrat?" called another. "Has he not a winter lodge and a summer burrow?"

"And the fishes?" said a third. "Does not the thorn-backed one build a nest as fine as any bird's?"

"Dear me, I don't know," cried Anne in a maze; "please talk a little slower or tell me over again." But the Water Spirits talked so fast and rushed about so that Anne knew that she must look for herself or ask some one who could keep still.

Presently something flew close to Anne's face, and she put up her hand in fright, for it was one of the great insects that are called Devil's Darning Needles, and are said to sew up your ears and put out your eyes if you make them angry.

" Pardon me, I was only taking a Mosquito off your nose," it squeaked, " and there is another on your ear ; allow me.   Let me introduce myself, as you are afraid of me, evidently mistaking me for some one else — perhaps a big stinging Wasp. I am Sir David Dragon Fly, the swiftest thing on wings and the bravest and most renowned Mosquito killer.

" A million Mosquitoes took wing this morning, and Heart of Nature sends us Dragons after them the minute they leave the water.   Where do Mosquitoes come from ?   The Village in the Pond, to be sure.   If there were no ponds and sluggish waterways, there would be no Mosquitoes."

" Do Mosquitoes have houses in this Village ? " asked Anne.

" No houses ; they wander about like tramps. In fact, most of the inhabitants of this Village carry their houses with them and camp where they choose, as the Water Spirits have told you ;

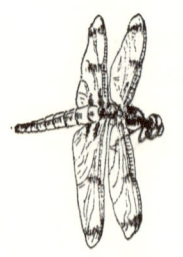

DRAGON-FLIES

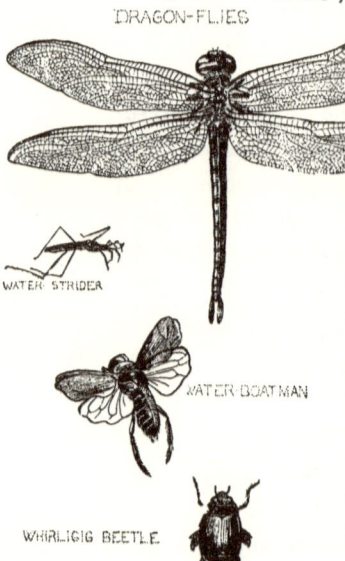

WATER STRIDER

WATER-BOATMAN

WHIRLIGIG BEETLE

WATER-SPIDER

we even do that in our family. Madam Mosquito lays her eggs on the roof of the water, then —"

"Roof of the water! What can you mean?" exclaimed Anne. "A roof is a stiff thing. Water all tumbles about loose; I'm sure it hasn't any roof!"

"*I'm* very sure it has. Look down there at Johnny Longlegs, the Water Strider; what is he walking on? And at that heedless, headlong family, the Whirligig Water Beetles; what are they walking on but the roof of the water?"

"They are floating," said Anne, hastily. Then as she stooped and looked closely at the long legs of the Strider and the turtle-like backs of the little Whirligig Beetles, she gave an exclamation of surprise.

"They are really walking," she cried, "and I can see the roof bend. It is a very weak roof, though; I wonder why that is?"

"Because we Water Spirits seldom stay still long enough for the roof to grow thick," answered the Nee-ba-naw-baigs. "One of our laws also is 'keep moving.' When we do rest long in one spot, this roof grows heavier, and House People call it scum and say evil things about it."

"What makes the roof, anyway?" asked Anne.

"Ask Wabeno, the Magician," laughed the Water Spirits, romping over the mill-dam, then calling and singing from the stream above the pond all in the same minute.

"Excuse me," said Anne to the Dragon Fly, who was darting impatiently to and fro, "you were telling me how Madam Mosquito lays her eggs, and I've been very rude in interrupting you; but I had to know the *why* about the roof of the water, and though I've seen it, I'm not sure of the why."

"As I was saying, Madam Mosquito lays her eggs on top of the water, and in all the changes the young Mosquitoes go through, from the time they leave the eggs until they are fully grown, they live squirming about on and under the roof of the water. Wrigglers, these half-made Mosquitoes are called, and if you'll look in a water barrel that has stood open to the sun you will very likely see some any day. The Mosquito's

skin serves it for a house and it changes this many
times, for as it grows the old skin is crowded, and
it is shed for another.   By and by, when wings,
sting, and everything else about the young Mosquito is ready, how do you suppose it changes
from a water wriggler to an air flyer?"

"Unfolds its wings and flies out of the water
into the air."

"What! with sopping wet wings?" asked the
Dragon Fly, scornfully.   "You must know that
one of the first 'Rules for Young Insects' is, —

> "'Your wings must be dry,
> Before you can fly.'

Wet wings are heavy, and we should fall through
the air like stones.   The Mosquito knows a thing
or two.   He crawls carefully out of his last skin
house, by way of a crack in the roof, and then
uses it for a float to rest upon until his fringe-
edged wings dry and he becomes used to his new
shape.   Then he stretches his wings and begins
his buzzy life.

"Now comes my work!   To and fro over ponds
and marshes I speed, snapping up these Mosquitoes
as they take their first flight, or, if I miss them
then, seizing them when they again approach the
water to lay their eggs."

"Please, Sir David Dragon Fly, why do Mosquitoes bite? They always seem to bite, while Spiders and Flies and other things only bite sometimes."

"What you call biting is merely helping themselves to food. They stick their sting into you to suck your blood. They don't know that it hurts you. Besides, Madam Mosquito is the only one who sucks blood or can sing the wing song. Master Mosquito is a poor harmless sort of thing; he dare not say a single word and has to be content with plant juice lemonade, for Heart of Nature does not allow him to eat meat soup like his wife."

"I wonder why it is that among insects and such things the man seems to be of so little account," said Anne, looking across the water with a puzzled expression. "The Bees live in a Queendom, and the males have no stings and are hustled out of the way very soon, and it's pretty much the same in Antville, and with the Mosquitoes it's even worse."

"Why? I dare not tell," said the Dragon Fly. "Ask Wabeno, the Magician."

At that moment a Kingfisher, that had been sitting motionless for some time on a dead Maple limb above the boat, dived deep into the pond and

u

returned with a luckless Perch, which he swallowed,
after making a great many faces.   As soon as the
circles that his plunge had made rippled away,
Anne saw that there was quite a commotion among
the Water People.   Minnows darted to and fro,
trying to hide under stones; a little Mud Turtle
slid off a log and bumped into a Snapping Turtle
going in an opposite direction; while some larger
fish hastened anxiously under an overhanging root,
and the Striderleg and Whirligig Beetle families
scattered suddenly and then began to whirl faster
than ever in a different place.

"What a fuss about nothing," laughed Anne.

"Nothing! do you call a water-quake nothing?" ·said the little Turtle as he regained his
place on the log, feeling very cross because he had
a shell-ache from the collision.

"A water-quake!   I never heard of such a
thing," said Anne, still laughing.

"Did you never hear of an earth-quake?"

"Certainly; it's when something inside the
earth blows up and shakes it, and sometimes it
spoils houses and kills people."

"Very well, House Child, a water-quake is
when something outside the water falls in and
shakes it, and sometimes it spoils houses and kills
people in the Village in the Pond," he mimicked.

Anne looked at the Turtle to see if he was making fun of her, but he was so solemn that she could not tell. She turned to find the Dragon Fly, but could not tell it from a dozen others that were darting about with wings spread wide like a Hawk when it seems to float on the air.

Presently, however, Sir David returned and lit on the rushes close to the boat.

"Where is your house?" asked Anne. "Do you, too, carry it with you?"

"Grown-up Dragon Flies have no houses, — we are Knights-errant; our young lie close on the bottom of the pond, each one in a little skin tent. Do you see those of us yonder, who, instead of catching Mosquitoes, swoop low over the water as if they would dive, like the Kingfisher? Those are the females, and as they touch the water they quickly lay their eggs under the roof, where they soon sink to the bottom, and, after going through as many masquerades as a Mosquito, the young Dragon splits the back of its last baby jacket and crawls up a plant stem into the air, where it dries its wings and is off, Mosquito hunting."

"If you Dragon Flies eat other insects, then you must be cannibals," said Anne, after thinking a moment.

"Hush! don't say that word here," warned Sir

David ; "almost everybody in the Village in the
Pond is a cannibal ; of course some families live
on plant juice lemonade, like Mosquito men, but
the rest! — Look quickly now; see how that Perch
has just gobbled up a Minnow, and round the corner of the root that narrow, sly Pickerel is waiting to grab the Perch."

"Oh dear me, he has caught it too, and bitten
it in two ! " cried Anne, changing her position so
suddenly, in order to see better, that the boat
slapped the water vigorously, making ripples and
spoiling the view altogether.

"Another water-quake," scolded the Turtle, but
when Anne looked again both Pickerel and Perch
had disappeared and
the other fish were
gossiping under
the root as
before.

" Do you know what has become of Dahinda,
the big Bull Frog, that used to live here ?   I
mean the one who used to beat the bass drum.
I haven't heard him this summer."

The Dragon Fly had gone, but the Turtle answered, " Dahinda is dead ; he died yesterday."

" Was he old, or did a boy or a Kingfisher
catch him ? "

" Neither ; he foolishly went into a swallowing
match with a Frog only one size smaller than himself, and choked to death."

" How was that, and what did he swallow ? "

" Swallow ?   Why, he tried to swallow the
other Frog, to be sure.   When Dahinda stretched
his throat to its widest and found that the other
Frog was too much for him, he was too proud to
let go.   He wouldn't give the smaller Frog the
satisfaction of swaggering about the pond and
saying, ' Look at me ! I'm the big Frog that
Dahinda had to unswallow ! '   So Dahinda held
on and they are both dead.   Where are they ?
Over in the backwater pool where Dahinda lived;
a couple of big mud Eels are going up there now
to dine off them, so you see after all they won't
be wasted."

" Nothing goes to waste in my garden," whispered Heart of Nature's voice, coming from a soft

breeze that rippled the pond.   Everything lives
for some other thing, and all for the Plan."

"Yes, dear Heart of Nature; still if Dragon
Flies aren't good for anything but to kill Mos-
quitoes, and Mosquitoes only good to feed Dragon
Flies, why couldn't the Plan do without either?"

But Heart of Nature had sped past without answering, and a small green Frog under the boat's
stern croaked, "Ask Wabeno, the Magician," and
Anne turned to the Turtle again, who looked as if
it had more to say.

"Snakes choke themselves the same way, very
often," it continued; "only the other day, Flat,
one of my last year's children, came back from a
walk through the woods, his eyes popping out of
his head with fright. 'Oh, ma,' he cried, 'I've
seen a Snake running away, and it had two tails
and no head!'

"'Which way did it run?' I asked. 'Both
ways,' he said, without stopping to think.
'Humph!' said I, 'you're spinning fibs, I know;
ten to one it was two Snakes trying to swallow
each other'—and so it was. House Child, *it is a
safe thing to suspect people who tell you that they've
seen a Snake with two tails and no head!*" and the
Turtle took a dive to refresh her wisdom.

Meanwhile the fish under the root were having

a squabble.   A handsome White Perch was scolding some little Minnows, who were gaping about
and listening to what their big brothers were saying.   This Perch was a very handsome fish and
evidently knew it, for he turned his silvery sides
until they caught almost all the rainbow colours
from the water.   Near him was a Sunfish dressed
in dark green and blue, with a yellow vest, while
between them, and larger than either, was a Sucker
with a gray coat, pink waistcoat, and a pouting,
foolish looking mouth.

"You said it, I know you did," mumbled the
Sucker, looking at the Perch with flashing eyes,
the greatest sign of anger he could give.   "You
called me a toothless, mud-living, vegetable sucker
— the Minnows heard you and told the Water Rat,
and the Water Rat told Wazhusk, the Muskrat,
and he told me when he was mussel hunting and I
was going up the river to lay my eggs last month.
There now, what have you got to say about it?"

"That it's all true," said the White Perch,
turning his back so suddenly that the Sucker
gave a gasp and sank to the bottom of the pond
in sheer astonishment.

"Strange what gossips these stay-at-home fish
are," said the White Perch, patronizingly to the
Sunfish.   "Now we travellers who go down to

the sea to winter, and run up stream in spring, have too much to think of to talk about our neighbours."

"Wait until you have spent a winter or two in this pond, and you'll be glad to talk about anything," said the Sunfish. "Why, I've known the time when if a bit of watergrass put its arm around a straw that floated along, while they had a chat, my, what gossip there was as to whether the grass was bold or the straw spoke first; it was simply awful!"

"But I'm not going to stay here in winter; I'm going back to the sea."

"Oh no, you are not; the water in this pond is low in the fall and you can't get down over the dam; you'll have to stay here and take little runs up stream, the same as I do. Of course you could go down in the spring with the Eels, if it wasn't against Perch law. You will be comfortable and have plenty of food, but you'll soon gossip and mind your neighbour's business like the rest of us, mark my words! Now *I* can stay at home and be contented. We Sunfish have our grounds allotted us in this Pond Village and live our lives out in the same spots, and we run very little risk if we watch out well for Pickerel, for there is plenty of food and not much fishing."

"Get away, you Minnow, or I'll eat you!" called the White Perch to a little fish less than four inches long, that was trying to attract its attention. The Perch, by the way, was feeling very cross because it had just learned that it must probably stay in a pond.

"I'd like to see you try! I'm no Minnow, but a Stickleback — one of the cleverest fishes and best housekeepers in this village. Look at the three spikes on my back and another underneath to make sure, and have pity on your throat. Even Dahinda, in his best days, never caught but one of us."

"Housekeeping! Then you must have a house," interrupted Anne; "most fish seem to live anywhere and do not even have a nest to hold their eggs."

"Let us speak low so the others will not hear us, and then look," said the Stickleback. "This is my nest."

Close to the pond's shallow edge, under the bank, was a little muddy ball, shaped like an Oven-bird's nest, but it only looked about the size of a Humming-bird's; it was made of bits of hay all woven together with fine threads.

"How cute!" whispered Anne; "but how did you get the cobwebs under water? Did Water

Spiders spin them, and does your mate sit on the eggs like a bird ? I should think it would be a very wet slippery thing for a fish to do."

" No, my mate and I only watch the eggs and see that no one touches them, and we don't allow our children to leave the nest until they can care for themselves. As to the web, we spin it ourselves. You see, I was not boasting when I said we were the cleverest fishes in the Village."

" But *how* do you spin the web ? " persisted Anne.

" Ask Wabeno, the Magician," cried the Water Spirits. " The first thing we know, if we answer your questions, you will want to find all the water paths and even our passwords, and we shall have you splashing about making water-quakes and trying to live in our Village, and then if you drowned it would give the pond a bad name. I think you'd better go home ; you flap that boat about so you'll sink all the spawn and frighten the wits out of all the young fry in the pond."

" Fry ! and spawn ; what are they ? "

" Fry is the name for baby fish in a flock, and spawn is the name for fish eggs in a bunch."

" Oh, but dear Water Spirits, I want to know the names of all the plants and trees and people in your Village."

"Then you will have to consult a directory, for we don't know all these names ourselves, but if you—"

"Mistress, mistress!" barked Waddles, tracking along the path by which Anne had reached the pond, nose close to ground. "Mistress, come with me quick; Tommy is in trouble, we can't talk to him, and we need you. Call the Miller and follow me!"

*   *   *   *   *   *

After Anne had left the house that morning, Tommy returned after getting leave from his mother to go to the pond, "if," she said, "you take Anne's hand and are very careful."

He was very much disappointed, but as he had often been with Baldy and Obi to the mill he thought he knew the way, and started to follow Anne. The walk seemed very long and rather lonely, so he crawled under the first bars in the lane, thinking he should reach Anne sooner by following a cow path across lots.

"Poor little Tommy! He did not know that between the meadow and the pond lay an ugly bit of bog, water-holes, and treacherous grass. The place looked innocent enough, it was fun hopping over half-decayed tree trunks and sedge tussocks. Then his feet slipped and he went down flat into a mud-hole, struggled to get a footing, but stuck fast, kneeling up to his waist in mud and water.

At first he was too much frightened to cry. The Mosquitoes bit him, and Gnats and Midges almost blinded him; the more he struggled the faster he stuck. He saw that he could not exactly drown, but the poor little mite also realized that no one knew where he was. What if Whip's mate should come along! Then he began to sob in bitter loneliness and call as loud as he could for Lily and Anne.

*   *   *   *   *   *

Meanwhile Waddles thought he would take a walk, and, feeling very good-natured, invited Lumberlegs and Lily to go with him. He nosed about until he found Anne's trail, which at the start ran with Tommy's, and all three trotted amicably along until Waddles stopped suddenly at the place where Tommy had turned into the pasture.

"I don't understand this," he said; "mistress never lets Tommy go in that wild field by himself. I wonder which track we had better follow?"

"Let us follow missy," said Lumberlegs. "It's the best way to the pond, and I need a bath," he added.

" I shall follow my master," said Lily, decidedly. " As you say, Waddles, he ought not to be in that wild place alone. Will you nose the way as quick as you can ? I feel anxious, and my nose is not as keen as my ears."

Waddles started off in a fairly straight line, closely followed by Lumberlegs, while Lily ran as fast as her lame paw, which would always be stiff, would let her. In a few minutes Waddles began to zigzag and dash frantically in and out among the bushes, giving tongue to his loudest cry.

Lily stopped, cocked one ear, and said, " I hear master and he's calling me ; he's hurt or in trouble. Can't you stop fooling and lead straight, Waddles ? Oh, just let me get my teeth into whoever is hurting my master ! "

" Lead straight ! " shrieked Waddles. " Why, dog alive, how can I ? The trail is crooked and snarled. 'Ware ditch ! " And the three stopped short in time to save themselves from falling into the hole where Tommy was crouching, very weary by this time and almost ready to let his head fall against the bog grass and go to sleep.

" What shall we do ? " said Waddles, trembling with excitement, to Lily. " I can't step in there ; my legs are too short, and so are yours."

Lily, who was old and had seen much trouble in her life, took in the whole situation at a glance.

" If he understood our language, we could tell him what to do, but only Anne knows all we say. We must stop his getting in deeper, and call Anne. Then we must use our trades.

" Lumberlegs, your legs are longest, spread your feet wide, step into the hole and pull Tommy backward to the log. My trade is 'take hold and keep hold.' I will get flat on the log and hold him fast. Waddles, you find Anne and tell her to bring the Miller. Now to work, and don't forget, for I cannot open my mouth to speak when once I take my grip; " and as Lily looked at Tommy, Waddles saw that there were tears in her eyes — a fact that he never told any one, not even Anne, but he never begrudged her his old house after that.

Lumberlegs did as he was told, and pulled bravely for so young a dog, and Tommy helped all he could, and stopped sobbing when he saw his dog friends. Lily spread her thick body on the the log and, reaching her neck forward as far as possible, sniffed at Tommy's blouse and then closed her jaw over it at the belt, where she would not pinch the skin. It was a cruel strain upon her neck, but she " took hold and kept hold ! "

Waddles gave one short bark and dashed off toward the pond, baying wildly.

*   *   *   *   *   *

When Anne, the Miller, and Waddles returned, Lily was still keeping hold, and Tommy had managed to work one muddy arm around so that he could grasp the log.

" I'm afeard to tech him while that dog holds on," said the burly Miller.

" Lily understands," said Anne, and in a moment Tommy was safe on the dry grass, and Anne had kissed the Widow Dog square on her nose. Waddles in his joy upset the Miller by running between his legs, and Lumberlegs licked his face by mistake for Tommy's.

" I didn't fall over the mill-dam and be drowned anyway," gasped Tommy, trying to lick up his muddy tears, laughing and crying together. " Oh, Anne, I was doing to be careful and take tight hold of your hand, as mother said, dess as soon as I found you."

Anne, Tommy, and Lily went home together, but Waddles and Lumberlegs returned by way of the Horse Farm to tell the news to the Duchess. She was very polite, invited them to take a drink from her newly filled pail, and then gave them a dog biscuit and a chop bone apiece.

"I'm pleased with all of you," she said. "Lumberlegs, my son, you are a credit to your family. What did I tell you, the other day when you were disputing about what you were good for? Did I not tell you to watch out and let nothing go wrong at your house? Well, you've watched out and worked at your trades at the same time. Mark my words, children, an honest trade is a good thing for a dog to have, even if he doesn't have to work at it for a living. Now go home and take a nap, for I think you will have a good meat dinner to-day." They did.

XIII

The Shedding Dance

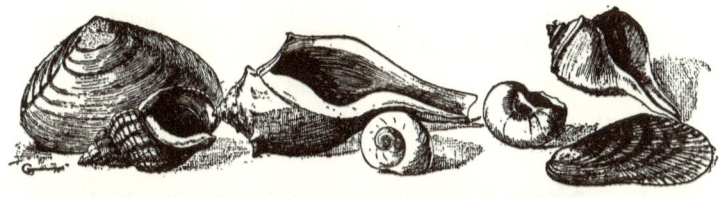

THE summer was as warm as the winter had been cold. Lumberlegs made a particularly deep earth hole under a spruce, where he spent most of the day. Lily patiently followed her master everywhere; while Waddles retired to the cellar, where he refreshed himself with drinks of ice-water from the pan under the refrigerator, which, with the aid of Lumberlegs, he was able to pull out; but, of course, forgetting to push it back again, the water from the refrigerator dripped on the floor. As he took several drinks every day his relations with the cook, who was responsible for keeping the pan in place, became strained and unpleasant.

"I'm glad he does be goin' with 'em to the

beach," she said one day in his hearing, "and I hopes he'll get his fill of water for wonst. I've no use whatever fer dogs as acts like people. If I don't mistake me, that Waddles does be queer in his mind; and I'm thinkin', someway, that he and Miss Anne do have speech together."

Waddles chuckled to himself, and immediately went off and "had speech with Miss Anne," for it was the first that he had heard about going to the beach. In fact, he had no idea of what a beach was like.

"It must have been decided this morning, then," said Anne as she listened; "and of course cook knows, because she has to be arranged with to keep house while we are gone."

"Anne! Anne!" cried Tommy, "father-mother's looking everywhere for you to tell you a surprise. But I can dust as well, for we're going to the water that Baldy's brother takes care of, before next Sunday! And it isn't deep at first, so I can't fall into it much, and sometimes we needn't wear shoes, and — and — we can dig holes anywhere, vely deep holes, and sit in 'em, too, and it won't be dirty or a mustn't be. And Obi's going to water my garden, and keep my stwashes from falling off the fence.

"Aren't you glad? don't you want to sit in

THE SONG OF THE SANDS

holes?" he added, pulling her hand as she did not speak. But this is what Anne was saying to herself: —

"The moon was new last night; I shall be there in time to see the Shedding Dance, for Kayoshk', the Sea Gull, said it happens 'when the midsummer moon is full'; now the only trouble will be to find the place where high and low tide meet."

The first thing Waddles did when he arrived at the shore was to wade in and take a good drink of water. Presently he walked out again and began to feel very giddy, and there was a bitter taste in his mouth. "Cook must have flavoured this water," he gasped, "just to spite me; it tastes like the kind that lives with the pork in the big stone pot at home, and I saw cook flavour that with white pebbles. Oh, it's awful! I think I'm poisoned!" He was not, however, and as soon as he had uneaten his dinner he felt better.

For the first week Anne spent her days on the beach; Tommy prattled and played, but she was content to sit under the shade of an old boat, sifting the sand through her fingers and wondering long wonderments. She fancied the sands sang songs about themselves, and every pebble seemed to have a story to tell. This one she fancied had been washed down the home river perhaps; it was like the rock of Wenona's Cliff; that one of a strange colour must have travelled a long distance with the tide.

Then she would look out across the sea at the streaks the current made, and the little circles where the fishes jumped, and sigh from very contentment.

"It's all lovely, and I don't know what I like best. I wonder if there is a village under the sea, like the Village in the Pond?"

" A country, not a village," said a voice from the drifted seaweeds that margined the water's edge; but it was the same voice that had sounded so long ago from the old oak.

"Dear Heart of Nature, are you here, too? Have you any gardens hereabouts?"

" Have I not often told you, House Child, that my garden is everywhere on earth and in sky and sea? Under yonder water roof lies a country full of peopled cities; its highways thread in and out between all the countries of the upper world; its mountain peaks rise and sometimes threaten the ships that pass over the water roof; its valleys have depths that no human gauge may fathom; its currents bring cold or heat to the countries they pass by; its gardens stretch from north to south, and through these gardens and highways swim and float and crawl and drift the People of the Sea."

"Sea People are good to eat, but are they useful for anything else, and do they have good times among themselves, or does everything eat something else the same as it does on land?" asked Anne.

"Everything lives for some other thing and all for the Plan. The land sends the sea its wastage; the Crab, the Welk, and the Starfish eat it up; the deep sea fishes eat these in their turn, and Heart of Man ensnares these fishes for his food, and so the wheel of use goes on revolving endlessly."

Anne sat very still, thinking; then she asked suddenly, "Won't you please tell me the exact place where high and low tide meet?" But Heart of Nature had gone.

"That's too bad," said Anne; "if I had only spoken quicker! Heart of Nature always gives me really truly answers to whys and never tells me to ask Wabeno, the Magician."

"Unless the whys are those that House People may not yet know, and then does Heart of Nature keep silence," came a whisper close to her ear.

*　　*　　*　　*　　*　　*

When the water was not too rough the lightkeeper, whom they named Rocky because he lived on a rock (Jeremiah, his real name, being, as Anne thought, too sad a name to say), used to row the children in his stout boat over to an island fringed with sand-plum bushes, where there were dainty shells, and where the queer little Fiddler Crabs, with one big and one little claw, scuttled sideways to their holes; not so quickly, however, but what Tommy caught some for his "quarium," which was a half-barrel that had drifted in, and had become buried to its rim in the sand.

As they rowed along, Tommy chattered to the old sailor, Waddles rested his chin on the boat's edge wondering every time it lurched what made his insides feel so loose, but Anne had only eyes for the shadowy things she could see through the clear water, — a forest of seaweed, then a Skate making faces at a Horseshoe Crab who was listening to a dispute between some Lobsters.

"Oh dear," she sighed, "if I only knew the spot where high and low tide meet!" Shawondasee danced along. "Do you know where it is?" she asked eagerly.

"I!" said Shawondasee, tickling the water into pretty ripples; "I think I knew once, but I forget. Why don't you ask Wabeno, the Magician?"

"It seems to me that every one says that, when I want to know the most important whys," sighed

Anne, twisting her handkerchief into knots; "for if I can't find the place, I might as well be at home, as far as seeing the Shedding Dance goes."

"Please, do crabs really dance and shed their shells?" she asked aloud of Rocky.

"Sartin they do; couldn't grow if they didn't, — that is, I mean they sheds 'em. I don't know about the dancin'; but I should think they might wrestle out uv the old shell that way like as any other. When do they do it? Well, little ones sheds as often as three or four times a year, I rekon 'cause they grow fast; but old ones don't shell out oftener 'n onct through July and August, — time fer 'em now, — and then soft fryin' crabs'll be plenty fer a considerable spell!

"What makes 'em soft? Why, 'cause the new shell takes time ter harden; it's a big lot bigger 'n the old one, and if it warn't soft it would split shellin' out o' the old one."

"I found a trab this morning and he had eyes and feet and everything, but he was empty and I put him in my quarium to see if he'd grow full again," said Tommy, "and there's lots of full trabs walking low down in that little river behind the beach."

"Yes, the crick's full on 'em, but they lies low and keeps under stones jest before sheddin'."

The moon grew rounder and rounder every
night, and as Anne watched it rising above the
water, it did not seem strange at all that it helped
to pull the tides up and down. In fact, she sometimes thought she could see it at work, yet even
the moon, intimate as it was with the tides, simply
smiled and could not tell her where high and low
tide meet.

As the night of full moon grew nearer and
Anne began to give up all hopes of seeing the
Shedding Dance, something happened and Waddles, as usual, was the cause of it. He had gone
up the creek early in the afternoon to follow a
very attractive smell, but it was nearly tea time
before Anne saw him hurrying along the beach
with hanging head, looking behind him every few
moments as if some one was chasing him. As he

drew near, she saw that a heavy object was dragging from his tail.

" Wicked people have tied a stone to Waddles
and tried to drown him ! " she cried, hastening to
his rescue. But they hadn't; a large bluish green
Crab held the poor tail in its vicelike grip.

"Let go this minute, or I'll bang you," said
Anne, picking up a stone; "don't you see how
you are hurting my dog?"

" If I let go, will you put me back in the creek?
I'm going to shed to-morrow, and I want to be in
a quiet place."

"I won't promise a thing," said Anne, made
angry by Waddles' pain. "Will you let go?
One — two — " Before she could say three the
Crab relaxed his grip, and Waddles released made
haste to reach the lighthouse and lick his pinched
tail in safety.

" Please put me back in the creek," said the
Crab, looking in all directions at once with its
bulging eyes.

" I won't, unless you tell me where high and low
tide meet," answered Anne, promptly.

"I suppose you wish to see the Shedding
Dance," said the Crab, evasively.

" Yes, I do," said Anne, feeling that her chance
had come at last.

"I cannot answer what you ask, but if you do what I tell you I will lend you my eyes, so that you can see the Shedding Dance without going into the water."

"Humph," thought Anne, "this is luck! How stupid I was not to remember that even if I found the place where the tides meet it would be sure to be a wet place! What must I do?" she said aloud.

"The tide will be low at sunset. Place me where the sand meets the rocks, then wait until the full moon comes up beyond the water."

"You are very kind," said Anne, clasping her hands and giving a little gasp of delight; "but don't you wish to go to the dance yourself?"

"I — dance?" said the Crab, with a shiver. "What a strange idea! I don't think you can understand about this dance, House Child. Who told you of it first?"

"Kayoshk', the Sea Gull, who said it always happens when the Crabs begin to shed their shells."

"True, but did Kayoshk' say that the Crabs danced?"

"N—o, I only thought they did, so as to shake their shells off."

"Dance to shake our shells off!" exclaimed the

Crab, turning up his eyes so far that they nearly broke off and twisted their necks badly. "You evidently have no idea of what a serious thing this shedding is to a crab. Suppose your own body, fingers, toes, and eyes even were covered with a crusty shell like mine, and you had to crawl out of it through a little hole under your chin, and leave this covering whole — would you consider it a dancing matter?"

"No, I'm sure I would not. I should be very sad and worried, and afraid of breaking and maybe leaving some toes or an eye in the old skin," said Anne, shuddering at the very idea. "How do you manage it? It seems impossible, for I thought until now that you only shed your back.

"You make me think of the Lobsters; they have an awful time in shedding, even if their shells do open nicely down their back. Why, sometimes they twist off their claws altogether, and they get so feeble that they can hardly even catch a mouthful of food."

"It is possible for us to shed because it is in the Plan, and Heart of Nature teaches us how to work. Before the time comes our flesh grows soft and watery, then we crawl out of the highways and battle-grounds under some stone or into a nook where we may not be seen.

"We give a mighty shrug to split our under shell, then claw by claw we pull and turn. Ugh! how the joints ache as we twist and wrench them, and how sore and tired we are when it is over! We lie as still as possible, waiting for our new armour to harden, for we are helpless against those bigger sea people who eat us.

"At this time House People call us Soft-shell Crabs, and when they catch us eat us skin and all; often we take revenge and give them stomach aches. Queer things House People are! If they could see the stuff we eat, they wouldn't care so much about us. We were made to eat the wastage of the sea, and only this year I helped to eat a pig that was drowned and came down the creek ; a dog, and —"

"Stop! don't tell me such horrid things!" cried Anne; "how dare you when you were trying only to-day to eat Waddles!"

"You needn't be so fierce," replied the Crab; "I don't eat live dogs. Isn't it much better for the Sea People to keep the shore swept clean than to leave these things lying about to decay and for people to step upon?"

"Y—e—s, I suppose so; but please tell me if the Crabs do not dance who does, and why is it called a Shedding Dance?"

"The other smaller Crabs and Sea People dance while we are shedding, because we are too weak to eat them; and the bigger ones that eat us dance because we are so easy to catch, and all the other things like the Sea-worms, Jellyfish, and Skates dance because they enjoy it, and it's quite the thing to do."

"Then there are other kinds of Crabs besides you, and you and your family are cannibals!"

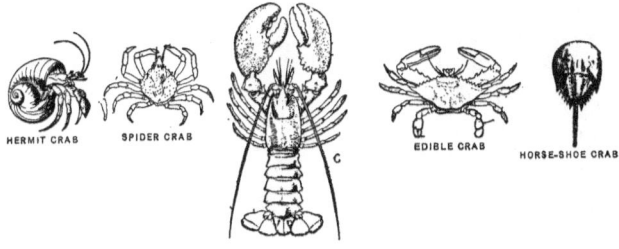

HERMIT CRAB   SPIDER CRAB   C   EDIBLE CRAB   HORSE-SHOE CRAB

"No, we are not cannon balls; they are round iron rocks and there is one down in the creek mud."

"Cannibals are different," corrected Anne; "they are people who eat the same kind of animals that they are themselves."

"Say that over again," said the Crab. "Um, ah! yes, I think we must be cannibals! We are a large family, though only a few of us live near this beach. Let me see," said he, counting on his

claws. "I'm the Blue Edible Crab — you can
always tell me for I'm twice as broad as I'm long;
then there's the Lady Crab, with the pretty
speckled coat, who lives in the sand; the Spider
Crab; the Fiddler, that you see on the sand
islands and creek meadows; the little Hermit,
who has no armour and so borrows an empty
winkle shell to live in lest the fishes snap his
tail off — besides a lot more."

"Do Crabs ever have tails?"

"Yes, we all do when we are young; when we
grow our armour we fold them up out of sight, that
is, all but the Hermit. There is a mite of a Crab,
also, that lives in the ears of Oysters, and so often
gets put in pickle with them and wears their
name; then there's the big Horseshoe Crab that
swims like a fish, and can turn somersaults, even
on land, by aid of his spike tail."

The tea bell sounded from the piazza and Anne
placed the Crab where she had been told, on the
narrow strip of beach below the light, and hurried
indoors.

*   *   *   *   *   *

A little before dark, when Tommy was being
put to bed, Anne crept down the ledge to where
Rocky was sitting on the edge of his boat smoking
his pipe.

It was a perfect night; the lighthouse kept scanning the sea with its wise, fiery eye, and in the east a silver line told where the moon was hiding.

"Are you going to stay out long, Rocky?" asked Anne, anxiously, "because father-mother said I might stay here to see the moon rise if you stay."

"Yes, I'll be about till the tide pulls up a spell; I want to net a mess o' bait to-night. Set down on that flat rock and you'll see nice; the sand's soft and tricky jest here below high water mark."

Anne laughed to herself; could anything be finer? The Crab was waiting under the edge of that very stone!

A silver rim began to peep above the water, and the light slipped along the ripples to the beach.

"Are you ready?" asked the Crab.

"Yes," whispered Anne.

"Shut your eyes, wish, and then open them, not forgetting to put on the Magic Spectacles."

*   *   *   *   *   *

A chilly sound of rushing water came in Anne's ears and something brushed against her face. She put out her hand to push it away and saw that she was sliding into the middle of a great field of eel grass; shapes were everywhere, and small fishes moved through the grass tops like birds among trees; there were the footprints in the sand where the Sandpipers had written their names at low tide, and above all was the water roof.

Then Anne noticed that what she put out as a hand was really a crab claw, also that her eyes stuck out on top, and that she could see backward as well as forward.

"Why!" she exclaimed, "my Blue Crab has shed its shell and lent it to me, eyes and all. I think, however, I'd better creep under this stone and see what will happen; for if I walk out in the open, something may eat me by mistake." Then, as she tried to turn, she found that the only way she could move was to slide half sideways.

"I think you are wise," said a sandy voice close by the stone; "it's dangerous for us to get into the whirl of the dance, for we may have to shed at any moment, and then when supper time comes who knows what Lobster might take a fancy to us."

Anne turned her eyes slowly and saw beside her a very handsome, almost round Crab, wearing white armour beautifully spotted with red and purple, and fringy-edged claws.

"Humph! this must be the Lady Crab," she

thought. At that instant the words "'Ware, Lobster!" were heard on every side. The Lady Crab backed down into the sand up to her eyes, and through a highway that ran between the eel grass and a rocky hill, thickly covered by a heavy forest of seaweeds, came a pair of good-sized Lobsters.

They stopped when almost opposite Anne's hiding-place; one crawled into the seaweed, tore some Mussels from the rocks, cracked them between one claw, and began to eat them greedily.

"Where were you last night?" asked the one who was not eating.

"In the lobster pot of that great land monster who lives on top of the rocks, who looks into the water every night with one red eye, but is blind by day."

"Oh!" thought Anne, "he is mixing up Rocky and

the lighthouse; I never thought before how strange the things on land would seem to Sea People, for I'm sure sea things seem very queer to me."

" How did you get out of the pot?" continued the talkative Lobster.

" Gave him a nip when he was tipping me into the big oyster shell he sails about in; he grabbed my best claw, and when I struggled it broke off. Look!" and the Lobster held up a stump.

" That's bad, but it will soon grow out again. Are you going to the dance to-night, or later on?"

" To-night; I feel it in my back that I, too, shall have to shed soon; my shell is horribly tight."

" Well, we are in a good place to look on. This year the dance forms around the edge of flat island only a little farther on, and the supper hunt goes from there well up the creek. Are you through? Then we had better move on."

" What is the supper hunt?" asked Anne.

" What ignorance!" sneered the Lady Crab; " as if every one of our tribe from Gull Grounds down to Alligator Point does not know that when the Fiddler Crabs stop playing, the dance ends, and they all go to the Place, and everybody catches some one else to eat for supper. It's obeying the first rule of the Sea People."

" What a horrid cruel party," said Anne with a

IN THE BOAT

shiver; "at the Forest Circus, even though Wild Cats and Rabbits were there together, *no one might eat any one else on the premises!*"

"I don't understand a thing you are talking about," said the Lady Crab. "Are you a foreigner washed up from some strange country? We often have such people washed here," snapping his claws, "but they don't live long."

"Yes, I *am* a foreigner," replied Anne, laughing softly; "but I was *wished*, not *washed*, here, and I advise you to keep your claws off me. What do you mean by the Place, and what is the First Rule of the Sea People?" and her voice sounded very loud as it echoed against the water roof.

"The Place — why, it is where high and low tide meet; the rule is, Eat and be eaten!" and then added to herself, "What a voice for a Crab! I wonder if this can be a Nee-ba-naw-baig spying about? I heard when I was up the creek that those Water Spirits could travel anywhere in any shape, and see through the biggest rocks and deepest sand."

Suddenly a strange sort of music sounded from the open space at the end of the highway. It moaned and squeaked and sounded like the fiddling of dry bows upon rusty strings. Anne forgot all about hiding, and made her way awkwardly

toward the open water, and the Lady Crab followed.

Upon a sunken island, half rock, half sand, sat
hundreds of Fiddler Crabs in a circle, playing away
for dear life, by using their big claw for a violin,
the little one for a bow. Around this island, circle
upon circle, as far as Anne could see by stretching
her eyes as much as possible, were ranged the Sea
People of the bay.

Nearest the island, clinging to the rocks, were
the Mussels : the plain, the Blue Mussel, the
smooth, and the Horse Mussel, who wears a rough
mane upon his shell. They kept step and time to
the music by opening and shutting their shells.

Behind these were ranged the various Clams in
family rows. The Little Necks had the place of
honour; then came the round Sea Clams that always keep down under the water roof; the long-
necked Beach Clams that love the sand; and the
long, thin Razor Clams that looked like change-
lings among their stouter brethren. The Clams
kept time to the music by clapping their shells
together like cymbals.

The Scallops swam gracefully along, opening
and shutting their shells in perfect rhythm, and
waving their pink and yellow inner mantles gracefully. They are very proud Shell-fish and have a

long pedigree; for is it not written in history that no less a person than Richard, the king, to whom a Lion once lent his heart, wore a Scallop shell on his helmet as a charm when he went to war? At least, that is the way the story is written in ocean history, and it came down to the Sea People through a very great-grandchild of the Lion, who, when bathing on a far-away beach, once told it to the ancestors of the Scallop Family, who first came to America in the good ship *Killer Whale*, which ship being wrecked by a lightning bolt (called by House People a harpoon) just before reaching land, the family camped on a convenient sandbar and became "early settlers" of the whole bay.

The brown Horseshoe Crabs did the most fantastic dancing, — one — two — three, swim, sink, — turn a somersault, — up and down the line.

In little groups and squads came other crawlers, — the Periwinkles, that know the song of the Ocean so well that if you put your ear to their empty shells even, you may hear them singing it; all the little borers that drill through the hard shells of their neighbours, and the useful Whelk that picks up the scraps left by the larger hunters.

Outside these crawlers trooped the moving flowers of the ocean with glistening bodies, — the

Sea Cucumber and Jellyfish, doing a skirt dance
with much waving of arms; the Sand Dollar,
turning cart wheels; the common Sea Urchin
humping like a hedgehog; while the cruel Star-
fishes, who hug their shelly brethren to death
that they may suck their blood, did the quaintest
five-step waltz imaginable.

Behind these creepers came the finny folk, —
the Skate, whose long black eggs with hooked
corners looking like seaweed bladders, all House
People know, coming first, followed by a myriad
different fishes.   These Skates dance with their
faces, and can take more steps with their mouths
than a centipede could with its legs.

"Where are the Oysters? I haven't seen one,"
said Anne to the Lady Crab presently, closing her
eyes, for the wavy motions of so many creatures
made her dizzy.

"What are you, anyway?" snapped the Crab.
"I think you must belong in fresh water; you

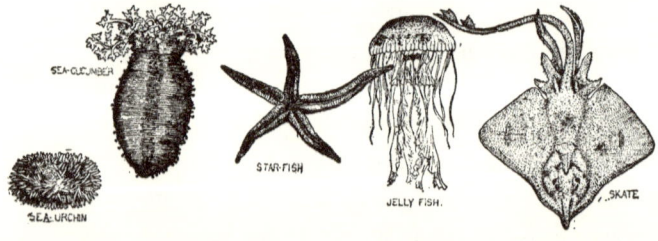

SEA-CUCUMBER

SEA-URCHIN

STAR-FISH

JELLY FISH.

SKATE

don't even know the Sea Alphabet, which says under letter R, ' No oyster shall go from home or take part in any festival in a month that has no R in it,' for these are their hatching months. Even House People know this rule and respect it, and seldom eat oysters in those R'less months."

" Months without an R," said Anne, musingly; " May, June, July, and August have no R's, to be sure, and this is July. It sounds true and is not a bad rule, either — something like not killing birds in the nesting season."

Meanwhile the even lines were breaking, and when Anne turned to see if she could count still more of the Sea People, the dancers were rising and falling like the waves themselves.

Suddenly the Fiddlers stopped their music and there was a rush and scuffle along the bottom. " To the Place! They are going to the Place, — 'ware Lobsters!" screamed the Lady Crab again, burying herself to the eyes.

Anne, knowing that this was her only chance of seeing the place where high and low water meet, tried to follow.

The scurrying grew louder and seemed to be coming nearer; a strange silver light mixed with the dancers who swirled about as if turning to water.

"My eyes! give me back my eyes!" cried the voice of the Blue Crab. "Quick, shut yours, Anne, rub them and off with the Magic Spectacles!"

Anne fumbled clumsily, hardly knowing whether she had fingers or claws.

The noise grew louder and the silvery lines of sea folk rolled and danced yet more wildly, some flying up into the air.

"Wind's comin' up squally with tide turn; jest got my bait in time," said Rocky's voice.

Anne rubbed her eyes hard. The boat grated over the pebbles and stuck its keel in the sand, and she saw that the water was rolling up the shallows, and the dashing white caps were dancing and shimmering in the moonlight.

"What's ailin'? Yer look skairt," said Rocky, noticing her confusion. "Seen suthin'? Full moon allers makes things in the water look black and extry queer."

"Nothing — that is — the Crab took back its eyes too soon and I couldn't get to the place where high and low tide meet."

"Yes, it's too soon fer Crabs," he replied, not exactly hearing what she said. "It's sheddin' time and we'll have soft ones soon, then after a spell, when they've hardened up, you and I and Tommy can go a-crabbin' for biters up the crick. There's a shed shell now, fust I've seen," and he stooped and picked the empty shell of the Blue Crab from under the rock and gave it to Anne.

She rose stiffly to her feet and looked first at the shell, then at Rocky, and out over the water with a puzzled gaze.

"What is it, little Owl?" said her father, who had come down the beach to find her. "What wonderful things have you seen in the water? I've been watching you for half an hour and you've scarcely moved."

Anne turned her face up to him in the moonlight, and smiling mischievously, held out the shell, saying : —

"Father dear, I mustn't tell you unless you can show me the place where high and low tide meet, because what I've seen is a very great secret between the Crab, who used to live in this shell, and me."

Then the lighthouse winked its red eye more wisely than ever.

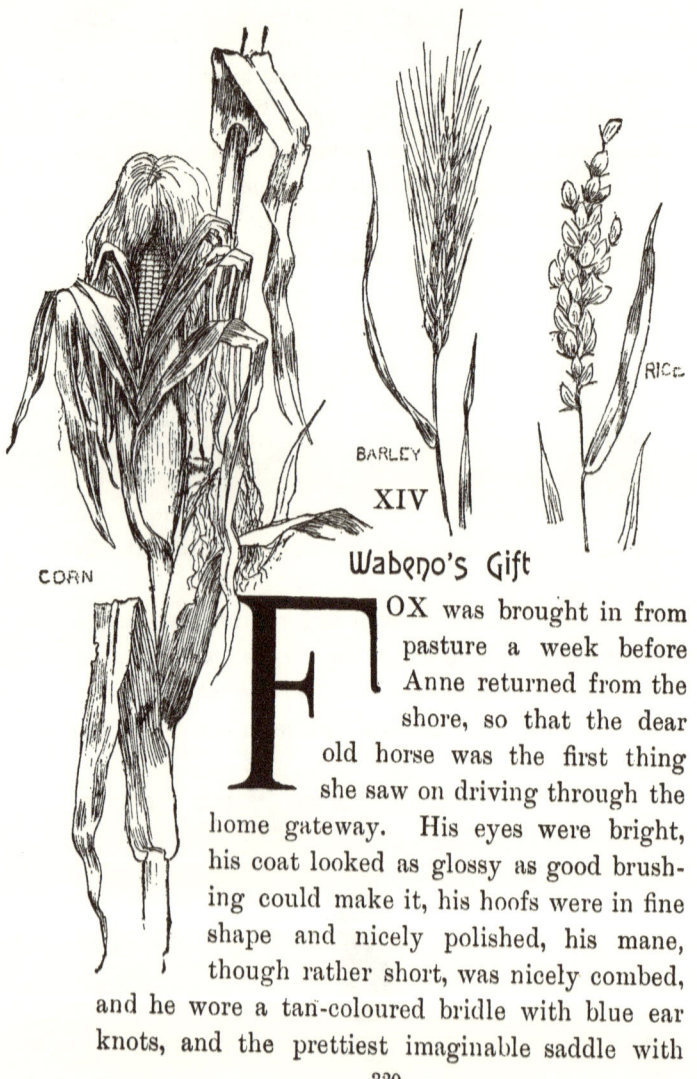

CORN

BARLEY

RICE

XIV

Wabeno's Gift

FOX was brought in from pasture a week before Anne returned from the shore, so that the dear old horse was the first thing she saw on driving through the home gateway. His eyes were bright, his coat looked as glossy as good brushing could make it, his hoofs were in fine shape and nicely polished, his mane, though rather short, was nicely combed, and he wore a tan-coloured bridle with blue ear knots, and the prettiest imaginable saddle with a blue cloth. As for his tail, it was such an admirable match for his mane, and so well fastened by the crupper, that no one would have imagined that it was not the original home-grown article.

Of course his legs were not as straight or his waist as slim as if he had not been through so many hardships, but what of that? If everything had gone well with him, he would not have come drifting back to the Horse Farm, Miss Jule would not have had the joy of curing him, or Anne of riding him.

Anne scrambled from the depot wagon almost before it stopped, and threw her arms first around Fox's neck and then hugged Miss Jule, who had been hiding in the shadow of the house, the better to see the meeting. Then Lumberlegs came bounding up bow-bowing with joy. He had grown so much that when he put his paws on Anne's shoulders to lick her nose, he looked quite over her head.

At this Waddles set up his most vigorous baying, Fox neighed, and for a moment nobody could hear themselves even think.

As for Lily, she was too happy to make a sound, but throwing herself at her little master's feet she licked his dusty shoes.

*　　*　　*　　*　　*　　*

After having been away for nearly two months, of course there was a great deal for the children to see on their return, and they made fresh discoveries every day.

Their gardens had overgrown all bounds. Anne's still looked very pretty, thanks to Obi's care in weeding it and keeping the sweet peas from going to seed; but Tommy's was a wreck. The onions at the corners had sent up long flower stalks, which had gone to seed and tumbled over, and the peas and beans were yellow and full of dry pods. The squash vines, however, were magnificent and covered the fence, while the yellow crooknecks peeped from between the big rough leaves.

" It will soon be time to take up my geraniums to keep in my window," said Anne, as they were looking at their gardens one September morning. " You haven't anything to pick or take up, Tommy; wouldn't you like one of my Fuchsias and a Heliotrope ? "

" Yes, I've lots to pick, — beans and peas and everything ! Course they're rather dry to cook for us, but I tan feed them to the hungry quail birds next winter; and oh, Anne, do help me tount my stwashes ! Obi says there is 'leven or fifteen; I've dot 'nough to make a whole flock of lovely ornaments for Miss Jule, and, Anne, what do you fink? If you'll help me put their feathers on, I'll div you one for yourself."

*　　*　　*　　*　　*　　*

One afternoon Anne strolled down to the potato field where she had found Bek-wuk, the Arrowhead. The potatoes had been dug, the ground ploughed, and Baldy was preparing to sow it with wheat from the bag that stood by the stone fence. The other home fields and those that belonged to the Horse Farm were empty, the wheat, rye, and oats that had grown in them having long ago been reaped, and the buzz of the threshing-machine sounded from the great barn. Even the corn in the valley fields was being gathered into stacks like wigwams.

A Crow flew awkwardly overhead, perched on the fence, and reaching over pecked inquisitively at the bag of wheat, giving a squawk and jump when he discovered Anne. It was the one-eyed Crow with the lame wing.

"Oh, ho! is that you, Kaw Ondaig? What have you been doing all summer, and how dared the other Crows come back from the mountain where the Bird Brotherhood sent them? There are Crows in every field as far as I can see, besides those that are talking way over in the Miller's wood."

"How have I been? Very well and comfortable, plenty to eat and no harrying. I was so honest down at the Farm that, until the corn ripened, I almost forgot that I was a Crow. As for the rest of the tribe, do you not remember that they were only banished during the song birds' nesting season, and that is over long since? They have come back to the cornfields for their tithe of the harvest."

"Yes, of course, to steal corn when there are no more nests to rob. I would not be so kind as the Bird Brotherhood; if I had my way, the Crows should go away for good."

"House People cannot drive us away," screamed the old Crow, flapping his wings boldly; "they shoot and harry us, tempt us with poisoned food, and still we are here at the corn harvest — it is our right; Wabeno gave it to us through our ancestor, Kaw-kaw, the northern Raven. Yes, ask Wabeno, the Magician, and he will tell you that it is so."

Anne felt a little abashed at Kaw Ondaig's fierceness, and, climbing over the fence to the first cornfield, she threw herself down in the shade of one of the stacks, nestling backward among the long leaves until she seemed to be sitting in the doorway of a wigwam.

The Crows came flapping and calling about her, and Mudjekeewis, the West Wind, whispered and gossiped about the field, while from a far corner a Quail family were making their way to glean their supper among the oat stubble.

"I don't believe that Wabeno ever told the Crows that they could take corn every year," said Anne aloud.

"Yes, he did," said Mudjekeewis; "I was there and heard him say so myself. To be sure, it was very long ago, on the very day when Wabeno gave the gift of corn to the Red Brothers."

"Ah, so you are back again! Don't be in a hurry, Mudjekeewis, but come and rest in this nice tent, and tell me about the Red Brothers and Wabeno. Was corn a very great gift to them?"

"Yes, Mondamin, Maize, or, as you say, corn, meant bread to them; bread when the buffalo were gone, bread when all wild game failed. House Child, do you know that in all the corners of the world where I have been bread is the greatest gift of earth to man?"

"Of course, bread is a 'must be,' but we do not make ours of corn meal."

"Different grains for different lands," said the Wind; "grains for heat and grains for cold, and of all the grains —"

"I am the King," whispered the Wheat that Baldy was sowing, to the Wind that helped scatter it. "No man knows from whence I came or what country gave me birth; before man could be I was, and if I should disappear man would follow. The world waits each harvest to know how I have thriven, that it may measure its strength. I am hearty myself; I need deep, sharp soil to eat and from which to rear my proud head on a straight, stiff stalk."

"I am more humble," called the scattered Rye in the thresher; "the bread I yield is dark and coarse, truly, but the ploughman loves it. I can grow anywhere, and on my straws the well-fed cattle sleep sound o' winter nights, while I give them dreams of summer pasturing."

"I am Monomin, the magic grain," said the Oats that the Quail were gleaning. "I whisper to the tired, hungry horse, 'Up and away!' and fire returns to his eye and strength to his limbs as he feels me stirring within him. Then in bleak, northern lands I give the people vital heat and life in bread and porridge."

"There are two other grains that I know well,"

said Mudjekeewis, "Rice, the bread of
the most far-away East, and Barley
that lives and thrives from north to
south and is swallowed both as bread
and as beer. The Wheat spoke truly,
in the strength of the Corn Brotherhood lies the strength of the world."

"I want to hear where our corn came
from and how Wabeno gave it to
the Red Brothers," said Anne.
"Come back, please, and tell me
the story."

"How and whence Mondamin,
or Indian corn, came?" said Mudjekeewis, sinking to the ground and
breathing lightly. "How came
it? That I can answer. Whence?
That is my friend's, Wabeno's, secret.
Even of the manner of its coming
there are many legends. I tell you
only what I know, and if any doubt
my tale, as you repeat it, only say,
'Mudjekeewis told me this, let it suf-
fice,'" and the Wind's voice sank to
a whisper.

"In a pleasant country lived an Indian with his
squaw and family; but it was a hungry land, so

z

what signified beautiful valleys if no buffaloes grazed in them, or deep silent woods if no deer and wild fowl were sheltered there ?

" It was early spring. The Indian had no grown sons to go on the far-away hunting trail; his children were young and wailed with hunger as the dried fish and meat began to fail, and it was not yet time for the spring shad running.

" The oldest child was a youth upon whose time-stick were cut the notches of fourteen winters, and in his heart he longed to help his parents, but knew not how.

" When an Indian boy has lived fourteen winters, he is no longer called a child ; his play days are put away from him, divided from his manhood by a fasting time of seven days. During these days the boy lives alone on the wood edge in a hut his mother builds. Alone with Heart of Nature and the Great Spirit, which is the name the Red Brothers give Heart of God; alone, with time to think. If the boy was held worthy in this fasting Wabeno would send Wagoose, the Dream Fox, to him with a dream which, being read aright, would bring good to all the people of his tribe.

" This boy, called Penaisee — little bird — by the tribe, because he could make almost every bird note with his flute of hollow reeds, longed for

the fasting time to come
in the hope that he might
see in a dream how to
bring plenty again to his
people.

"When the Willows
began to grow green at
the tips, flowers whitened
the meadows, and he
saw his mother
steal to the wood
edge and weave to-
gether a rude wigwam,
he knew the fasting
time had come, and he
hastened to keep it glad-
ly. The silence only
elated him at first. He
went about peeping here
and there, gathering arm-
fuls of blossoms and heaping them on the ground
for a bed, where he spent
the first night looking
at the stars and watch-
ing for Wabeno and the
Dream Fox. For five days he wandered thus,

watching each night, nothing but water passing his lips, until his body grew spent and his eyes hollow with hunger, and, picking with his last strength a branch of Dogwood blossoms, he staggered to his wigwam in despair, saying : 'Wabeno will not give a dream. I shall starve and my people also.'

"This was at twilight on the sixth day. Then we Winds took pity on Penaisee and whispered to him counsel : 'Lie down, Penaisee, little bird, and close the outward eyes, for by them never may Wabeno be seen ; it is the inward eye, open only in sleep, that may see the Dream Fox's picture book. Sleep, Penaisee, sleep and wait !'

"Penaisee obeyed, and as the light of the full Planting Moon crept round and looked him in the face, he saw coming between the trees the mystic figure of Wabeno, clad in strange green leaves, while Kaw-kaw, the Raven, flew near him, Wa-goose following.

"Raising one hand, Wabeno struck the magic drum, which gave a strange rattling noise, while with the other he made passes in the air. On he walked, straight into the wigwam, which grew higher that it might receive him. Then he stooped by Penaisee, touched him upon the ears and lips to signify that he was to listen, but not speak.

"Next Wabeno unfastened the skin that covered his magic drum and, lo! the bowl was filled with round pale yellow kernels like small rough pebbles. Laying these on the ground he carefully covered his drum again and spoke, while at his words the Whippoorwill hushed its calling and the Night-hawk paused in mid air, with spread wings, in sheer amazement.

"'Penaisee,' he said, 'I know your wish and your need. Because your wish is not for yourself alone, I listen. For my gift I give these magic seeds from out my magic drum. Sleep yet another night, then arise and with a crooked stick make holes a stride apart in yonder open ground. In each hole put three kernels, one for me, one for thee, and one for Wagoose, the Dream Fox. Cover them and watch the growth. For two moons draw the earth upward about what grows and keep wasting weeds away. At midsummer full moon, when your fasting lodge is empty, will I come and touch the flowers that grow upon the stalks to make them fruitful.'

"Then Wabeno stooped, and picking up a spray of Dogwood blossoms, laid them on the boy's eyes, saying: 'This shall be a sign to you. Yearly when these flowers bloom it is the time to sow the seed of Mondamin, Wabeno's gift.'

"Then Kaw-kaw, the Raven, croaked sadly, 'Wabeno, master, I starve. Why do you give away the magic seeds?' And Wabeno, smiling, said, 'Penaisee, forget not my comrade Kaw-kaw; but in the harvest time that as yet you know not of, let him also share my gift with you.'

"Then Wagoose walked down the moonbeams and unrolled a birch bark scroll, and on it, as Penaisee gazed, was painted the picture of a field of corn, with Wabeno walking in the moonlight touching the filling ears.

"Penaisee remained asleep, and on the seventh dawn when he awoke he found the magic kernels where Wabeno placed them. Then feeling fresh strength within him, he made the holes a stride apart and covered the kernels well with earth; then, turning, gave morning greeting to the Sun, and by its first rays he saw his father standing by the lodge bearing a dish of food. Neither spoke, but each one understood.

"Every moon did Penaisee draw the earth around the stout green stalks, and as he toiled he grew in stature like the corn stalks, taller than any of his race. When the moon before the Moon of Falling Leaves arrived, he sent a message to the tribe to come and gather in the ears and to receive Wabeno's gift of bread. On

WABENO IN THE MAIZE FIELD

that day Wabeno whispered, 'Let the boy no
longer be called Penaisee, a little bird, but Wendigo, the giant.' And ever after that moon was
called by all the tribe, Mondamin, or the Maize
Moon."

*   *   *   *   *   *

Anne looked across the fields. The wind arose
from the corn stack beside her and followed her
thoughts afar.

"I'm so happy and it's all so beautiful, the fields
and the sky and the animals and father-mother
and Tommy and — everything — Oh, how I wish
Heart of Nature would give me the magic crystals,
so that I could see the other Heart too!"

"Be content, House Child," said the familiar
voice close to her heart, "you see more than you
may yet understand. You have the precious crystals in your keeping; for it is only by looking
through the eyes of Heart of Nature and Heart of
Man that on this earth you may see Heart of God!"

Tommy ran up and put his arm around his
sister. She looked at him and then across the
fields with a new light in her eyes. "I understand, dear Heart of Nature," she whispered.

*   *   *   *   *   *

"Anne, please Anne, look at me and listen,"
begged Tommy, pulling at her hand. "Baldy says

my stwashes are hard and ripe, and the big, white rooster's going to be made into soup, and I've dot all his fevvers, and I've dot twelve black beans for eyes, and mother says I can sit up till eight o'clock and make those lovely stwash deese for Miss Jule, 'cause to-morrow is her birfday, and she's going to have a party. A nice little party wifout any best clothes, just for you and me and Lily and Lumber-legs and Waddles and her dogs and Fox! You will help me, won't you, Anne?" he said, peering anxiously into her face, "betause it's going to be vely hard to make their tails and eyes stick on."

"Of course I will," said Anne, laying her cheek on his curly head.

"Why don't stwashes grow fevvers?"

"Because birds are the only feathered things."

"But why?"

"I cannot tell," said Anne, laughing. "You must ask Wabeno, the Magician."

THE END

GLOSSARY

Amoe. The Honey Bee.
Annemee'kee. Thunder.
Apuk'wa. The Bulrush.
Askuta-squash. The Squash or Gourd.

Bek'wuk. The Arrow.

Chi-kaug. The Skunk.
Coon Moon. February.
Corn Moon. August.

Dahin'da. The Bullfrog.
Deer Moon. October.
Dibik'gezis. The Night Sun, the Moon.

Ghee'zis. The Sun.
Gitche Manito. The Great Spirit, God.
Gitche-ah-mo. The Honey Bee.
Goose Moon. April.

Hard Moon. January.

Iskodah. A Comet.

Kabibonok'ka. The North Wind.
Kayoshk'. The Sea Gull.
Keeway'din. Northwest or Home Wind.

Ko'ko'ko'ho. The Great Horned Owl.

Little Oo-oo. The Screech Owl.

Mai-mai. The Woodcock.
Ma'ma. The Woodpecker.
Midsummer Moon. July.
Mon'da'min. Maize, Indian Corn.
Mon'o'min. Oats.
Moon of Falling Leaves. September.
Moon of Leaves. May.
Moon of Snow Blindness. March.
Moon of Snow Shoes. December.

Nee'ba-naw-baigs. Water Spirits.

O-o-chug. The House Fly.
Ondaig. The Crow.
Owais'sa. The Bluebird.
Opin. The Potato.

Pau-puk-kee-wis. The Storm Fool.
Peboan. Winter.
Penai-see. Little Bird, Hummingbird.

Planting Moon. May.

Puk-Wudj'ies. Little Vanishing People.

Shaw-shaw. The Swallow.

Shawonda'see. The South Wind.

Sugge'ma. The Mosquito.

Wabasso. The White Rabbit, the North.

Wabeno. The Magician.

Wabun-An'nung. The Morning Star.

Wabun. The East Wind.

Wa'wa. The Wild Goose.

Wa'goose. The Dream Fox.

Wawa-sa-mo. Lightning.

Waz'husk. The Muskrat.

Weeng. The Spirit of Sleep.

Wendigo. A Giant.

www.ingramcontent.com/pod-product-compliance
Lightning Source LLC
Chambersburg PA
CBHW022143010726
47493CB00002B/325